4-PLAY

Irvine Welsh is the author of *Trainspotting* (1994), *Marabou Stork Nightmares* (1995), *Ecstasy* (1996), *Filth* (1998) and *Glue* (2001).

Harry Gibson was born in Cowley, the car factory bit of Oxford. He likes dressing up and arsing about, so he became an actor, mostly at Glasgow Citizens' Theatre, where he is now learning how to direct plays.

Keith Wyatt is a writer and actor living and working between Montreal and London. Previous writing credits include theatre and film works made in Canada and the UK. At present he is collaborating with Irvine Welsh on an adaptation of *Ecstasy* for the screen. He is also working on an original stage production and his first novel, entitled *Confessions of a Courtesy Clerk.*

4-PLAY

Trainspotting by Harry Gibson
Marabou Stork Nightmares by Harry Gibson
Ecstasy by Keith Wyatt
Filth by Harry Gibson

BASED ON THE NOVELS AND NOVELLAS OF

Irvine Welsh

VINTAGE

Published by Vintage 2001

2 4 6 8 10 9 7 5 3 1

First published in Great Britain in 2001 by Vintage

Vintage
Random House, 20 Vauxhall Bridge Road,
London SW1V 2SA

Random House Australia (Pty) Limited
20 Alfred Street, Milsons Points, Sydney,
New South Wales 2061, Australia

Random House New Zealand Limited
18 Poland Road, Glenfield,
Auckland 10, New Zealand

Random House (Pty) Limited
Endulini, 5A Jubilee Road, Parktown 2193, South Africa

The Random House Group Limited Reg. No. 954009
www.randomhouse.co.uk

A CIP catalogue record for this book is available from the British Library

ISBN 0 09 942643 9

A VINTAGE ORIGINAL

Papers used by Random House are natural, recyclable products made from
wood grown in sustainable forests; the manufacturing processes conform to
the environmental regulations of the country of origin

Typeset by SX Composing DTP, Rayleigh, Essex
Printed and bound in Great Britain by
Bookmarque Limited, Croydon, Surrey

CONTENTS

Introduction

Irvine Welsh was interviewed by Kano in the Café Thyssen, Brouwersgracht, Amsterdam, shortly after the play of *Filth* came out. There was a supplementary interview by phone a year later to update things for the purpose of this introduction.

Q: They plays: what are they about then?

A: Have you no seen them?

Q: Some of them, but I'm wanting you to tell me. Thought that was what you wanted. You sais 'interview me, but aboot they plays'.

A: Fair enough, so let me answer that question in a round about way. There's a tired cliché-ridden thesis around that theatre, especially in Britain, is dull and boring. Unfortunately, it's also true. It's one of the most bourgeois of art forms in the UK, which would seem to make it dull by default. The British bourgeoisie seem to be the very antithesis of that word it seems obligatory for them to relentlessly drool, 'cool', which since its appropriation by the New Labour crew, has become one of the most offensive words in the English language. It's almost obligatory now for any public-school person working in the arts to effect a working-class accent and try to fraternise (at least for a while) with as many rough diamonds as possible. Television, newspapers and magazines are full of public-school boys and girls mockneying it up as much as they can get away with. It's become quite impressive to hear young or youngish punters in London actually speak with proper, unabashed posh accents. It's a reverse form of snobbery that a lot of gifted toffs now have to play at being gadges or geezers with the complicity of a hungry media who then take great pleasure in outing them, rather than just being who they are. But this level of artifice, required almost everywhere else, hasn't yet reached the theatre. We haven't even got a mod-bourgeois, imperialist view of our own culture, stylised and sold back at us. Mostly theatre is still about lovies, darlings and absolute sweethearts, and in some ways it's admirable, but in others it's such a shame.

Q: Why is it? They cannae help being posh and liking theatre.

A: Multicultural societies need multicultural art, mate, not just a few poncey toffs telling us what we can and can't see.

Q: Aye, awright, but you've no answered the question. What are the plays aboot?

A: Let me finish with this first but, cause I think you have to look at theatre in a broader sense, about what's happening elsewhere. For example, I was over in New York recently, where the theatre scene is infinitely better. In one weekend I saw Debbie Harry in a Sarah Kane play, Philip Seymour Hoffman direct a new play called *Jesus Got On The A Train*, a play by 23rd Street Theatre Company based on the writings of Charles Bukowski, and Stephen Berkoff's *Shakespeare's Villains*, all within a few square miles. In London it would take donkey's years to get through a haul like that.

Q: So that means that you're a theatre lover, going to all that in one weekend like a ponce instead of spending time in a Lower East Side crack den like a real Scotsman would do!

A: (*Laughs*) You're such a cunt, Kano . . . aye, I'm a closet theatre lover. I like the idea of it, live-acting performance on stage, it's just the reality that so often depresses. It was just before Christmas and I was trying to cut down on alcohol and drugs. Only a rehab case would be that obsessive about shows.

Q: So, ye gaunny tell me what they plays are aboot or are ye no?

A: Eh, I've really been through aw this, loads of times, with the books. I think it might be better to ask the people who did the adaptations . . .

Q: I don't know them, and I dinnae see any of them here. (*Laughs*) You'll have to do.

A: Thanks.

Q: Okay then, tell me how it all came about.

A: I never thought about having my books adapted for the stage, or film, for that matter, and it's a source of great pride that so many very able people have adapted, want to adapt or are in the process of adapting my stuff for stage and screen.

Q: Aye, right. Who were the cunts that adapted the plays? How did it come aboot?

A: (*Laughs*) The cunts were . . . *Trainspotting* was the first to get the treatment, starting a relationship with the Citizens in Glasgow which has continued over the years. Harry Gibsons adaptation was originally directed by Ian Brown, then of Edinburgh's Traverse, on the small stage at the Citizens. Since then I've seen many versions of it all over the world, the latest an incredible operatic-style piece in Portuguese which I stumbled on to by chance in Lisbon.

Q: Aye, you just happened tae be stumbling in Lisbon and ye fell ower it, likes?

A: Aye, that was about it. Gen up! But back to *Trainspotting*, the original cast was Susan Vidler, Ewen Bremner, Jim Cunningham and Malcolm Shields, who was an excellent Begbie. I remember the sheer shock in rehearsals hearing actors performing my own words back to me. I went on to come across their paths again, Susan in the *Trainspotting* film and in my play *Hole*, Ewen in the films *Trainspotting* and *Acid House*, Jim in *Marabou Stork Nightmares* and Malcolm in *Hole* and the *Acid House* film.

**Q: *Trainspotting* was barry. The film, likes.
Never read the book.**

A: Buy it then, ya tight cunt.

**Q: I choried *The Acid House*. From the English
bookshop here. No the big yin, the Waterstone's or
Smith's but that wee one. You know the place, the
cunt there looks at you as if you've robbed
something before you have. So you think, might as
well. Is that still open? I've not been past that way
in ages.**

A: Probably shut cause of you thieving all the stock.
Anyway, where were we? Aye, *Marabou Stork Nightmares* was
the next book to be adapted, again by Harry Gibson, for the
stage, likes. I couldn't really see how it would work but I
thought he did an excellent job. *Marabou*'s my favourite of
all my books though in sales terms it's the runt of the litter.
I'm also quite precious about it, having knocked back a
couple of approaches to turn it into film. I wasn't keen on
what the people involved had in mind. Back to the play
though, the set was elaborate, and you need a big cast,
which makes it costly to put on. My best memory was of Jim
Cunningham losing his voice on the opening night, shame
for Jim, but it gave me the excuse to get away early and get
drunk with some old Weedgie pals in the Victoria Bar. I
hope the *MSN* play comes back, because it's ambitious and
good, deserves to.

Q: Aye . . . (*Yawns*)

A: (*Laughs*) Stop the fuckin yawning. I need to go over this
bit for people that are interested in theatre, and that. So
next up came *Filth*, again adapted by Harry Gibson. This
was a Tam Dean Burn tour de force. Tam plays thirty-three
parts in this one-man show and he captivates and rivets the
audience from start to end. As I write this, *Filth*'s back at the
Citizens for another run. *Filth*'s probably been my best-
received book, both here and abroad. I had a look at *The
Oxford Book of English Literature*, which it called it 'poorly

received'. I just thought: what the fuck are the cunts on about? It was a number-one best-seller in the UK, and according to the publishers, the fastest-selling trade paperback ever, so that begs the question: poorly received by whom?

Q: Aye, the play was good, with the boy fae Clerie. Somebody says the book was awright n aw.

A: Those up-their-own-arse critics. The trivial, dull pretentious shite which . . . but we're going round in circles again.

Q: But you get paid for it. You've just got a chip on your shoulder, mate, it hus tae be said. No every cunt's gaunny like what ye dae, ye cannae expect that.

A: That's beside the fuckin point. I just like things to be done properly, that's all. Say 'I think it's shite', or 'I think he's a cunt', if you want, but at least get the fucking facts straight. The book *wasn't* poorly received by the public, and it got some great reviews as well, some of the best I've ever had. Why the fuck say it wis if it fuckin well wisnae? If you're setting yourself up as an authority, get the facts right and don't confuse them with your opinions.

Q: Thought you never read reviews!

A: I read the ones they use on the paperback's dust jacket a year later, like 'fantastic', 'superb' and all that stuff.

Q: That's a load ay fucking shite! *Every* book's got that sort ay crap on it. People ken that that means fuck all. And ye didnae answer my question.

A: What? What question?

Q: You get paid for it, for they plays, dae ye no?

A: Eh . . . aye.

Q: Every time some cunt pits on one of this plays, does aw the work, Welshy there gets paid. And you dinnae dae *any* work for it al all?

A: Admittedly, but . . .

Q: So it's like you get paid twice; once for writing the book, and once when somebody else puts it on as a play. Ye think that's right?

A: Aye. I fuckin well wrote the thing, so it *is* right.

Q: But the play must help the book, help that sell mair copies. So it's like you get paid for daein nothing.

A: Suppose it is. Fuckin great really!

Q: Glad tae hear it. So get tae the fuckin bar then, ya cunt.

A: Fuck you, it's your fuckin round, ya paupin bastard.

Q: (*Laughs*) Lager?

A: A black Russian.

Q: Aye, sure. You'll git lager and like it.

Pause.

Q: Bet ye thir's loads ay poofs in the theatre.

A: Tons.

Q: Must be plenty fanny n aw but. Posh birds n that.

A: Tons.

Q: Thir's still a bit oan the tape . . . well, you think that you've got enough for this intro then?

A: Aye. Wait. I never mentioned Keith Wyatt and *Ecstasy*, did I?

Q: Aye. *Ecstasy* wasnae very good. The book, that is.

A: The ideas were good, they were just badly written. I was trying out different voices and it didn't work out. The third one was okay, but it made a better play. That's why I really love Keith's version of it. It made writing the thing worthwhile. It being a number-one best-seller made it worthwhile as well, I suppose, but artistically, the play delivered the book for me. I liked the other adaptations, but I liked *Trainspotting, Marabou* and *Filth* as books. I don't like *Ecstasy* as a book, so my expectations of it as a play weren't high. I saw it at the Edinburgh Fringe and I thought it would be studenty shite; some Canadians doing *Ecstasy* as a play. I was wrong. It was about the best adaptation/interpretation of my stuff for stage I've seen, and I've seen different productions all over the world. It was so fucking clubby, man, it was like being there. I was with my pal Debs from London, and my poet mate Paul Reekie who was even leering at the lassies the way he does in clubs. I was so blown away, I went out to celebrate with the cast. The Canadian crowd even came with us to Hibs v St Mirren at Easter Road.

Q: Now *that* must be time to stop.

A: Aye, awright.

Q: Is this aw gaunnae be in the book as we've said it?

A: Aw aye, well, I'll obviously tart mine up tae make me look cool and articulate, and fuck about with yours tae make you look a right cunt. (*Laughs*)

Q: Thought ye might.

Irvine Welsh's

Trainspotting

Adapted by Harry Gibson

Characters

Most of them are in their 20s.

Drunk, *50, Franco Begbie's father*

Three mates:
Mark Renton, *unemployed, university drop-out, junky*
Tommy Murphy, *unemployed, into drink, E and clubbing*
Franco Begbie, *petty criminal, heavy drinker, cunt*

June, *unemployed, pregnant by Franco*
Lizzie MacIntosh, *unemployed, Tommy's ex-girlfriend*
Alison, *waitress, mother of Dawn by Sick Boy, junky*
Lassie *in pub*
Boy *in pub*
Johnny Swan, *40s, drug-dealer*
Simon 'Sick Boy' Williamson, *rent boy, junky*
Mrs Renton, *40s, Mark's Mother*

Optional:
Lizzie, *as a schoolgirl*
Morag 'Jam Rag' Henderson, *as a schoolgirl*

Doublings

The play was written to be performed by four actors:
Mark, Boy
Drunk, Tommy, Simon, Morag
Franco, Johnny, Mother
June, Lizzie, Alison, Lassie

Set

The usual *Trainspotting* stage set turns out to be the ruins of old Leith Central Station (final scene). Designs suggest that the space is somehow underground, with a subway-train tunnel underneath. The occasional roar, lights and dust of a subway train passing serve as a rough way of changing the scene.

Historical Notes

The 'usual set' works well, but naturally anything is possible. The music suggested in this text is not, of course, obligatory. I've directed the show five times and seen it done by others in Edinburgh, Dresden, Iceland and Paris: each theatrical culture spins it differently. The Edinburgh lads did a punk version, virtually in one lighting state, with little sense of changing scene: the set was essentially a lavatory. The four actors – looking very mean and speedy – stayed on stage most of the time. It ended with the Lord's Prayer (growing from Franco's final 'Ma faither') shouted defiantly by all of them. The stark concentration of that fine version was at the other extreme from what I saw in Dresden, an eight-actor three-hour mishmash of bits from the book, the play, the movie and far too many hours of workshop games. It was chaos; and got seventeen curtain calls! The Icelanders created a broken-brick room increasingly invaded by a sort of mythworld which made me think of trolls; Tommy was an idiot boy and Mother was a frightening Nordic witch wielding a giant spoon. It was high on epic, low on street credibility. The Parisians played on a couple of huge scaffolding climbing frames, and rushed around having tons of fun acting out almost every character mentioned in the text – as if they were all still children. It was crazily engaging . . . but pretty soulless. Nonetheless, I stole one of their ideas and staged the Toronto version using two eight-foot-high mobile scaffolding towers which were draped with old curtains and washing lines, moving on a sort of parking lot with giant spike-marks, flanked by two big piles of garbage that included everything that could possibly come in handy, including a plaster statue of the Blessed Virgin and a practical washing machine. It was an eye-candied, almost Christmas-pantomime version, but it was probably too much fun. In New York I created the darkest version ever, in an all-black brickwork set with lots of haze and smoke, which seemed to stun the old and left the young 'n' stylish looking pretty fucked up. I think I made it all too dirty, cos the Broadway critics came down slummin . . . and hurried back uptown writhing with disgust.

Anyway, I reckon that it pays to do it pretty simply, without trying too hard to make it be more than it is. It is not what critics call 'a well-made play'; back in 1994 we simply aimed to get it on, small and quick, because we thought highly of Irvine Welsh's stuff and wanted to see whether it could work on stage. The cult status of the book, and then the gloriously Monkees-style movie, blew up everything out of proportion and made a lot of folk expect too much of the show. It's a rough sketch of a rough lifestyle, not a full-blown drug-abuse drama with a lot of sentimental character-work and a poignant redemptive ending.

Printed here is the New York version.

Harry Gibson

*Music: The Chemical Brothers, 'Where Do I Begin?' (beginning) from
the album* Dig Your Own Hole, *Virgin Records Ltd.*

> *Sunday morning I'm waking up.*
> *Can't even focus on a coffee cup.*
> *Don't even know whose bed I'm in.*
> *Where do I start, where do I begin?*

Mark

Mark   Aw . . . fuck! Ah woke up in a strange bed, in a
strange room, covered in ma own mess. Ah'd pished the
bed. Ah'd puked up in the bed. Ah'd shat mahself in the
bed. O fuck.
Ah slide oot o bed. Ah pick up the duvet. Ah look down.
The bed is a total fucking mess. The wee pink carnations on
a white background are drownin in toxic brown pollution.
Ah huv to gather it up in the bottom sheet – like a fish
supper – and then wrap it up in the duvet cover, sorta crush
it into a ball, makin sure thir's no leakage, ken, and stow it
under the bed. Then ah turn the mattress over to hide the
damp patch. Then ah see mahself in a mirror: Jesus Christ!
Ah steal outa the bedroom into the toilet to shower the crap
off my chest, thighs n arse. The toilet is – nice. Who the fuck
do ah know with a nice toilet? O no. Gail Houston! Ah'm in
Gail Houston's mother's house. O! How did ah get here?
Who brought us here? Who the fuck undressed us? I
remember fuck all after the pub . . . the mushrooms . . .
dope . . . speed . . . acid . . . coke . . . space cake. Fuck. N
that was before the football match. Where Gail Houston
came into the picture I'm no awfy sure.
We'd been going oot fir six weeks but we'd no had sex. See,
she hud said she did not want oor relationship t start oot
oan a physical basis, as that wid be how it wid principally be
defined from then on in. She read this in *Cosmopolitan*, ken.
So six weeks oan ah've got a pair of bollocks like
watermelons. There was probably a fair bit of spunk in that

bed alongside the piss, shite n puke. Anywey, ah've just got down under the bare duvet on the bare mattress hopin fir a wee bit o sleep, when the door opens. Gail comes into the room. It is morning.

'You were in some state last night then! What happened to the bedcovers?'

Eh . . . a wee accident, Gail.

Ah'm no sure she completely understands but ahm no wanting to paint hur a picture. She wrinkles her nose and says to never mind n come downstairs – 'We're just gonna huv some breakfast.' She sweeps oot.

Breakfast?!

Ah get up n get dressed n creep doon the stairs – taking ma bundle with me as ah want to take it hame and get it cleaned. Ken? Right. Gail's parents are sitting at the kitchen table. The sounds n smells ay a traditional Scottish Sunday breakfast fry-up are un-fuckin-speakable: lumps of slaughtered and aborted animals lie twitching in a pool of boiling cow-fat: the sausages remind me of things ah want to forget.

'Well someone was in a state last night!' says Gail's ma, but teasingly, ken. Ah flushed wi embarrassment.

Mr Houston, sitting at the kitchen table, tries tae smooth things over fir us. 'Ah well, it does ye good tae cut loose once in a while.'

'It would do this one good tae be tied up once in a while,' sais Gail. (A wee bit o bondage wid do me fine.)

Er . . . Mrs Houston, ah sais, pointing tae ma fish supper, ah made a bit ay a mess ay the sheet n the duvet cover. Ah'm going tae take thum home n clean thum. Ah'll bring thum back tomorrow.

'Aw, don't you worry about that, son. Ah'll just stick them in the washing machine!' – She does not understand. – 'You sit down and get some breakfast.'

Naw, but, eh . . . a really bad mess. Ah feel embarrassed enough. Ah'd like tae take them home.

'Dearie dear!' Mr Houston laughs – uncomprehendingly.

'Now no, you sit down, son, ah'll see tae them!'

Mrs Houston powers across the flair towards us, n makes a grab fir ma bundle. She widnae be denied. Ah pull it to me, to my chest; but Mrs Houston is fast as fuck n deceptively strong. She got a good grip and pulled against me. The sheets flew up in the air – n a pungent shower of shite, alcoholic sick n vile piss splashed oot across the scene. Mrs Houston stands mortified, for a few seconds, before runnin heaving to the sink. Brown flecks of runny shite sit oan Mr Houston's glasses, face n white shirt.

'God sake, God sake!' Mr Houston croaks . . . as Mrs Houston boaks. Ah'm trying to mop some ay the mess back intae the sheets . . .

Mark, Tommy

Tommy   Hey! [*OR*: 'Oh to, oh to be, oh to be a Hibee!' (*i.e., the Hibernian Football Club chant*). **Mark** *joins in.*]

Mark   Tommy! [*OR*: Tommy. (*i.e., introduces him to the audience.*)]

Tommy   Mind the time ah went wi Laura McEwan?

Mark   Laura McEwan?! (*To audience*) A girl wi an awesome sexual reputation.

Tommy   One night in a Grassmarket pub she jist grabs me and takes me hame.

Mark   Aye well, what can ye dae?

Tommy   What can ah dae? She says 'Ah want you tae take ma arse virginity. Fuck me in the arse. Ah've nivir done it that wey before.'
Eh (ah sez) yeah, that sounds barry . . . But there were some other things she wanted tae dae wi me first. She binds ma ankles together wi Sellytape. Wuv nae clothes oan ken. Wuv stripped oaf. Ah'm leyin oan the bed. Right. She's bound ma ankles tegither wi Sellytape. And, uh, ma wrists. She's bound them wi Sellytape an aw.

Mark   So how you gaunnae fuck er in the erse if ye don't mind ma askin?

Tommy   She sais 'Ah'm doin this because ah don't want you to hurt me, understand? We do it from the side.'

Mark   Fuck off!

Tommy   'The minute ah start tae feel pain it's fuckin over. Right? Because naebody hurts me. No fuckin guy ivir hurts me. Ye understand me?'

Yeah, sound, likesay, sound. Ah dinnae want tae hurt enywan. Enywey, ah'm lying there, trussed up oan the bed, naked likes, n she's rubbing her crotch n seyin 'You're beootiful!' Ah'd nivir been telt before that ah wis beautiful.

She gives us a blow job. Whooo . . . awww . . . (*etc.*)

And just before ah was about to come – she stops! N she leaves the room. She leaves me lyin there, tied up wi Sellytape and a dick like a pickaxe handle! Ah started tae get a wee bit paranoid. Laura hud a long-term partner called Roy – committed tae a psychiatric hoaspital. She comes back in the bedroom n she's goat somethin in her hand.

'Ah want you to dae us in the arse now. So ah'm gaunnae Vaseline your dick heavily so that it doesnae hurt me when you put it in. My muscles'll be tight, cause this is new tae me, but ah'll try tae relax.'

She's smokin a joint at the time. Mebbe a wee bit stoaned. Cos it wisnae Vaseline she found in the bathroom cupboard, it was Vick's Vapour Rub. Aaargh! Ah thought the tip ay ma penis hud been sliced oaf!

'Fuck. Sorry!' She helps us off the bed, she helps us into the toilet. Ah'm hoppin along shedding tears ay pain! She fills the sink with water, and then she's off to find a pair of scissors tae cut the fucking Sellytape. Ah struggle up on ta the sink and try tae lower ma dick into the water. Fuck! (*Falls.*) Ah woke up in hospital. Ah'd six stitches in ma head, Sellytape burns oan ma ankels n a hoat dog between ma legs.

So don't you cry over Gail Houston, cos I never did get tae shag the arse off Laura McEwan.

Mark, Tommy, Franco

Franco   Yah smert cunt! Put my name down for a game o' pool, willya? We've a while before the train. (*He pisses.*)

Mark   Ma first day at primary school, the teacher sais tae us, 'You will sit beside Francis Begbie.' It wis the same story at secondary. Ah only did well at school tae get intae an O-level class tae git away fae Begbie. Didnae work.

Franco   Anywey the other fuckin week ah wis in here [*OR name a pub*] wi Tommy, fir a game ay pool, ken, n this cunt Jakey comes into the pub. Ah remembered the cunt, fuckin sure n ah did. Ah used tae think he wis a fuckin hard cunt back in fuckin school, ken? Ah remember smashin loads ay crabs tae bits wi stones wi that cunt doon the fuckin harbour, ken? He nivir recognised us. Didnae fuckin ken us fae Adam, the cunt.
Anywey Jakey's goat a mate wi um, a plukey-faced wide-o, and he goes to pit his fuckin money doon fir the balls – oan the table. Fir the pool, ken? But, sittin in the corner, there's this wee specky gadge, an he's already got his name up, chalked up, oan the board, ken? But he wid've just fuckin sat there n said fuck all if ah hudnae fuckin spoke like. Ah says to the plukey cunt 'That cunt's fuckin next, mate', pointin tae the wee specky gadge. Ah wis fuckin game fir a swedge. If the cunts hud've fuckin come ahead it wis nae problem like. Ah mean, you ken me, ah'm no the type ay cunt thit goes lookin fir fuckin bothir likes, but ah wis the cunt wi the fuckin pool cue in ma hand, n the plukey cunt could have the fat end ay it in his pus if he wanted like.
So the wee specky cunt's pit his fuckin money in, n he's rackin up the baws n that, ken? The plukey cunt jist sits doon n says fuck all. Ah kept ma eye oan the hard cunt, or at least he wis a fuckin hard cunt at the school, ken. The

cunt nivir sais a fuckin wurd. Kept his fuckin mooth shut awright, the cunt. Tommy says tae us 'Hi Franco is that boy getting lippy?' Ye ken Tommy; dinnae get us wrong, ah lap the cunt up, but he's fuckin scoobied whin it comes tae a pagger. He's pished ootay his fuckin heid n he kin hardly haud the fuckin pool cue. (This is fuckin half past eleven oan a Wednesday mornin wir talking aboot here.) They fuckin heard um like, these cunts, but they nivir fuckin sais nowt again. The plukey cunt and the so-called hard cunt. Ah nivir fuckin rated the plukey cunt, but ah wis fuckin disappointed in the hard cunt, or the so-called hard cunt, like. He wisnae a fuckin hard cunt. A fuckin shitein cunt if the truth be telt, ken. Big fucking disappointment tae me, the cunt, ah kin fuckin tell ye.

Mark   Begbie is a cunt ay the first order, nae doubt about that. The big problem is, he's a mate an aw. Ye cannae really relax in his company, specially if he's hud a bevvy.

Franco   Specially if ah've had a bevvy.

Mark   Ay, yir status could change suddenly fae great mate intae persecuted victim. So we indulge the radge, tell him he's the big man, laugh at his murderous jokes. Ye know how it goes: ye laugh with the rest o the cunts because ye'are feart no to, ye'are feart tae stand oot fae the crowd; ye'are just a wee fucken coward. But then, aw the lies ye tell and the bullshit ye make up tae curry favour, it makes a great apprenticeship for a storyteller.

Ah mind the time me and Begbie wir lyin in the field at the bottom ay the school running track. We were lyin doon there so's we could see the lassies racin in their wee shorts n blouses. We were lyin oan oor stomachs, heids propped up oan elbays n hands, watching Lizzie MacIntosh pitting up a game race against the lanky strides ay big Morag –

Both   Jam Rag!

Mark   Henderson.

[*Optional:* **Morag** *and* **Lizzie** *run, slow-mo, over the stage.* Chariots of Fire.]

Mark   Anywey ah hears this heavy breathin and turns tae notice Begbie slowly swivelling his hips, starin at the lassies, gaun –

Franco   That wee Lizzie MacIntosh . . . total wee ride . . . fuckin shag the erse ofay that any day ay the week . . . the fuckin erse oan it . . . the fuckin tits oan it . . .

Mark   Then he goes aw rigid and his erse is twitchin and his face faws doon intae the grass. Ah reach out n pull Begbie ower oantay his back, exposing his knob, which is drippin wi spunk and dirty wi earth. The cunt had slyly dug a hole in the turf wi his flick knife, and hud been fuckin the field. 'Ya dirty cunt, Franco!' Begbie jist pits his knob away, zips up, and then grabs a handful ay spunk n earth and –

Franco *rubs earth in his face.*

Mark (*riled; then a climbdown*)   Whit dae ye dae? Ken, friendship wi Begbie is an ideal preparation for relating tae women. Ye learn sensitivity tae th'ither person's changing needs.

Franco   Wummen!

Mark   Cannae live wi em . . . Cannae live withoot em.

Franco   See ma heid was fuckin nippin this morning, ah kin fuckin tell ye. There's two boatils ay Beck's in the fridge an ah down the cunts in double quick time an ah feel better right awey. Ah go back ben the bedroom and she's still fuckin sleeping . . .

Mark   June?

Franco   Aye, June. Lazy fat cunt. Jist cause she's huvin a fuckin bairn, thinks it gies her the right tae lie aroond aw fuckin day. Ah've goat tae pack a bag an ah'm lookin fir ma fuckin jeans n she's jist waking up.

Flashback.

Franco, June

June (*off*)   Frank!

Franco   That cunt hud better huv washed ma fuckin 501s.

June (*entering from bed*)   Frank, what are ye daein? Whair ur ye goan?

Franco   Ah'm ootay here. Whair the fuck's they soacks? Everythin takes twice as fuckin long whin yir hung-ower –

June   Whair ur ye goan?

Franco   N ah kind do withoot this cunt nippin ma fuckin heid.

June   Whair?

Franco   Ah telt ye, ah've goat tae fuckin nash. Ah pulled a bit ay business oaf n ah'm disappearing fir a couple ay weeks. Any polis cunts come tae the door, yuv no seen us fir yonks. Ye think ah'm oan the fuckin rigs, right? Yuv no seen us, mind.

June   But whair ur ye gaun, Frank? Whair ur ye fuckin well gaun?

Franco   That's fir me tae ken n you tae find oot. What ye dinnae fuckin well ken they cannae fuckin well beat oot ay ye.

June   Ye cannae jist fuckin go like that, ya bastard! (*Etc.*)

Franco *boots her in the fanny.*

Franco   Nae cunt talks tae us like that. That's the fuckin rules ay the game, take it or fuckin leave it.

June   The bairn! The bairn!

Franco   The bairn! The bairn! Shut yir fuckin mooth aboot the fuckin bairn. It's probably no even mah fuckin bairn anywey. Shavin gear . . .

June   Get the doaktir.

Franco   Ah'm fuckin late, ah've nae time. 'Syir fault. See if ah'm fuckin late fir thit train . . .

June   Ah hurt, ah hurt . . . Get the doaktir . . .

Franco   Goat tae fuckin nash.

June   The bairn . . .

Franco   Ah've hud bairns before, wi other lassies. Ah ken whit it's aw aboot. She thinks it's aw gaunnae be fuckin great whin the bairn comes, but she's in fir a fuckin shock. Ah kin tell ye aw aboot fuckin bairns. Pain in the fucking –

June   Fraank!

Franco   'Time fir a sharp exit.' [*OR 'It's Miller time!'*]

June   Fraaank!!

Tommy, Boy, Lassie

Tommy (*clutching his face*)   Did you see that? Pure fuckin mental! Ah'm sittin in the bar wi Davie Mitchell, ken. Wir just oot fir a quick drink. N this boy is huvin words wi a lassie he's with:

Boy   Cause ah fuckin sais! That's fuckin how!

Tommy   N he hits her.

Boy *hits* **Lassie**.

Tommy   No a fuckin slap or nowt like that, but a punch. Naebody bothers. A guy at the bar wi red hair n a ring through his nose looks ower n smiles, then turns back tae watch the darts match. No one ay the boys playin darts turns roond. Whin ah git tae the bar tae get us a couplay pints in, thuv started again. Ah kin hear thum.

Lassie   Gaun then. Dae it again. Gaun then!

Boy *hits* **Lassie**.

Tommy   Blood spurts fae her mooth.

Lassie   Hit us again, fuckin big man. Gaun then!

Boy *hits* **Lassie**. **Lassie** *screams and then starts crying* . . .

Tommy   The red-heided cunt catches ma eye n smiles.
'Lovers' tiff,' he sais. Ah look ower tae the barman, an auld
guy wi grey hair n a droopy moustache. He sais 'They
should be daein that kind ay arguin in the hoose, no in a
pub.'
'Never, ever hit a lassie,' ma faither often telt us. 'It's the
lowest scum thit dae that, son,' he sais. This cunt that's
hittin the lassie fits the bill: he's goat greasy black hair, a
thin white face n a wee black mustache: ferret-faced fucker.
Ah dinnae want tae be here. Ah jist came oot fir a quiet
drink wi Davie. Only a couple, ah promised him, tae git um
tae come. Lizzie's away to her mother's. 'Ah'm no comin
back, Tommy,' she sais. So ah came fir a pint.
The lassie's eyes are swollen n shuttin. Her jaw's swollen n
aw, and her mooth is still bleedin. She's a skinny lassie n she
looks like she'd snap intae pieces if he hit her again. Still, she
carries oan . . .

Lassie   That's yir answer. That's eywis yir answer.

Boy   Shut it! Ah'm tellin ye! Shut the fuck up!

Lassie   Whit ye gaunnae dae?

Boy   Ya facking – (*Fist up.*)

Tommy   Hoah! That's enough, mate. Leave it. Yir oot ay
order.

Boy   It's nane ay your fuckin business! You keep oot ay
this!

Tommy   Ah'm makin it ma fuckin business. Whit you
gaunnae fuckin dae aboot it?

Boy   You want yir mooth punched?

Tommy   Think ah'm gaunnay jist sit here n lit ye dae it? Fuckin wide-o! Ootside then, cunt. Cumaun!

Lassie (*attacking* **Tommy**)   That's ma man! That's ma fackin man yir talkin tae!

Tommy *goes down.*

Lassie   That's mah man . . . (*She goes down.*)

Franco, Mark, Tommy, June

Franco   Fucked if ah'm gaunnae stey wi that fuckin June eftir the bairn's here. Ivir since she's been huvin that bairn, she thinks she kin git fuckin lippy wi us. Nae cunt gets lippy wi me, bairn or nae fuckin bairn. She kens that, n she still gits fuckin smert. See if anything's happened tae that fuckin bairn . . . That cunt's dead if she's made us hurt that fuckin bairn. (*Exits.*)

June *staggers off, hurt.*

Tommy *staggers off, drunk.*

Mark

Music: The Chemical Brothers: 'Private Psychedelic Reel'.

Mark   'Choose life!' Ay, choose mortgage payments, choose cars, choose dishwashers. Choose sittin on a couch watching mind-numbin spirit-crushin game shows, stuffin junk food intae yer mooth. Choose rottin way at the enday it all, pishing n shitein yir life away, a total fuckin embarrassment to the selfish screwed-up brats ye've spawned to replace yirselves! Choose life? Ah chose not tae choose life. Ah chose somethin else.

He searches for heroin. None left. He's getting sick . . .

Ah've had a long-standing problem wi heroin addiction. Ah
feel it's important to be honest and mention this to you. Ye
become restless n uneasy, weak n irritable, yur nose n eyes
start tae run, yur yawnin, yur tremblin, sweatin n sneezin.
Yur limbs ache n yur pupils dilate . . . yur ootay yir box.

Mark, Simon

Music: The Chemical Brothers: 'Where Do I Begin' (conclusion).

Mark   Right. Wir in ma flat. Who was with me? No
Tommy, he wisnae intae the skag.

Enter **Simon**, *suffering* . . .

Sick Boy! Simon Sick Boy Williamson! We cried him 'Sick
Boy' no because he was always sick with junk withdrawal
but because he was one sick cunt. Wir watching a Jean-
Claude Van Damme video.

Simon   But what wir waitin for is another fuckin fix, a trip
to see the Mother Superior, fuckin quick n all!

Mark   Wir getting sick. But ah'm hangin in there, waiting
for Jean-Claude to get down to some serious swedgin.

Simon   Mark. I've got to see the Mother Superior!
Maaark!

Mark   Aw, haud on a second.

Simon   Ah've goat tae fuckin move, man.

Mark   Ah jist want tae see Jean-Claude smash the
fuckin –

Simon (*taking control*)   Let's fuckin go!

Mark   Ah willnae get to watch it noo!

Simon   Y can watch it the night.

Mark   'Sdue back now. They'll gie us back charges at the shop.

Simon   Fucksake! I'll gie ye the money to get it back oot! Fifty measly fuckin pence!

Mark   That's no the fuckin point!

Simon   The point is, ah'm really fuckin sufferin here n you are draggin yir feet deliberately.

Mark   Ah'm no!

Simon   Fling yer fuckin jaykit oan well!

Both   Taxi!

Simon   Supposed to be a fuckin taxi rank here!

Mark   Supposed to be August but I'm fuckin freezin ma balls off here. I'm no sick yet, but I can feel it coming, it's in the post that's for sure.

Simon   The taxis are aw up kerb-crawlin fir rich Edinburgh Festival cunts too fuckin lazy tae walk a hundred fuckin yards fae one poxy church hall tae another fir their fuckin drama shows.

Mark   Simon . . .

Simon   Money-grabbin bastards.

Mark   These guys, Simon, ah think . . .

Simon   Lowest form of vermin on God's earth.

Mark   These boys huv been waiting for a taxi before us, Si –

Simon   Taxi!!!

Mark   He charges straight out into the middle of the walk screaming 'Taxi!!' and a guy in a black, purple and aqua shell suit [*OR a green baseball cap; whatever*] shouts: (as **Boy**) 'Whit's the fuckin score?'

Simon   Fuck off, ya plukey-faced wee hing-oot. Git a fuckin ride! Cummon, Mark!

Mark (*as* **Boy**)   'Cummoan ya crappin bastards!'

Simon   Cummoan!

Mark   We piled into the taxi. Gob splattered against the side window. The driver wisnae amused. (*To* **Simon**) See what yuv done now, ya big-moothed cunt? Next time one ay us is walking hame on oor Jack Jones we get hassle fae these wee radges.

Simon   Yir no feart ay they wee fuckin saps, ur ye?

Mark   Aye, aye, ah am, if ah'm oan ma tod n ah get set oan by a squad ay fuckin shell suits. Ye think ah'm Jean-Claude Van fuckin Damme? Fuckin doss cunt.

Simon   Ay want tae see Mother Superior n ah dinnae gie a fuck aboot any cunt else. Goat that? Watch ma fuckin lips.

Mark   Wir here.

Simon   Boot fuckin time.

Mark, Simon, Johnny, Alison

Music: 'Shine on You Crazy Diamond' (Part 1) by Pink Floyd.

Mark   Up there was Johnny Swan. As we hit the stairs tae Johnny's gaff, ah'm getting bad cramps. Soon ah'm dripping like a saturated sponge wi the effort. Sick Boy was probably worse. At the toapay the stair ah find him slouched against the banister. Ah thought he wis gaunnae spew intae the stairwell. 'Awright, Si?' He waves us away, shaking his heid and screwing his eyes up. Ah sais nae mair. The doorbell was shatterin.

Bell.

***Enter* Johnny** *and* **Alison.**

Johnny Swan! Mother Superior! We cried him 'Mother Superior' because of the length of time he'd had his habit. The cunt was bombed outay his box.

Johnny   Ahaww! Ah've goat wan Sick Boy here an another sick boy there an that makes two sick fuckin boys!

Mark   He'd once been a really good mate of mines. We used to play football together. Now he's just a dealer. He sais tae us once:

Johnny   Nae friends in this game. Jist associates.

Mark   Aye, right. See, the real junky doesnae gie a fuck aboot anybody else. Nae friends . . . Alison was there.

Alison   Mark, ye smert cunt. Y'awright?

Mark   Alison was cookin. Sick Boy wis sittin up cloas tae her, never taking his eyes oaf the contents ay the spoon she wis heatin over a candle. Johnny bends doon in front ay Sick Boy, pulls his face tae him and kisses him, hard, on the lips. Sick Boy pushes him away, trembling. 'Fuck off! Doss cunt!' cries the sick boy.

Simon   Doss cunt!

Mark   Johnny an Ali laughed loudly. O, ah wid huv laughed loudly n aw, if ah hudnae felt each bone in ma body wis being crushed in a vice n set aboot wi a blunt hacksaw. Sick Boy picks up the rubber tube and tourniquays Ali above her elbow. Then he taps up a big blue vein oan her thin ash-white arm.

Simon   Y want me to do it?

Mark   She nodded. Alison nodded. He droaps a filter intae the spoon n blaws oan it, before sucking up about five mls through the needle, intae the barrel ay the syringe. He's goat a fuckin huge blue vein tapped up, which seems tae been almost coming through Ali's airm. He pierces her flesh and injects a wee bit slowly, before sucking blood back intae the chamber. Her lips are quivering as she gazes pleadingly at him for a second or two . . . His face looks ugly, leering, reptilian, before he slams the cocktail towards her brain! She pulls back her heid, shuts her eyes and opens her mooth, givin oot an orgasmic groan.

Alison *gives oot an orgasmic groan* . . .

Mark   She says . . . (**Alison** *still groaning* . . .) She says –

Alison   That beats any meat injection! That beats any fuckin cock in the world!   ·

Mark   Sick Boy's eyes are now innocent and full ay wonder, his expression like a bairn thit's come through oan Christmas morning tae a pile ay gift-wrapped presents stacked under a tree. Simon and Alison baith look strangely beautiful and pure in the flickering candlelight. 'That beats any meat injection. That beats any fucking cock in the world.' Aye . . .

Then Johnny helps Sick Boy tae cook up and shoot home. Seeing Sick Boy's thick juicy dark-blue wiring, Johnny holds back the syringe and croons gently . . .

(**Johnny** *croons a songline. Originally: 'You're so vein. I bet y think this hit is aboot ye.' Many others are possible.*)

Mark   Just as Sick Boy is aboot tae scream, Johnny spikes a vein, draws some blood back intae the barrel, and fires the life-giving life-taking elixir home. Sick Boy hugs Swanney tightly . . . then eases off, keeping his airms aroond him. They were relaxed, like lovers in a post-coital embrace . . . Then ah went to take a shot. Took us ages to find a good vein. Ma boys don't live as close to the surface as most people's. When it came, I savoured the hit. Ali wis right. Take yir best orgasm, multiply the feeling by twenty, n yir still fucking miles off the place. Ma dry cracking bones are soothed and liquified by my beautiful heroin's tender caresses . . .

Alison *and* **Simon** *go off.*

Mark   Alison and Sick Boy got up and trooped outay the room thegither. They looked bored and passionless, but when they didnae come back, ah knew that they'd be shagging in the bedroom. What dae ye dae . . .?

Enter **Alison** *screaming . . .*

Mark   Alison comes intae the room screamin. It's horrible. Ah cannae handle this.

Alison (*incoherent*)   The bairn's away, the barin's away . . .

Mark   We ken thit something really bad has happened because Alison has come ben the room, screamin!

Alison (*incoherent*)   Dawn! O my God! O fuckin God!

Mark   Johnny moves ontae the couch, sittin a few feet fae Alison. Ah thought that he wid touch her. Ah hoped he would. Ah'm willing um tae do it – But he jist stares at her. So ah sais . . . ah sais whit ah always say when somethin bad happens: 'Ah'm cookin up in a bit.'

Alison (*incoherent*)   It's ma fault, it's ma fault . . .

Johnny   Eh . . . Ali . . . likesay, Mark's cookin up, eh . . . ye ken, likesay eh . . . he's um . . . ye shouldnae . . . whit –

Mark   Sick Boy comes back through. His boady's strainin as if against an invisible leash.

Simon   Fuck . . .

Mark   His voice reminds us –

Simon   . . . some fuckin life, eh?

Mark   – ay the demon in *The Exorcist*.

Simon   Something like this happens . . .

Mark   It shits us up.

Simon   . . . What the fuck dae ye dae? Eh?

Johnny   What's wrong, Si? What's the fuckin score?

Simon   The gig's fucked. It's aw fuckin fucked!

Mark   He moans, in a high desperate whine. It was like a dug that hud been run ower and wis waiting fir some cunt tae pit it oot ay its misery.

Alison   The bairn's away. The bairn's away.

In the bedroom . . .

Mark   We get up and go through tae the bedroom. Ah can feel death in the room before ah even see the bairn. It wis lyin face doon in its cot. It, naw, she, wis cauld n deid, blue aroond the eyes. Ah didnae huv tae touch her tae ken. Lyin their like a wee doll at the bottom ay some kid's wardrobe.

Simon   That wee . . .

Johnny   So fuckin small.

Mark   Wee Dawn.

Johnny   Fuckin shame.

Simon   Wee Dawn.

Johnny   Fuckin sin, man.

Mark   Ah'm fuckin right ootay here, man. Ah cannae fuckin handle this –

Simon   Nae cunt's leavin here the now!

Johnny   Stay cool, man. Stay cool . . .

Simon   Wuv goat fuckin gear stashed here. This street's been crawlin wi the fuckin DS for weeks now. We fucking charge oaf now, we aw fuckin go doon. Thir's polis bastards every-fucking-where ootside.

Johnny   Aye, aye, but mibbe we should aw git the fuck ootay here, n Alison can git the ambulance or polis once wuv tidied up and fucked oaf.

Mark   Mibbe wuv goat tae stick wi Alison, likesay. Like, mates n that. Ken?

Johnny   The way ah see it is thit it's Alison's bairn, ken? Mibbe if she looked eftir it right, it might not be deid. How should we get involved?

Mark   Hate tae say it, bit Johnny's goat a point. Ah'm starting tae hurt really bad. Ah jist want tae take a shoat and fuck off.

Johnny   Who gave her the bairn?

Mark   Jimmy McGilvary, wiz it no?

Simon   Shite it fuckin wis.

Johnny (*to* **Mark**)   Dinnae you play mister fuckin innocent!

Mark   Eh?! Moan tae fuck! Whit you oan about?

Johnny   You wir thair . . . Boab Sullivan's perty.

Mark   Naw, man, ah've nivir been wi Alison.

Johnny   How come ye wir crashed oot wi her in the mornin at Sully's perty?'

Mark   Ah wis fucked, man. Ootay ma box. Ah couldnae huv goat a stiff nek wi a doorstep as a pillay.

Simon   Naw . . .

Mark   Ah cannae remember the last time ah hud a ride.

Simon   Naw . . .

Mark   Sick Boy!

Simon *puts a hand oan the deid bairn's cauld cheek. Under the shades, tears fill his eyes.*

Simon   Ah'm nivir touchin that shite again. Ah'm clean fae now oan.

Johnny   C'moan, Si. Dinnae jump tae the wrong conclusions. Whit happened tae the bairn's nowt tae dae wi the skag. Ach, it's no Alison's fault either. She loved the bairn. 'Snaebody's fault. Cot death. Ken? Happens aw the time.

Mark   Yeah, likesay, cot death, man.
Ah feel thit ah love thum aw.
Ah want tae tell thum.
Ah try . . .
But it comes oot as: 'Ah'm cookin!'

Simon   Fucksake! (*Attacks* **Mark**.)

Johnny *intervenes.*

Simon *leaves.*

Johnny (*to* **Mark**)   Doss cunt! (*Pursuing* **Simon**) Si!

Mark   That's me.
Ah go back in the livin room. Alison's nivir moved. Ah feel thit ah should mibbe go and comfort her, pit my airm aroond her. But ma bones feel twisted and scraped. Ah couldnae touch anybody right now. Instead ah babble. 'Really sorry, Ali. Naebody's fault though. Cot death n that. Wee Dawn. Barry wee bairn. Fuckin shame. Fuckin sin, man, ah'm tellin ye.' Alison lifts her heid up and looks at us.

Alison   Ye cookin, Mark? Ah need a shot. Ah really need a fuckin shot. C'moan, Marky, cook us up a shot.

Music: 'The Drugs Don't Work' by the Verve . . .

Mark *gives* **Alison** *a shot.* **Alison** *curls up.*

Mark

Mark   Ten tins ay Heinz tomato soup. Eight tins ay mushroom soup. All tae be consumed cold. One large tube ay vanilla ice cream – which will melt and be drunk. Two boatils ay Milk of Magnesia, one boatil ay paracetamol, one packet ay Rinstead mouth pastilles, one boatil ay multivitamins, five litres ay mineral water, twelve Lucozade isotonic drinks. And some magazines: soft porn, *Viz*, *Scottish Football Today*, the *Punter*, etc. The most important item hus already been procured from a visit tae the parental home . . . ma ma's bottle ay Valium.

It's going tae be a hard week. Ma room is bare and uncarpeted. There's a mattress in the middle ay the flair with a sleeping bag oan it, an electric fire and a telly. Ah've goat three brown plastic buckets wi a mixture ay disinfectant and water; one for ma pish, one for ma shite and one for ma puke. You've got tae know what it's like tae try comin off the skag before ye can actually dae it. You can only learn through failure, and what ye learn is the importance ay preparation.

Sound: distant ambulance . . .

It starts as it generally does, with a slight nausea in the pit ay ma stomach and an irrational panic attack. As soon as ah become aware ay the sickness gripping me, it effortlessly moves from the uncomfortable tae the unbearable. A toothache starts tae spread fae ma teeth intae ma jaws and ma eye sockets. And then the sweat arrives . . . and then the shivers, covering ma back like a thin layer ay frost oan a car roof. An need, ah need, ah need!

In twenty minutes ah wis in Muirhouse. Oan the bus an auld boot gies us the evil eye. No doubt ah'm fuckin boggin n lookin a real mess. Doesnae bother us. A lassie sits across fae us listening tae her Walkman. Is she good-looking? Whae cares? She's listenin ta Bowie – 'Golden Years'. (*Sings:*) 'Don't let me hear you say life's takin you nowhere – Angel . . .' Ah've goat every album Bowie ever made. The fuckin lot. Ah dinnae gie a fuck aboot him or his music. Ah only care aboot one thing.

Some auld cunt is fartin and shitein at the driver aboot bus numbers and routes and times. Get the fuck oan or fuck off n die ya foostie auld cunt! Ah almost choke in rage at her selfish pettiness and the bus driver's pathetic indulgence of the cunt. When she finally gits oan the auld fucker has the cheek tae have a gob oan her like a cat's erse. Ah will her to have a brain haemorrhage . . .

Ah'm gaunnae miss ma stoap! No. Ah get oaf at the shopping centre, the steel-shuttered units which huv nivir been let and the car park where cars huv nivir been parked fir twenty years. Ah slide along the wall. Ma guts are starting tae go: ah feel a queasy shifting in ma constipation. Ah arrive at the skag merchant's door. He'll see ah'm suffering, and he'll gie us crap, cause the cunt knows ah'd walk oan ma hands and knees through broken glass tae use his shite fir toothpaste. But ah still love him. Ah huv tae. He's the boy holdin. He's holdin. Ah pull oot some crumpled notes fae ma poackits and flatten them oot oan the coffee table. He snaffles them and produces two wee hard bomb-shaped things wi a waxy coat oan them. Ah'd nivir seen the likes ay them before. 'What the fuck's this shite?!'

'Opium. Opium suppositories.'

'What the fuck dae ah dae wi these?'

'Dae ye really want me to tell ye? They melt through yir system, take away the pain, help ye git oaf the junk, right? That's the cunts they use in hoaspitals fir fucksakes.'

So . . . ah excuse masel, retire tae the toilet and insert them up ma erse. As ah leave he sais tae me:

'It'll take time.'

And ah sais 'You're tellin me: fir aw the good they've done so far ah might as well huv stuck thum up ma erse.'

But by the time ah hit the bottom ay the stair ah'm feeling better. The ache in ma body doesnae bother us. It feels like ah'm meltin inside. Ah huvnae shat fir aboot five or six days. As ah pass through the shopping centre ah fart. Fuck . . .

Ah huv tae take immediate action. There's a bookies in the shopping centre wi a toilet in the back. Ah dive in the smoke-filled shoap and head straight tae the bog. What a fuckin scene. Two guys standing in the doorway ay the toilet, just pishing intae the place which has a good inch ay stagnant urine covering the flair. Ah look across hopefully tae the cubicle.

'Bog's fuckin blocked, mate. Ye'll no be able ta shite in that.'

Ah look sternly at him: 'Ah've goat tae fuckin go, mate. It looks fuckin awfay in thair, but it's either that or ma fuckin keks.' So . . .

The bowl, the seatless bowl, is filled wi broon water n toilet paper n lumps ay floating shite. Ah whip oaf ma keks and sit on the cold wet porcelain shunky . . . and ah empty ma guts: ma bowel, stomach, intestines, spleen, liver, kidneys, heart, lungs and fucking brains are aw falling through ma ersehole intae that bowl.

Then ah realise what ah've done. Ah sit frozen fir a moment. But only a moment. Ah roll up ma shirtsleeves. There are scabby needlemarks along ma arms. But . . . ah plunge ma hands and forearms intae the broon water. Ah slosh around down there and get one ay ma bombs back straight away. Ah rub off some shite that's attached tae it. A wee bit melted but still largely intact. Ah stick it oan top ay the cistern. Locating the other takes several long dredges through the shite ay many good Muirhoose punters. Ah gag once, but eventually ah get ma lump ay white gold back, even better preserved than the first. Ma broon-stained airm reminds us ay the classic T-shirt tan: ah hud tae go right aroond the bend. Ah wis tempted tae swallay the suppositories, but ah rejected this notion almost as soon as it crossed ma mind. They were probably safer back where they came from. Home they went. And home ah went.

It was a swelterin hot day. Summer!

Somebody said it was the first day of the Edinburgh Festival. 'Certainly got the weather for it.' Aye, right.

'Choose life!' Fuck . . .

More heroin appears. He shoots up.

Mark, Tommy, Lizzie, Alison

Music: 'Roads' by Portishead.

Dumbshow: **Lizzie** *leaves* **Tommy**. **Tommy**, *lost, turns to* **Mark**.

Mark   Tommy . . .

Tommy   Ah split up wi Lizzie,

Mark   Ye pished oaf aboot it?

Tommy   Dinnae ken. If ah'm honest, ah'll miss the sex maist. That n like, jist huvin somebody, ken?

Mark   Lizzie MacIntosh. Ah telt ye the time me and Begbie wir lyin watching the lassies racin? Naw, doesnae matter.

Tommy *picks up the syringe* . . .

Tommy   What does it dae fir ye, Mark?

Mark   Don't start on me! Ah ken ah'm killin mahself n ah huv tae pack it in cause ah kin live ma life withoot it n aw that: ye've telt us before, Tam, jist ike ma auld lady.

Tommy   Naw, tell us.

Mark   Ah dinnae really know, Tam, ah jist dinnae.

Tommy   Ah want tae ken . . .

Mark   Life's boring n futile. We start oaf wi high hopes, n then we bottle it. We realise we're all gaunnae die withoot finding out the big answers. Basically, we live a short, disappointing life, and then we die. We fill up oor lives wi shite, things like careers and relationships, tae delude oorselves that it isnae aw totally pointless. Smack's an honest drug, because it strips away the delusions. Wi smack, whin ye feel good, ye feel immortal. Whin ye feel bad – ye see the misery o the world as it really is. Real life . . .

Tommy   Shite. Pure shite.

Mark   It's also a fuckin good kick.

Tommy   Gies a go. Gies a hit.

Mark   Fuck off, Tommy.

Tommy   Ye sais it's a good kick. Ah pure wantae try it.

Mark   Ye dinnae. C'moan, Tommy, take ma word fir it.

Tommy   Ah've goat the hireys. C'moan. (*Money.*) Cook us up a shot.

Mark   Tommy . . . fucksake, man . . .

Tommy   Ah'm tellin ye, c'moan. Supposed tae be fuckin mates, ya cunt. Cook us up a shot. Ah kin fuckin handle it. One fuckin shot isnae gaunnae hurt us. C'moan.

Mark *takes the money, and gives* **Tommy** *a shot . . .*

Alison   'Life's boring n futile. We start oaf wi high hopes, n then we bottle it. We realise we're all gaunnae die withoot finding out the big answers. Basically, we live a short, disappointing life, and then we die. We fill up oor lives wi shite, things like careers and relationships, tae delude oorselves that it isnae aw totally pointless. Smack's an honest drug.' Shite. Pure shite.
He droaps a filter intae the spoon n blaws oan it, before sucking up the smack through the needle intae the barrel ay the syringe . . . He's goat a fuckin huge blue vein tapped up . . . He pierces the flesh and injects a wee bit, slowly, before sucking blood back intae the barrel . . . His lips are quivering as he gazes pleadingly at him for a second or two . . . And then . . . he fires the life-giving . . . life-taking . . .

Music: 'Roads' returns, distantly . . . in echo . . .

The shot and its effects bring **Mark** *and* **Tommy** *in close contact. For a while, it has the look of love . . .*

Alison   Their eyes are innocent and full ay wonder, like a bairn's thit's come through on Christmas morning tae a pile ay gift-wrapped presents stacked under a tree. (*She is fighting* *tears . . .*) They both look strangely beautiful in the candlelight.

Tommy   This is pure fucking brilliant, Mark . . . ah'm fuckin buzzin here . . . ah'm just pure buzzin . . .

Mark   See . . . some cunts are so predisposed to smack.

Alison *is crying . . .*

Mark (*to* **Alison**)   Ah cleaned the fuckin needle!

Music: 'How can it feel this wrong?' and starts fading . . .

Mark   See ma problem is, whenever ah get something that ah thought ah wanted, girlfriend, flat, joab, education, money, whitevir, it jist seems sae dull n sterile that ah cannae value it any mair. Junk's different though. Ye cannae turn yir back on it so easy. It willnae let ye. Tryin to manage a junk habit is the ultimate challenge. Ah mean . . . it's real.

Tommy *retches.*

Music gone.

Mark   Yuv done it, mate. That's you got the set now. Dope, acid, speed, E, mushies, Vallies, smack, the fucking lot. Knock it on the heid. Make that the first n last time.

Tommy   Too fuckin right.

Mark   Split up wi Lizzie then?

Tommy   Ah just pure wish Lizzie wid always be like she is in bed.

Mark   Shag extraordinaire?

Tommy   Sweet and beautiful. Ah know ah shouldnae be tellin aboot it, man, but . . . God . . . hur in bed . . . ah'm addicted tae having sex wi her. God . . . Yellow silk pillowcases . . . they ones Davie gied us . . .

Mark   Ah wis with him when he knocked them off.

Tommy   Her hair on the pillow . . .

Mark   British Home Stores . . .

Tommy   Ah love daein it fae behind . . .

Mark   But she's kicked ye intae touch!

Tommy   Ah forgot her birthday. Ah mean ah goat ma ticket fir the Iggy Pop gig when ah goat ma giro n that wis me pure skint. Ah mean it wis the ticket or a birthday present fir Lizzie. Nae contest.

Mark *laughs* . . .

Tommy   Ah thought she'd understand. It's ma ain fault. Ah should've said nothin aboot the ticket. Ah get too excited . . . ah pure open ma big mooth far too wide.

Lizzie   So, ye'd rather go tae a concert wi Davie fuckin Mitchell than the pictures wi me?'

Mark   The rhetorical question!

Tommy   That's pure Lizzie.

Mark   The stock-in-trade weapon of burds n psychos.

Tommy   She's goat this . . . outrage.

Mark   She's goat a tongue like a sailor.

Tommy   She calls me all the fuck-ups under the sun.

Lizzie   All the fuck-ups under the sun!

Mark   The pure viciousness ay hur expression . . .

Tommy   Ye can see her point.

Mark   . . . will corrode her beauty before it's time.

Tommy   Ah'm jist auld fuck-the-wind.

Mark   But her pretty head resting on the yellow silk pillowcase . . .

Tommy   Daein it fae behind . . .

Lizzie   'Daein it fae behind . . .'

Tommy   Ah loved her but.

Lizzie and **Mark** *exchange looks.*

Mark   Aye, well, make that the first and last time.

Tommy   Too fuckin right. Too fuckin right!

They laugh and tussle . . .

Lizzie   Men! Why don't they just fuck each other?

Tommy   Love . . .

Mark   Love . . .

Tommy (*sings*)   '. . . me do. You know –'

Both   '– I love you. I'll always be true. So please . . . love me do-oo.'

Alison *arrives. The boys sit up.*

Alison   Mark says that love doesnae exist. Like God. But I've goat some White Doves!

Tommy   Eckies!

Alison/Tommy   Excellent!

Mark   Alison, Alison, most Ecstasy hasnae goat any MDMA in it.

Alison   This gear is pure freaky but.

Mark   It's just part speed part acid.

Tommy   Lurve!

Alison/Tommy   Lurve!

Mark   Love is like religion. The state wants ye tae believe in that kinday crap so's they kin control ye, n fuck yer heid up.

Alison/Tommy (*sing*)   'Love, love me do. You know . . .'

Mark   Ach, let's do it!

All (*taking the tablets*)   For the fans!

Alison   Let's float ootay here n cross over tae the Meadows.

Tommy   Aye, let's hit the Meadows. Thuv goat a big theatre tent and a funfair.

Music: fairground mix . . .

They go to the fair . . . They go on rides . . . Thrills! They end up lying in the grass . . .

Music fades to distance . . .

Mark   Tam! There's a fuckin squirrel at yir feet.

Tommy   Aw, magic! Wee silvery thing . . .

Alison   C'moan . . .

Mark   Kill the cunt! (*He throws a stone.*)

Tommy   Naw!

Mark   Goan!

Tommy   Leave it man! Squirrel's botherin nae cunt! (*They grapple.*)

Alison (*like a mum with naughty kids*)   Naw, look, see, they wifies, they're lookin at ye!

Mark   C'moan ye wee bastard!

Tommy   Naw, he's daein his ain thing!

Alison   Mark, Tam, c'moan!

Mark   Where the fuck did it go tae?

Alison   See they posh wifies, I'm tellin ye!

Mark (*for the wifies*)   C'moan, Tam, wrap the squirrel in Cellophane so's it doesnae split whin ye fuck it!

Mark *and* **Alison** *cackle . . .*

Mark   What's that foostie-minged fucker starin at? Whit ye cruisin us fir, ye tearoom hags? Ah'd rather stick it between a couple ay sandin blocks, doll!

Alison   Fahk aff! You'd shag the crack ay dawn if it hud hairs oan it!

Mark   Ah could shag a hairy donut the night!

Tussle. Shrieks. **Alison** *and* **Mark** *run off.*

Mark (*returning*)   C'moan, Tam. Fucksakes, man, what is it?

Tommy   Youse wir guannae kill that squirrel.

Mark   'Sony a fuckin squirrel, Tam. Thir vermin.

Tommy   It's mibbe nae mair vermin thin you or me, likesay. Whae's tae say what's vermin? They posh wifies think people like us ur vermin, likesay, does that make it right thit they should kill us?

Mark   Sorry, Tommy. 'Sony a squirrel. Sorry, mate. Ah ken how ye feel aboot animals . . .

Tommy   It's wrong, man . . . Ye cannae love yirsel if ye want tae hurt things like that . . .

Mark   Ah jist, like, ye ken whit ah mean, Tommy, it's like . . .

Tommy   Ah mean . . . what hope is thir?

Mark   . . . fuck, ah'm fucked up, Tommy. Ah dinnae ken.

Tommy   The squirrel's likes fuckin lovely . . .

Mark   Aw the fightin . . . aw the gear . . . the drugs . . .

Tommy   . . . he's daein his ain thing . . . he's free.

Mark   Ah dinnae ken what ah'm daein wi ma life . . . it's aw jist a mess, Tommy. Ah dinnae ken whit the fuckin score is. Sorry, man. Sorry . . .

They hug.

Yir one ay the best, man. Remember that. That's no the drink or the drugs talkin, that's me talkin. It's jist that y get called aw the poofs under the sun if ye tell another guy y love um n yir no pissed.

Alison   Look at mah nipples! They feel fuckin weird! Nay cunt's got nipples like mines!

General chest baring and nipple exploration. **Alison** *and* **Mark** *pinch* **Tommy**'s *nipples.* **Alison** *chases* **Tommy** . . .

Mark   Ah love you guys!

All hug.

Alison   Pinch mah nipples!

They do. All exeunt shrieking . . .
Music: 'Fable (Message)' from Dreamland *by Robert Miles.*
Enter a squirrel . . . exit squirrel.

Interval.

Requiem Aeternam

Mark

Britten's War Requiem: *'Requiem Aeternam' . . . mix to train passing . . . distant gunfire.*
Through haze or smoke, light falls on a coffin covered with a Union Jack. Maybe there is a photo of Billy on top . . .

Radio voice   Another soldier has been shot and killed in Northern Ireland. Lance Corporal William Renton of the Royal Scots Dragoon Guards was twenty-seven. He came from Leith in Edinburgh. The Northern Ireland Secretary condemned the killing as a loathsome and cowardly act. This brings the total number of deaths associated with terrorism in Northern Ireland this year to forty-two. The Economy: the markets closed today at an all-time high, the FTSE index . . .

The night before the funeral.

Mark *enters drunk but grimly coherent, wearing a white shirt hanging out over black jeans.*

Mark   Billy Boy. Billy Boy. Ah remember you: sittin oan top of me. Me helplessly pinned tae the floor. Windpipe constricted to the width of a straw. Praying, as the oxygen drained from ma lungs and brain, that Ma would get back from the shops before you crushed the life oot of ma skinny body. The smell o piss from your genitals . . . the damp patch oan yer short troosers. Was it that exciting, Billy? Ah hope so. Ah cannae really grudge ye it now. Ye always had a problem that way; sudden discharges of faeces and urine that used tae drive Ma tae distraction. So on patrol in Crossmaglen, ye left your armoured car tae examine a road block. Then POW! ZAP! BANG! and ye were deid. ' "He died a hero," they say.' In fact he died a spare prick in a uniform, walking along a country road wi his rifle in his hand, an ignorant tool ay imperialism. That was the biggest crime: you understood fuck all aboot it. You died as you lived: completely fuckin scoobied. You made the *News at Ten*, but. Three minutes ay fame, like a fuckin advert. And some ruling-class cunt, a minister ay some description, says in his cut-glass accent how you were 'a brave young man', and your murderers will be 'ruthlessly hunted down'. Aye, and so they fuckin should be, Billy. All the wey tae the Houses ay fuckin Parliament!

Ken whit the daft cunt turns roond n sais tae us? He goes 'Ah cannae fuckin stick civvy street. Bein in the army, it's like bein a junky.' Just like being a junky . . .

He tucks in shirt, gets out a black tie and half ties it . . .

In the cemetery.

It's weird standin round a grave. Davie Mitchell's here. Jist outay prison. Tommy n aw. (*Stares.*) Tommy's lookin like death . . .

Ma cousin Nina looks intensely shaftable. She's goat long dark hair blowing in the wind and is wearing an ankle-length black coat. Seems tae be a bit ay a Goth. Ah give her a broad wink and she smiles, embarrassed. Ma father's been clocking this and he steams ower tae me. 'Wahn fuckin bit ay crap oot ay you n that's us finished. Right?' His eyes were tired, sunk deep intae their sockets. There was a sad unsettling vulnerability about him ah'd never seen before. Ah wanted tae say so much tae the man. 'Da . . .' But ah resented him fir allowing this circus tae take place. 'Leave it to us,' the softly spoken Army Welfare Officer told Ma. Leave it to us. Ah seethed when ah saw that fuckin Union Jack oan his coffin. (*Rips off the tie.*)

After the funeral.

At the piss-up after we buried him, one ay his squaddy mates sidles up tae me. (*Cockney sentiment:*) 'You were 'is bruvver,' he sais, choppers hingin oot tae dry. Every cunt's eyes focus oan us. 'Billy n me nivir agreed oan that much,' ah sais, 'but one thing we hud in common wis thit we both liked a good bevvy and a good crack. If he can see us now,

he'll be laughin his heid oaf at us standin here aw moosey-
faced. He'll be saying "Enjoy yirsels, fir God sake!"' Ay,
stick tae the clichés. It's the best way tae strike a chord
without compromising too much wi the sickenin hypocrisy
which fills the room. Decency! Ah gie thum all a beery grin.
But ma Uncle Cha-Cha Charlie sees through ma game.

'Listen, son, if you don't get on yir fuckin bike, I'm gonna
tan your jaw. If it wisnae fir yir father thair, ah'd've done it
a long time ago. Yir brother wis ten times the man yull ivir
be, ya fuckin junky. If you knew the misery you've caused
your ma n da –'

'You can speak frankly,' ah cut in.

'Oh, ah'll speak frankly aw right, ye smert cunt. Ah'll knock
ye through that fuckin waw.'

His chunky tattooed fist – the one called HATE – was just a
few inches fae ma face. Ma grip tensed oan the whisky gless
ah wis haudin. If he moved he wis gittin this gless. 'If ye did
gie us a kickin,' ah sais, 'ye'd be daein us a favour. Ah'd jist
huv a wank aboot it later on. We drop-oot university junkies
are kinky that wey. Cause that's aw you're worth, ya fuckin
trash. Ye want tae go ootside, just say the fuckin word.' The
room seemed tae shrink tae the size ay Billy's coffin. The
cunt pushed us gently in the chest, with a fist called LOVE.

'Wuv had wahn funeral in the family the day, wir no wantin
another yin.'

Good story . . . (*He untucks and unbuttons the shirt.*)

Ah went tae the toilet. Sharon wis comin oot. Sharon,
Billy, ur ye listenin? Her face was flushed n bloated with
alcohol . . . and pregnancy. Sharon n me huv mibbe spoken
about half a dozen sentences tae each other, ivir. So ah sais
tae her 'You n me need tae huv a wee blether likes.' N ah
usher her intae the toilet n loak the door behind us. Strange
how death brings the living together. Ah start tae feel her up
. . . while rabbitin a load of shite aboot how we huv tae stick
thegither at a time like this. Ah'm feelin her lump n gaun
oan aboot how much responsibility ah felt taewards ma
unborn niece or nephew. We start kissin, and ah move ma
hand doon, feeling the panty lines through the cotton

material ay her maternity dress. Ah wis soon fingerin her
fanny, and she hud goat me prick oot ay ma troosers. Ah wis
still bullshittin, tellin her that ah'd always admired her as a
person and a woman, which she disnae really need tae hear
because she's gaun doon oan us, bit it's somehow comfortin
tae say. She gies a good blow job. N ah wis thinking, if only
Billy could see us now. It wis the first good thoughts aboot
ye ah'd hud, y cunt. Ah withdraw jist before comin, and
guide Sharon intae the doggy position. Ah love deain it fae
behind. She has a powerful ivy smell. It's a wee bit like
throwing the proverbial sausage up a tunnel, but ah find ma
stroke and she tightens up. They say that a shag is good for
an unborn child, circulation of blood or that. Ah can see
mahsel, stickin it in the bairn's mooth –

A knock on the door! Auntie Effie's high nasal voice:

'Whit yes daein in thair?'

''Sawright, Sharon's bein sick. Too much bevvy in her
condition.'

'Ur you seein tae her, son?'

'Aye . . . ah'm seein tae hur.'

'Awright well.'

Ah blurt oot ma muck n pull oot. Ah gently push hur
prostrate, helping her turn ower, and scoop her huge milky
tits oot ay her dress. Ah snuggle intae them like a bairn. She
starts strokin ma heid. Ah feel wonderful, so at peace.

'That wis fuckin barry.'

'Will we keep seein each other now, then, eh?'

Fucksake!

'Wuv tae git up, Sharon, git cleaned up, likes, ken? They
widnae understand if they caught us. Ah know that you're a
good lassie, Sharon, but they dinnae understand fuck all.'

'Ah ken you're a nice laddie.'

She was caught in this git-a-man git-a-bairn git-a-hoose
shite that lassies get drummed intae them; mashed tattie fir
brains.

Ah took her back tae ma flat. We jist talked. She telt us a
load ay things thit ah wanted tae hear, things ma ma n
faither never knew, and wid hate tae know. How you were a

cunt tae her, Billy. How ye battered her, humiliated her,
and generally treated her like a piece of shite. 'Whit did ye
stey wi um fir?' ah asked. And she sais . . . she sais 'He wis
ma felly. Ye eywis think it'll be different, thit ye kin change
thum, thit ye kin make a difference.' Aw Billy?!

He kicks the coffin. It collapses into planks and chairs.

Music: a loan piper plays 'Amazing Grace' . . .

Aw fucksakes! Billy! Ah didnae –

He pulls off his shirt and shoots up . . .

'If ye did gie us a kickin, ye'd be daein us a favour. Ah'd jist
have a wank aboot it later on. We drop-oot junkies are
kinky that wey. Cause that's aw you're worth, ya fuckin
trash. Ye want tae go ootside, just say the fuckin word.' The
room seemed tae shrink tae the size ay Billy's coffin. 'Wuv
had wahn funeral in the family the day, wir no wan –' Ah!
Ah! Fu- fu-

He blacks out.

Blackout.

Dies Irae

Mother, Mark

Mother   Ah'll help ye, son! Ah'll help ye fight this disease!

Lights up.

Sound: 'Amazing Grace' is playing on the radio . . .

Mark *is slumped on the floor or in a chair.* **Mother** *tucks a duvet
round him.*

Mother   Ah've loast one laddie already, ah'm no losin
another yin! Ye'll stay here wi me n yir faither until yir
better. Wir gonnae beat this, son, wir gonnae beat it.

She switches off the radio.

They played that at the funeral. 'Amazin Grace'. (*Exits.*)

Mark   Ma heid struggles to piece togither how ah goat here. Ah can remember Johnny Swan's place . . . then feeling like ah wis gaunnae die. Then Johnny n Alison takin us doon the stairs, gittin us intae a taxi n bombin up tae the Infirmary. Overdose. Takes yer breath away. They must've given thum ma ma's address. N here ah am. In the junky's limbo, too sick tae sleep, too tired tae stay awake. A twilight zone where nothin's real. 'I'll help ye, son! Wir gonnae beat this disease . . .'

Mother (*brings tray*)   Ye'll git through it though, son. Doctor Mathews sais it's jist really like a bad flu. (*Exits.*)

Mark   When wis the last time auld Mathews hud cauld turkey? Ah'd like tae lock that dangerous auld radge in a padded cell fir a fortnight, and gie um a couple ay injections ay diamorphine a day, then leave the cunt fir a few days. He'd be beggin us fir it eftir that. Ah'd jist shake ma heid and say 'Take it easy, mate. What's the fuckin problem? It's jist like a bad flu.' Did he gie us temazepam?

Mother (*brings ketchup*)   Naw! Ah telt um, nane o that rubbish. Ye wir worse comin oaf that thin ye wir wi heroin. Ye wir in a hell ay a state. Nae mair drugs.

Mark   Mibbe ah could go back tae the clinic, Ma?

Mother   Naw! Nae clinics. Nae methadone. That made ye worse, son, ye said so yirsel. (*Exits.*)

Mark   Aw Christ! Dinnae let this be happenin tae me . . .

Mother (*brings meal*)   Ye lied tae us, son. Tae yir ain mother n faither. Ye took that methadone n still went oot scorin. Fae now oan, son, it's a clean brek. Yir stayin here whair ah kin keep an eye oan ye.

She gives him a plate piled with mince and mashed potatoes.

Ah've lost one laddie already. Ah'm no losin another yin!
(*She has a wee private weep* . . .)

Mark   Ma . . . ah've telt ye . . . ah don't eat meat.

Mother   Aw! Ye eywis liked yir mince n tatties!
That's whair ye've gone wrong, son, no eating the right
things. Ye need meat. It's good steak mince. (*With a forkful of
mince:*) Come on, son, make a tunnel for the choo-choo . . .
remember?

Mark   No Mummy no!

Mark *takes a fit and crashes to the floor.*

Sound: loud train . . . Lights: weird . . .

Mother *transforms into* **Franco**.

In a hospital.

Sound: Steady train, interior . . .

Franco   Oan the train gaun doon tae London, Mark sits
doon beside two burds. Fuckin tidy n aw. Good fuckin
choice. 'These seats are free until Darlington,' he sais,
lookin at the fuckin reservation cairds stickin oot the tops ay
the seats. Fuckin liberty, so it is. It should be first come, first
fuckin served. Aw this bookin seats shite . . . ah'll gie the
cunts bookin seats. Ah fuckin grabs the cairds n sticks thum
in ma tail – 'Thir fuckin free the whole wey doon now,' ah
sais, smilin at one ay the burds. Too fuckin right n aw. Sixty
quid a ticket. No shy they British Rail cunts, uh?

He steals a look at **Mark**. *He is telling the story to get* **Mark** *to
snap out of a coma. He speaks louder, to the whole train.*

If ah had ma fuckin wey, the train wouldnae stoap for aw
they cunts thit've booked fae Berwick n aw they fuckin
places; it wid jist be Edinburgh tae London that wid be it,
end ay fuckin story!!! Aw they cunts wi backpacks n luggage
n bairns' fuckin go-carts. Shouldnae huv bairns oan a fuckin
train. Ah speak ma fuckin mind, whitivit any cunt sais!
Mark jist shrugs his shoodirs. He keeps lookin ower at the

burds, thir likesay American, ken. Problem wi that smert cunt is thit he jist cannae really fuckin relate tae burds. Ye wait oan that cunt tae make the first fuckin move, ye'll be waitin a long fuckin time. Ah fuckin show the smert cunt how it's done. 'No fuckin shy, they British Rail cunts, eh?' ah sais, nudgin the burd next tae us.

Mark (*not moving. Canadian girl:*)   'Pardawn?'

Franco   Foreign cunts. 'Whair's it yis come fae then?'

Mark (*Canadian girl*)   'Excuse me, I don't really understand yew.'

Franco   Foreign cunts've got trouble wi the Queen's fuckin English, ken. Ye huv tae speak louder, slower, mair posh likes. 'WHERE . . . DAE . . . YEZ . . . COME . . . FAE?'

Mark (*Canadian girl*)   'Toronto.'

Franco   'Tirawnto. That wis the Lone Ranger's mate, wis it no?' The burds jist look it us. Some punters dinnae understand the Scottish sense ay humour.

Mark (*Canadian girl*)   'Where are you from?'

Franco   – other burd asks us. 'Total wee ride . . . fuckin shag the erse ofay that any day ay the week . . . the fuckin erse oan it . . . the fuckin tits oan it . . .' (*In danger of mounting Mark . . .*) Where . . . are . . . you . . . from . . .?

Mark (*sitting up*)   'Edinburgh.'

Sound: train effect stops.

Lights: normal . . .

Franco   Ah! Aw ready tae steam in now once Franco breks the fuckin ice! 'Edinburgh'!

Mark *lost but found . . .* **Franco** *moved but tough . . .*

Franco (*fondly*)   Cunt.

Mark *clings to* **Franco** . . .

Franco (*a surge of protectiveness, anger, compassion* . . .) These burds are gaun oantay us aboot how fuckin beautiful Edinburgh is, and how lovely the fuckin castle is oan the hill ower the gairdins n aw that shite. That's aw they tourist cunts ken though, the castle n Princes Street, n the High Street. Like whin Tommy's auntie came ower fae that wee village oan that island oaf the west coast, with all her bairns. The wifey goes up tae the council fir a hoose. The council sais tae her 'Whair's it ye want tae fuckin stey, like?' The wifey sais –

Mark (*wifey*)   'Ah want a wee hoose oan Princes Street lookin ontay the castle.'

Franco   Aye! This wifey's fuckin scoobied likes, speaks the fuckin Gaelic as a first language, disnae even ken that much English. Perr cunt jist liked the look ay the street whin she came oaf the train, thoat the whole fuckin place wis like that. The cunts at the council jist laugh n stick the cunt in one ay they fuckin rabbit hutches in West Granton, thit nae cunt else wants. Instead ay a view ay the castle, she's goat a view ay the gasworks. That's how it fuckin works in real life, if ye urnae a rich cunt wi a big fuckin hoose n plenty poppy. (*Tears in his eyes*) Real life uh?

Mark   Ya get knocked down.

Franco   But ye get up again.

Mark   Thir nivir gonna keep ye down!

Franco   I get knocked down.

Mark   But ah get up again.

Both   They're never gonna keep me down!

Sound: add Chumbawumba's 'Tubthumping'.

They link up and go off singing along with the song . . .

Offertorium

Alison

*Enter **Alison** as waitress.*

*Sound: Chumbawumba keeps going till **Alison** looks up to the control box pleadingly. Then it changes to quiet jazz, e.g. Miles Davis: 'There Is No Greater Love'.*

During her speech, she cleans the stage.

Alison   Ah'm workin. In a restaurant bar. It's one o they quiet nights. Ma manager, Graham, is in the kitchen preparing food that he hopes somebody will eat. Three guys come intae the restaurant. Obviously drunk. They sit doon at a table n order.

(*London lad accent:*)   'A couple of bottles of your best piss!' English settlers. Ah smile at them, though. Ye huv tae learn tae treat people as people. One sais tae another: 'What d'you call a good-looking girl in Scotland?'

N another wan sais: 'A tourist!'

Then wan sais, gesturing in ma direction: 'I dunno though. I wouldn't kick that out of bed!'

Doss prick. Ah cannae afford tae lose this joab. Ah need the money.

'Orroit, darlin?' he sais, studying the menu: dark-haired skinny wanker wi a long fringe. 'Orroit?' Ah dinnae need this shite. Takin the order is a nightmare. Thir havin a loud conversation aboot careers, computers, marketing, life in the fast lane . . . in between trying tae humiliate me. The skinny wanker actually asks us whit time ah finish, n the rest make whooping noises and dae drum rolls on the table. D'ye undersand how ah feel? Whin ah get in the kitchen ah'm shakin wi rage. 'Can ye no git these fuckin arseholes ootay here?' ah sais tae Graham.

'Business, Alison, business,' he says. 'The customer, ma dear, is always right – even if he is a knob-end.'

'Ah wish thit Louise or Marisa was on tonight, another woman tae talk tae. Ah'm smack-bang in the middle ay a heavy period n ah'm feelin that scraped out n drained awey.

She has finished cleaning up now.

Ah go tae the toilet n change tampons, wrapping the used one up in some toilet paper. A couple of thum's ordered orange and tomato soup. Ah stroll into the kitchen. Graham's busy at the microwave. So ah take the bloodied tampon and lower it intae the first bowl ay soup. Like a tea bag. Ah squeeze it with a fork. A couplay strands ay black uteral lining float in the soup, before being dissolved wi a healthy stir. Ah deliver the pâté starter and the two orange and tomato soups tae the table, making sure that the skinny gelled-up fuckwit has goat the spiked one. 'More wine!' the fat, fair-heided prick petulantly booms at us. They're talking about how terribly hoat it is in Hawaii, makes ye sweat like a pig. More wine? Ah go back tae the lavvy and fill a saucepan wi urine. Ma urine has that stagnant, cloudy look which suggests a urinary tract infection. Ah add some tae the carafe ay wine. Looks a bit cloudy but they're so smashed they winnae notice. Ah pour some more ay ma pish ontae the fish. It's a fennel sauce, ah think. It's a fanny sauce now. But they pricks eat and drink everything withoot even noticing! It's hard tae shite ontae a piece of paper. No, it is. Ah jist manage a wee runny turd, which ah take through and whizz up wi some cream in the liquidiser, and then merge wi the chocolate sauce heating away in the pan. Profiteroles. Profiteroles all round! It's a loat easier tae keep smilin now. Ah feel charged wi a great power! The fat bastard hus drawn the really short straw. His ice cream is laced wi rat poison. No, ground-up traces of broken glass . . . Naw . . . Too radge . . . It's all too mad . . . (*It was just a story* . . .) What fucken planet are we oan?

Sanctus

Alison, Tommy, Franco, Mark

Music: 'The Road to Hell' by Chris Rea from same-name album.
When the music reaches the drone effect, the drone is looped and then
plays under the whole scene . . .

Alison   It's five o'clock in the morning. The old pub
between the brewery and the hospital has just opened up.
It's raining.

Enter **Tommy**, *suffering . . .*

Tommy   Laura McEwan. Lorra McEwaaan! Sounds
barry likesay. 'Ah don't want ye tae hurt me . . . the minute
ah start tae feel pain it's fuckin over.' Oooh!

He sees **Alison**.

Lizzie . . . Ah split up wi Lizzie!

Enter **Franco** *and* **Mark**, *staggering drunk . . .*

Franco   . . . so ah'm oan toap ay this burd, ken, cowpin it
likes, gaun fuckin radge, n it's fuckin screamin likes n ah
thinks fuck me this dirty cow's right intae it likes –

Tommy   Fuckin weird, man . . .

Franco   Fuck off!

Mark   Tam?

Franco   Fuckin junky . . .

Mark   Tam! How ye daein, man?

Tommy   Fuckin weird . . . you n me . . .

Mark   Whit ye drinkin?

Tommy   Naw . . . Goat any smack?

Mark   Fucksake, Tommy. Forget it, man. Leave it alane while ye still can.

Tommy   Ah can handle it. Are ye cairryin?

Mark   Ah'm clean now.

Tommy   Aw . . .

Mark *gives* **Tommy** *money* . . . **Tommy** *leaves.*

Franco   'Kin junkie! Anywey ah thinks fuck me this dirty cow's right intae it likes, but it pushes us oaf, ken n she's bleedin ootay her fanny ken, like it's fuckin rag week, n ah'm aboot tae say, that disnae bother me, specially no wi a fuckin root oan like ah hud, ah'm fuckin tellin ye. Anywey, it turns oot thit the cunt is huvin a fuckin miscarriage thair n then! Is that no funny?

Mark   How's June?

Franco   Who?

Alison   'June,' he said, 'how's June?' Remember? 'Who?'

Franco   How's Alison . . . eh?

Mark   Wee Dawn, wee Dawn . . . Fucking shame, cot death . . .

Franco   Ach, the bairn wid huv died ay fuckin AIDS if it hudnae died ay coat death. Easier fuckin death fir a bairn.

Mark   She didnae huv HIV!

Franco   O. Whae's tae fuckin say? Whae's tae fuckin say?!

Mark (*caving in*)   Nae cunt really kens . . .

Franco   Aye, right . . . (*He falls on his arse and flakes out.*)

Alison   Ye can lose them at any time. Before they're even born. Even eftir thir born, ye lose them. Ma Auntie Jeannie sais thit eftir they're seven you lose them. Then jist whin ye think ye've adjusted, it happens again when they're fourteen. And then . . . then the heroin. 'Ah'll help ye, son, ah'll help ye fight this disease. Wir gaunnae beat it, son, wir gaunnae beat it.' But the bairn's away, the bairn's away.

Music: drone fades.

Agnus Dei

Alison, Mark, Tommy, Franco

Tommy *enters naked, with a lit candle. He cooks up.*

Alison   O! O son . . .! O son . . . Hail Mary full of grace, the Lord is with thee, blessed art thou among women and blessed is the fruit of thy womb, Jesus. Holy Mary, Mother of God, pray for us sinners now and in the hour of our death . . .

Tommy *shoots into his penis.*

Alison   Nawww!

Tommy *collapses.*

Alison   Mark. Ye smert cunt. Ken thit Tommy's sick?!

Mark   Aye. Ah heard.

Alison   Go n fuckin see the cunt. Go n fuckin see the cunt!

Mark   How ye feelin?

Tommy   No bad. Cold but.

Mark (*puts his coat round his shoulders*)   Yir lookin well.

Tommy   Ah'm gaunnae die.

Mark   Sometime in the next fifteen years. Ye can step out in the street under a fuckin bus. Want tae talk aboot it?

Tommy   No really. See whit they painted oan ma door?

Mark   Wee fuckin saps.

Tommy   'Junky'. 'Plaguer'.

Mark   Draftpak kids, thull harass anybody.

Tommy   You took the test?

Mark   Aye.

Tommy   Clear?

Mark   Aye.

Tommy   You used mair than me. And ye shared works. Sick Boy's, Spud's, Swanney's . . . Davie's fir fucksake. Tell us ye nivir used Davie Mitchell's works!

Mark   Ah nivir shared, Tommy.

Tommy   Bullshit! Cunt! You fuckin shared!

Mark   Ah nivir shared . . .

Tommy   Ah used tae sit n huv a bevvy wi Franco an a laugh at yis, call yis aw the daft cunts under the sun, fuckin junky. Then ah split fae Lizzie, mind? Went tae your bit. Ah asked ye fir a hit. Ah thoat, fuck it, ah'll try anythin once. Been tryin it once ivir since.

Mark   See . . . some cunts are so . . . predisposed tae smack.

Tommy   Ah dinnae ken whit tae fuckin dae, Mark. Whit am ah gaunnae dae?

Mark   Really sorry, Tommy . . .

Tommy   Goat any gear?

Mark   Ah'm clean now, Tommy.

Tommy   Sub us then, mate. Ah'm expectin a rent cheque.

Mark *puts down money.* **Tommy** *takes it and leaves, throwing the coat back at* **Mark**.

Mark   Aw Tommy. Aw fucksakes. Ah didnae –

Ah wanted tae say 'Git oan wi yir life. It's aw ye can dae. Look eftir yirself.' But he willnae live fifteen, ten or even five years before he's crushed by pneumonia or cancer. He's blown things wi his ma n she's chucked him oot n he's here, in a fuckin rabbit hutch. Fifteen thousand people oan the waitin list but naebody wanted this one. It's a prison. He'll nae survive the winter. I'm sorry, man. Ah'm so fuckin sorry.

Music: the drone returns . . .

Franco   Ah'm fuckin Lee Marvin! Let's git some scran – and then hit a decent fuckin boozer. Cummoan.

Mark *blows out* **Tommy**'s *candle.*

Franco   Cummoan!

Franco *and* **Mark** *leave.*

Libera Me

Alison

Alison   Whair ur ye gaun? Whair ur ye gaun?

Music: the drone gets louder and louder . . .

'Gaun tae the match, gaun tae the gig, gaun tae the pub wi mah mates, gaun doon tae London fir a few days, goat tae nash, gaun tae the airmy, tae Belfast, intae Bosnia, tae get doon tae some serious swedgin, ah wis fuckin game fir a swedge, cummon ye crappin bastards! Ye big-moothed cunt, yecuntchy, yecuntchy, cunt, cunt, cunt –

Music: drone cuts out.

Lights: daylight.

Alison   Ah'm walkin down the street, n ah meet up wi
Lizzie. N these guys, workies, up oan their scaffolding,
whistle at us.
'Awright, doll?'
Lizzie's been doon tae see about her rent arrears n she's
pretty mad, like, tense n that, cos she turns oan the guy:
'Huv you goat a girlfriend?' she shouts. 'Ah doubt it,
because yir a fat ugly prick!'
Aye! The guy looks at her wi real hate, I mean, now he's
goat a reason tae hate her, no jist cos she's a woman ken.
The guy's mates are gaun 'Whoooah, whoooah!' eggin him
oan.
'Fuck off ya boot,' he snarls.
But she disnae, she stands her ground. 'O, ah wis a doll a
minute ago,' she cries, 'but now ah've telt ye tae fuck oaf
ah'm a boot. Well, you're still a fat ugly prick, son, and
that's no gaunnae change!'
(*Aussie*) 'And so say all of us!' – Australian lassie, wi a
backpack. A pair of thum. A few folk have stopped tae check
oot the hassle.
'Fuckin dykes!' another guy shouts.
Noo, that gets right oan ma tits, getting called a dyke jist cos
ah object tae bein hassled by revolting ignorant radges. 'If
all guys wir as repulsive as you, ah'd be fuckin proud tae be
a lesbian, son!' Did ah really say that? Crazy!
(*Aussie*) 'You guys have obviously got a problem. Why don't
you just go and fuck each other?'
Quite a crowd has now gathered. Two auld wifies are
listening in. 'That's terrible,' says one, 'lassies talkin like that
tae the laddies.'
'Och,' says the other wan, 'it's guid tae see lassies stickin up
fir thirsels. Wish it happened in ma day. Aye,' – she sais tae
me – 'ah wish ah wis your age again, hen, ah'd dae it aw
different, ah kin tell ye.'
The guys are looking embarrassed, really shit up by the
crowd. The foreman comes out. 'Back inside, yous!' And
they go, like sheep. And we aw let oot a cheer. It wis
brilliant! Magic!

Me and Lizzie and the two Aussies and the two wifies all end up in the Café Rio havin cups ay tea thegither. The Aussies actually turned oot tae be New Zealanders, Veronica and Jane. They *were* lesbians! Travelling round the world thegither. Ah'd love tae gie that a go. Me and Lizzie. Too mad.

We take them back tae ma flat fir a smoke ay hash. N we sit there slaggin oaf men — stupid inadequate creatures wi flat bodies and weird heids and dangling tubes. All thir guid fir is the odd shag.

Sometimes ah wish ah wis gay. Dae it aw different.

What planet are we oan?

Requiescant in Pace

Alison, Franco, Mark, Drunk

Sound: a ghostly train passes, echoing . . .

Franco   Lesh go fir a pish!

Alison   Three men meet in the ruins of old Leith Central Station. Franco, Mark and the old drunkard who sleeps there.

Franco   Some size ay a station this wis. Git a train tae anywhere fae here at one time, so they sais.

Mark (*nothing left to say any more . . .*)   Aye.

Franco   If it still hud fuckin trains, ah'd be oan one ah kin tell ye, oot ay this fuckin dive.

Mark   Aye.

Franco   Real life, uh?

Drunk   What yis up tae lads? What yis up tae? Ye trainspottin, ur ye?

Franco   Aye. That's right!

Drunk   Ah well, ah'll leave yis tae it.

Franco *grabs him, peers at his face and decks him.*

Drunk   Trainspottin . . .

Mark   Ah seen hum before.

Franco   Ma father.

Mark   Whit?

Franco   He's ma father. He's ma fuckin shitein father!

[Ending #1]

Mark and **Franco** *piss . . . on the drunk . . . and laugh with joy . . .*
Franco *falls on his arse.*

Mark   Tommy . . .

Alison (*sings*)
    My life goes on in endless song
    Above earth's lamentation,
    I hear the real though far-off hymn
    That hails a new creation.
    Through all the tumult and the strife
    I hear its music ringing,
    It sounds an echo in my soul:
    How can I keep from singing?

    What though the tempest loudly roars,
    I hear the truth, it liveth.
    And though the darkness round me close,
    Songs in the night it giveth.
    No storm can shake my inmost calm,
    While to that rock I'm clinging.
    Since love is lord of heaven and earth
    How can I keep from singing?

[*Optional music: 'Last Train to Gran Central' by the KLF, during
which lights fade slowly to black . . . Then calls . . .*]

[Ending #2]

Mark *pisses earlier in the scene, as he says, 'Aye . . . Aye . . .'*
Franco *alone pisses on his father . . . and* **Mark** *edges away . . .*

There is a typewriter on stage. **Mark** *ends up sitting at it, by*
Alison, *who's smoking, drinking coffee, whatever. For the first time*
we see a more or less normal domestic moment . . .

Mark *types a word.*

Mark   'Trainspotting'. (*Thinks.*) 'Ah woke up in a strange
bed, in a strange room, covered in ma own mess . . .' (*He
glances at* **Alison**.)

Alison *manages a smile . . .*

Mark *types away . . .*

Music . . .

Fadeout . . .

End.

Irvine Welsh's

Marabou Stork Nightmares

Adapted by Harry Gibson

Characters

The play may be performed by any number of actors.

The first version did not include Dorrie and was played by five actors, one playing all the female roles. The revival added a sixth to play Dorrie only. This version can be played by seven (one non-speaking), doubling as follows.

1
Doctor 1
John Strang
Winston
Tony Strang
Lexo
Hammy
Paramedic

2
Doctor 2
Verity Strang
Nurse
Dorrie

3
Roy Strang

4
Male nurse 1
Bernard Strang
Cabbie
Demps
Gilly
Alan
Paramedic

5
Male nurse 2
Gordon Strang
Sandy
Ozzy
Skelly
Brian
Paramedic

6
Kim Strang
Caroline
Kirsty

7
Boys
Policeman
Barmen

Author's Notes

I wrote and directed this adaptation of Irvine Welsh's novel (published 1995) for the Citizens Theatre Company, Glasgow, who first performed it on 1 March 1996 with designs by Suzanne Field and lighting by Michael Lancaster. I directed a revised version at the Haymarket Theatre, Leicester, in September 1996, designed by Charles Cusick-Smith with lighting by Chris Ellis. The cast was as follows:

Roy	James Cunningham
Sandy, **Gordon**, **Ozzy**, *etc.*	Stuart Bowman/Gavin Marshall (Leic)
Bernard, **Demps**, *etc.*	Christopher Delaney
John, **Tony**, **Lexo**, *etc.*	John Kazek
Vet, **Kim**, **Kirsty**, *etc.*	Joanna Macleod
Dorothy	Lenny McEwan (Leic)

It was peformed in the main 700-seat auditorium on a single large set with moving parts, representing Roy's hospital room, the Strang living room, a dream African landscape, the veranda of Uncle Gordon's house in Johannesburg, a camp in the African bush, an exterior concourse in a Muirhouse housing estate, a nightclub interior, roof garden and car park, waste ground on Crammond Island, a courtroom, the Leith riverside, the bedroom in Roy's flat, 'a place between heaven and earth', etc. Flying and traps were used, and sound and light plots were elaborate. The epic style perfectly evoked the multiple layers of reality at work within Roy's coma-dream: the colour and the spectacle worked along with the humour to relieve the intensity of the subject matter. The sell-out productions received rave reviews, though some critics were troubled by the violence.

No doubt it can be performed more simply, in a studio theatre, and I would be happy to revise the script.

Harry Gibson

Music used in the productions included:

Ballads

Nat King Cole singing *Nature Boy*
Matt Munro singing *Born Free*
Elaine Paige singing *Nobody Does It Better*
Dinah Washington singing *Mad About the Boy* and
    What a Difference a Day Makes

Classical

Janacek's *Cunning Little Vixen* Suite (Andante II)
Taverner's *The Protecting Veil* (Section 1)
Wagner's *Ride of the Valkyries*

Dance

React 2 Rhythm: *Intoxication*
Robert Miles: *Uncle Bob's Burley House*
Underworld: *Born Slippy* (Pete Tong remix)

Radio/TV/Film

Housewives' Choice (signature tune)
Casualty (signature tune)
Inspector Morse (Painful Admissions)
Indiana Jones (main theme)
Once Upon a Time in America (Friendship & Love)
Vertigo (Prelude & Rooftop)

Tribal

Balinese choric chant: *Ketjak*
Burundi drumming
Ghanaian songs

Part One

Doctor 1 Mr Strang has been in a vegetative state for nearly two years now. We try to reach him but . . .

Doctor 2 Okay, Roy?

Doctor 1 Roy, I'm shining this torch in your eyes.

Doctor 2 Pupil dilation seems more evident.

Doctor 1 We're definitely getting some sort of reaction.

Doctor 2 I wouldn't be surprised if he could hear us.

Doctors Roy . . . Roy . . . Roy . . .

Roy Fuck oaf n die, ya cunts!

Doctor 1 There's definitely increased sign of brain activity.

Doctor 2 I wouldn't be surprised if he could hear us.

Roy They're tryin tae disturb me, tryin tae wake me. They willnae let this sleeping dog lie. When the cunts start this shite it makes things get aw distorted. I lose control.

Nurse 1 Good morning, Nurse Norton!

Nurse 2 Good morning, Nurse Devine!

Nurses Morning, Roy!

Nurse 2 He's looking brighter this morning, Nurse Devine.

Nurse 1 Yes, you're brighter this morning, Roy lovey . . .

Nurse 2 Time for Number Twos!

Roy O, git ootay ma fuckin erse!

Nurse 1 Clench your teeth and open wide!

Roy Tryin tae stick another tube up ma fuckin – Aaargh!

Nurse 2   Sposed tae be in a fuckin coma, ya cunt!

Roy   Aahh . . .

Nurse 1   Ya love it don't ya, ye wee poof, up yir fuckin erse!

Roy   Mammehhhh! . . .
O fuck! Thir here!
Daddy, nice to see you. Is it fuck.
Mummy, aw Mummy! Fuck off and die.
Thir always fuckin here.
Dae they no have proper fuckin visitin hours in this hoaspital?

John   Awright, son? How ye daein? Eh? Awright? Disnae seem two whole years yuv been in yir vegetative state, Roy. Two years since yer accident. Like ah sais your accident, Roy.

Vet *sobs.*

John   That's us in another final, Roy. One-nil. Another final. Barry goal an aw. Darren Jackson.

Vet   Japs!

John   Whit?

Vet *stares.*

John   Whit's wrong, Vet?

Vet   There's a Jap ower there, John.

John   It's just a nurse, Vet, just a nurse. Probably no even a Jap. Probably a Chinky or somethin.
Eh, son? Just a nurse ah'm sayin, son. Eh, Roy?

Vet   A Chunky?

John   Ay the wee Chinky nurse. Nice lassie. Eh, son? Looking better the day though, son. Mair colour. Like ah sais, eh Vet, like ah sais Roy's goat mair aboot um.

Vet They nivir git it. Every other poor bugger gits it, but they nivir git it.

John Eh? Whit ye oan aboot?

Vet AIDS. Ye nivir se Japs wi AIDS. Here wuv goat it. In America thuv goat it. In India thuv goat it. In Africa thuv got it. Oor Bernard might huv it. No thaim, though. They nivir git it.

John Chinky nurse. Nice wee lassie.

Vet Ken how? Ken how they nivir git it.

John Vet, this husnae goat nowt tae dae wi –

Vet Cause they inventit it! They inventit the disease! Soas they could take ower the world!

John You fuckin stupit or somethin? Talkin like that in front ay Roy! Ye dinnae ken whit the laddie kin hear, how it effects um! Like ah sais, ye fuckin stupit?

Vet Aw son! Awww! (*Runs off crying . . .*)

John Ah'm askin ye! Ye fuckin stupit? (*Runs after her . . .*)

Roy Ah grew up in what was not so much a family as a genetic disaster. Ma old man was a total basket case. The old girl was, if anything, worse. Before they were due to get married she had a sort of mental breakdown. Her first mental breakdown. Now it's hard to tell when she's *not* having one. Her father had been a prisoner of war in a Japanese camp. He had gone a bit loopy. He filled her head with tales of Jap atrocities. Then she had read a book in which it was claimed that the Yellow Peril would take over the world. Ah nivir stood a chance.

Vet (*singing*) The minute you walked in the joint –

Roy Fucksake.

Vet I could see you were a man of distinction,
    A real big spender. Good-looking, so refined –
    Wouldn't you like to know what's going on in my –

John Whit ar ye daein, Vet? Whit the fuck are ye pleyin at?

Vet Mind they sais, John, mind they sais that ah could sing tae him, mind he eywis liked us singing 'Big Spender' when he was a bairn. Ah could make up a tape ay me singing 'Big Spender', John, get Tony to play the guitar n that, pit it oan ays headphones, John, git through tay the laddie's brain n that . . . Aw Christ!

Roy Fucksake, I don't want to be part of your ugly world! I want to go deeper, deeper . . . Africa . . . Africa! Sandy! Sandeee!

Sandy *enters impressively and does cool things . . .*

Roy It was just me and Sandy, Sandy Jamieson, just us, on this journey through this strange land . . . Sandy is a former professional footballer. But now he is an experienced hunter of man-eating beasts.

Sandy Gosh, Roy, this is a strange little performance.

Roy Down here inside my secret world, Sandy Jamieson is my best friend . . .

Sandy Here we are, old chap . . .

Roy . . . the best friend I've ever had!

Sandy . . . in deepest, darkest Africa . . .

Roy We're here to hunt the stork . . .

Sandy . . . steaming down the strong brown river . . .

Roy . . . the evil ugly marabou!

Sandy The marabou is a dangerous and formidable opponent, and we're alone and isolated in hostile terrain.

Roy Gosh!

Sandy These waters are infested with sharks.

Roy Golly!

Sandy   And the bloody boat's sinking!

Roy   Jeepers!

Sandy   Good thinking, Roy! Jeep! Jeep!

Both   Go, go, go! (*They make racing-car sounds . . .*)

Sandy   I say Roy, look out, the dog, the dog!

Roy   Winston!

They hit the dog and drive on, laughing crazily . . .

Sandy   The marabou stork is one of the major dangers to the pretty pink flamingo. The stork walks along the shore causing flamingo flocks to panic. It then makes a short flight and stabs a selected flamingo in the back. Once disabled, the flamingo is drowned and then torn to pieces and eaten by one or several marabous in three to four minutes. Bad bastards.

Roy   Sandy! Look!

Sandy   Marabou! They were standing in the rubbish by the lakeside: the black wings, the reddish throat . . . the legs stained white with dried excrement . . . the scabs of dried blood round the base of the long sharp bill.

Roy   I feel sick . . . It's horrible . . .

Sandy   Just lie perfectly still . . .

Roy   Holy cow!

Sandy   They're flying!

Squawking . . .

We're under attack!

Roy   Cover me, cover me! Aargh! Hib boys, ya fuckin cunts, Europe's numero uno! Fucking ratshaggin bastards!

Both   Whoah! Nyaah! (*They are on a helicopter, probably made from a rotary clothes airer . . .*)

Sandy   Marabou coming in at six o'clock!

Roy   Fire missiles!

Sandy   Lock on!

Roy   Fire, fire, fire!

Sandy   It's no good, there's too many of them! Eject!

Both   Eject, eject!

They parachute down . . .

Sandy   Damn and flipping blast!

Roy   Ya cunts!

Both   Game over.

Sandy   I'm all sweaty now.

Roy   It was just me and Sandy. Just boys . . .

Sandy   Let's go for a dip in the lake.

Roy   Just the two of us . . .

Sandy   Roy old chap –

Roy   . . . Why?

Sandy   You coming? Are you? Coming? (*He starts to strip . . .*)

Music: 'Mad About the Boy'.

Roy   Naw. It wisnae like that. It wisnae – like – that! (*He dives back into bed . . .*)

Gordon (*South African*)   Roy? Are you sleeping, Roy?

Ozzy (*Muirhouse*)   In Muirhouse nay cunt can hear ye scream.

Ambulance siren.

John   Awright. We're away now, son. Yir ma n me. Like ah sais that's us away now, Roy. Cheerio, son!

Vet   Cheerio, Roy! Cheerio, darlin . . .

John   Like yir ma sais, that's us sayin cheerio. Seeya the morn, son. Ah'll be in in the morn. Cheerio, Roy!

Vet   Hey Big Spender, spend a little time with me, eh? (*She leaves, sobbing.*)

John   That's some fuckin woman. Your mother. A fuckin great woman. The best yir ever likely tae find. Youse remember that. Whativir else yis dae, yis eywis treat that fuckin woman wi respect, like ah sais, respect. Cos that's the best fuckin woman yis are ever likely tae see in yir fucking life. Your fuckin Mother!
Ah ken what they cunts think ay us. Ah ken aw they cunts. Ken what they are? Ah'll fuckin tell ye what they are. Rubbish. Not fuckin quoted. JOHN STRANG'S MA NAME! FUCK YIS AW, YA CUNTS! ANY BASTARD IN THIS FUCKIN SCHEME'S GOAT ANYTHING TAE SAY TAE ME OR MA FAIMLAY, YIS KIN SAY IT TAE MA FUCKIN FACE! CUNTS!

Roy   I was born in a block of flats.
Five storeys of rabbit hutches.
Concrete stairs n balconies.
Dimpled glass n wire doors.
We lived in a concentration camp for the poor.
Inside our house it was chaos.

Glass smash.

Vet   Aw, Christ!

Roy   My old man was a basket case, completely away wi it.

John   ANY BASTARD IN THIS FUCKIN SCHEME'S GOAT ANYTHING TAE SAY TAE ME OR MA FAIMLAY, YIS KIN SAY IT TAE MA FUCKIN FACE!

Roy   He patrolled the area late at night with a shotgun under his big brown fur coat accompanied by his faithful Alsatian, an ugly evil beast called Winston.

Winston (John*) pads on stage.*

Roy   I was eight years old when it happened: when I was attacked – for the first time. I was watching a *Superboy* cartoon on the television. I decided that Winston was Krypto the Superdog and I tied a towel to his collar to simulate Krypto's cape. The beast freaked out and turned on me, savaging my leg. Aaargh! The cunt savaged my leg so badly that I needed skin grafts at the hoaspital.

Ambulance siren.

Winston/John   Ruf! Royf! Roy! ROY!

Roy   The old man was terrified –

John   Son, see, dinnae tell nae cunt it was Winston.

Roy   He pleaded. He threatened.

John   Like ah sais dinnae you tell nae cunt it was Winston.

Roy   He was terrified in case they took the dog away.

John   It's all they fucking stray dogs oan the green. Ought to be fuckin exterminated! Dinnae you tell nae cunt. Fuckin disgrace! Environmental health hazard! Ought to be fuckin exterminated . . .

Roy   Ah needed skin grafts! After that I walked with a limp. I walk with a slight limp to this day. Only now . . . I don't walk at all. Down here in the comforts of my vegetative state. I'll stay down here out of the way, where they can't get to me. At least till I work it all out. It hasn't been so easy recently. Characters and events have been intruding into my mind, psychic gatecrashers breaking in on my private party. This is what I have instead of a life. I grew up in a concentration camp for the poor. I did the normal things kids did, I played fitba, Japs and Commandos, mucked about on bikes, hung around stairs bored, battered smaller/weaker kids, got battered by bigger/stronger kids. There was always fights with stanes in the scheme. The first thing I learned tae dae was tae fling a stane. That was what you did as a kid in Muirhoose, you flung stanes; flung them at radges, at windaes, at buses. It was something to do. In the summer, I loved catching bees . . .

We'd fill auld Squeezy detergent bottles with water and skoosh the bee as it sucked at the nectar on the flower. The trick was for the boys to train a couple of jets on the bee at the same time and blast it to fuck. The water weighed down its wings. Then we'd scoop the drenched bees into a jar and then dig little prison cells for them in the softer material between the sections of brick at the ramp at the bottom of our block of flats. We used iced-lolly sticks as the doors. We had a concentration camp for bees, a tiny Scottish housing scheme. For bees.

Sometimes me n my pals used to go out of the scheme. Occasionally we'd walk to snobby bits like Barnton, Crammond or Blackhall. The polis would always come round and make us go hame though. Other times, we would think about running away and going camping, like in the Enid Blyton books. Gosh, Sandy, some hungry Horace has scoffed all the biscuits! But we'd usually just get as far as the beach, watching birds. Then we'd get fed up and go hame. Aw I wanted tae dae was watch birds. I got an interest in birds. Used to get loads ay books on them fae the library. I got it from my auld man I suppose. He was really interested in birds as well. Nature freak. We both loved the nature documentaries on the telly.

John   Africay!

Roy   He was never so happy as when programmes about exotic birds came on the box, and he was very knowledgeable on the subject. John Strang was a man who knew the difference between a cinnamon bracken warbler and the brown woodland variety.

John   See that! Bullshit! A Luhder's bush shrike, the boy sais! That's a Doherty's bush shrike! Like ah sais, a Doherty's bush shrike! Jist as well ah'm tapin this oan the video!

Roy   We were the first family in the district to have all the key consumer goods as they came on to the market: colour television, video recorder, satellite dish. Dad thought that they made us different from the other families in the scheme, a cut above the rest.

John   Middle class.

Roy   In fact, they just proved we were typical schemies.

John   Meant fir better things.

Roy   Meant fir better things. Aye.
I was embarrassed when any of the other kids came roond to the hoose. Most of them seemed to have better hooses than us, it was like we were the scruffs. We nivir hud much money. Ma da wis a security guard and Ma did school dinners. Not at my school, thank fuck.

Vet   Your tea, Roy.

Roy   My older brother Tony was a dark swarthy ape, totally ruled by his hormones.

Vet   Your tea, Tony.

Roy   Any time we were out and Tony saw a young lassie, he would mutter 'Ah'd shag the fuckin erse ofay that.'

Tony   'Ah'd shag the fuckin erse ofay that any day o the week.'

Roy   I heard it so often that for a long time I believed that sexual intercourse required rear entry.
Speaking of which . . .

Bernard *enters singing 'Do You Really Want to Hurt Me?'*

Roy   . . . my younger brother Bernard could mince before he could walk.

Tony   Total fucking embarrassment!

Roy   Tony was awright. He battered me a few times, but he also battered anyone who messed with me. Unless they

were his mates. But Bernard I hated. He just stayed in the
hoose and played with my wee sister Kim.

Kim (*head round door*)   Hiya, Roy! Hiya, Bernard!

Roy   Bernard was like Kim. Bernard was a girl.

Bernard   To persecute me for my sexuality
is to pander to the slavedeck of false illusion
when the tapes play mixed messages
through mediums yet to be discovered.

Roy   Whit?

Bernard   To persecute me for my sexuality
is to pander to the slavedeck of false illusion
when the tapes play mixed messages
through mediums yet to be discovered.

Roy   A primary-school teacher had once told ma ma that
Bernard was 'gifted'. So she gamely encouraged the wee
poof. After that he did fuck all for years except ponce about.

Vet   John, Tony, Roy, your tea for Christ sake!

Roy   As my dad worked in a security firm, he decided to
sort us out. At sixteen, Tony was out shaggin most of the
time, but wee Bernard and wee Roy were in no position to
defend ourselves. The old man bought us cheap plastic
boxing gloves . . .
He would suddenly set up a ring in the living room with
four confiscated traffic cones.

John   Tops off, cunts!

Bernard   No!

John   C'moan, boys. Get the gloves on.

Bernard *tries to escape.*

John   Bernard!

Vet   John, bichrist, your tea!

Roy   The boxing gloves were the kind that just tear your face up.

John (*supervising* **Bernard***'s stripdown*)   C'moan, c'moan!

Vet   Bugger!

Roy (*strips down*)   Bernard was older, bigger and heavier-handed.

Bernard   Da!

Roy   But I was more vicious.

Vet   Bugger!

John   'Moan lads!

Vet   Well, ah'm no wastin mine. (*Goes off with her tea.*)

John   Nay low punches. Nay heids. Break whin ah sey break. Shake hands. And come oot fightin.

Roy *and* **Bernard** *touch gloves and part.*

John (*to* **Roy**)   Remember you're a Strang, son. He's no. Yir fighting fir the Strang name. He's a fuckin crappin eyetie bastard. (*To* **Bernard**) Bernard!

Roy   Bernard and me were half-brothers. Before mairryin ma faither, Ma hud been wi an Italian male nurse. The wee poof wisnae a Strang at aw.

John   Right. (*Rings bell.*) Yo!

Bernard *steps warily forward.* **Roy** *dances to and fro . . .*

John (*soon impatient; to* **Roy**)   Punch um, punch um, son.

Roy *wades in.* **Bernard** *blocks and jabs back.* **Roy** *backs.* **Bernard** *eases off.* **Roy** *counter-attacks: they are soon locked together,* **Bernard** *slapping at* **Roy**. **Roy** *backs;* **Bernard** *keeps slapping . . .*

John   Bernard, dinnae fuckin slap um like a pansy! Keep that jab gaun!

Bernard *dithers.* **Roy** *swipes at him.* **Bernard**'s *mouth is hurt.*

John   Yes!

Bernard *flails back at* **Roy**. **Roy** *dances away.* **John** *roars, so* **Roy** *wades in again.* **Roy** *jabs* **Bernard**'s *face.*

John   Ya beauty!

Roy *backs but grins.* **Bernard** *covers his face.*

John   Cummoan! Box um, Roy, box um! Fuckin poof!

Bernard *reveals a bloody face.*

Roy   Fuckin poof . . .

Bernard *pitches blindly forward and locks with* **Roy**. **Roy** *gives body blows and* **John** *separates them.*

John   Keep that fuckin jab in ehs eye! Gaun!

Roy *cannons into the blinded* **Bernard** . . .

Roy   Queer-faced cunt! (. . . *And socks him.*)

Bernard *staggers.* **Roy** *hangs back.*

John   Poke ehs fuckin eye right oot!

Roy (*swiping*)   Take that ya fuckin sappy big poof!

Roy *triumphs too soon.* **Bernard** *charges into him and they crash into the dinner table. As* **Roy** *pushes him off, the cloth is yanked and plates and food fly across the floor.* **Bernard** *staggers back, bleeding;* **Roy** *sees and dithers.*

John   Finish um, finish um! Nae fuckin prisoners!

Bernard *sinks.*

Roy (*dancing over* **Bernard**)   Sappy big poof!

John   Cummoan, Bernard. Fucksake, stick up fir yirself.

But it is no good. **Bernard** *has given up.* **John** *rings his bell.*

Roy   It wasn't always like that. Sometimes it was me that goat it. Either way, these fights made Bernard and me fear Dad and hate each other.

Vet (*returning*)   Aw Christ!

Bernard   The situation that is life
sustainable, yet renewable
its elements building blocks
in a completed construction
yet which cannot be identified as such in isolation.

Vet   Bernard! (*Goes to wipe his bloody face.*)

Bernard   To persecute me for my sexuality –

Roy *blows fart.*

Bernard   You understand nowt.

Roy   Ah understand what's shite and what's no. Your poems areny shite, ah'll gie ye that. They'd have tae improve a hundred per cent tae be shite.

John   Ho-ho, he's goat ye there, Bernard, like ah sais, goat ye thair. Yill nivir beat Roy whin it comes tae words.

Bernard   I refuse to be drawn intae a war of words with stupid people.

John   Whae're you fuckin well callin stupid? Ah'm askin ye! TRY GITTIN A JOB INSTID AY DAEIN AW THAT POOFY POETRY SHITE THIT NAEBODY'S FUCKIN WELL INTRESTET IN!

Vet (*cleaning floor*)   John! Ye cannae keep gittin oantae the laddie. Leave um alane. At least ehs poetry's hermless.

Roy   Total fuckin embarrassment.

John   It's no natural, like ah sais, no fuckin natural. Fuckin buftie. Yir no tryin tae tell us that ye think it's natural tae huv sex wi another man? Jist as well eh nivir came fae me.

Vet   Might as well huv come fae you.

John   What's that meant tae mean? Eh? Ah'm askin ye! Whit's that meant tae mean?

Vet   Your fuckin faither, that's what that's meant tae mean.

Terrible silence.

John   Whit aboot ma faither?

Vet   He went that wey.

John   MA FAITHER DIDNAE GO ANY FUCKIN WEY! MA FAITHER WISNAE A WELL MAN! (*Grabs her.*)

Roy   Da! (*He leaps on* **John**.) Dinnae Da!

Struggle . . .

Vet (*runs off*)   Ya bugger!

Bernard (*running on; joins in*)   Stoap it! Stoap it!

Vet (*re-enters: throws water or confetti over them*)   Your faither went tae prison fir interferin wi young boys!

John *roars.*

Vet (*with carving knife*)   COME OAN THEN YA FUCKIN SHITE! AH'LL FUCKIN WELL KILL YE!

John *and* **Vet** *run off.*

Bernard   Da, dinnae! (*Exits after them.*)

Plate-glass smash . . . **Winston** *barking . . . ambulance sirens.*

Roy (*dives into bed*)   Naaw!

Midnight chimes . . .

Bernard *sweeps up and withdraws . . .*

John *and* **Vet** *return, singing, sharing a bottle of wine and a kebab.*

John   See us, Vet? Meant fir better things. Likesay, me wi a security job. Nae prospects. Like ah sais, meant fir better things. This country's gaun tae the dogs. Cannae even git yer fuckin bucket emptied. Winter ay, winter ay –

Vet   Discontent, John.

John   Aye, Vet, winter ay discontent. (*Sees wine label.*) Sooth Afrikay! That's the place! Sooth Afrikay. Barry country. Loads ay wildlife. Land ay opportunity. Ah'll take us oot thir, Vet. Fucken well sure n ah will. Oor Gordon wid put us up, nae danger.

Vet   Oor Gordon?

John   Gordon, oor Gordon. Ma brother, ma fuckin brother!

Vet   O . . . Gordon . . .

John   Sooth Africay!

Vet   Nae Japs . . .

John   Vet, thir's nae Japs in Sooth Afrikay.

Vet   Nane?

John   It's a white man's country, like ah sais, a white man's country. White is right oot thair, ah kid ye not. Land ay opportuity.

Vet   Somewhair ah kin get tae dry clathes.

John   Eh?

Vet   They Pearsons. Eywis in the dryin green.

John   Ah fuckin telt that cow! Ah fuckin telt hur! Ah sais tae her, nixt time ah fuckin see your washin in that fuckin dryin green whin ma wife's tryin tae wash, the whole fuckin loat's gaun doon the fuckin shute intae the rubbish!

Vet *soothes him . . . which gets sexual . . .*

John   Fuckin ignorant some people, like ah sais, fuckin ignorant. But see in Sooth Afrikay, Vet, we'd huv a big hoose like Gordon's. Dry oor clathes in the sun, in a real fuckin gairdin.

Vet   O, it wid be nice tae huv a real back gairdin. Wi flowers n vegetables.

John   Oooaahh . . . Sooth Africay . . .

Vet   Aw, John . . . Whooooah!

They go off.

Bernard *comes forward.*

Bernard   They fuck you up, your mum and dad.
They may not mean to but they do.
They fill you with the faults they had
And add some extra just for you.

But they were fucked up in their turn
By fools in old style hats and coats,
Who half the time were soppy-stern
And half at one another's throats.

Man hands on misery to man.
It deepens like a coastal shelf.
Get out as early as you can,
And don't have any kids yourself.

Roy   Fuck off and die! Ah don't want to, ah don't want to –

A jet comes screaming into land . . .

'Born Free . . .'

Gordon's 'Boy' *sets up . . .*

John, **Vet**, **Bernard**, *and* **Roy** *arrive with sunhats and suitcases.*

Roy (*with binoculars and childlike wonder*)   Africa! Africa!

John   Meant fir better things. Like ah sais . . .

Vet   It's the City ay Gold, John. City ay Gold bichrist.

John   White man's country, like ah sais . . .

Vet   Nae Japs.

John   . . . white man's country!

Roy   N will we live in a big hoose like they ones in Barnton, Dad?

John   Bigger than thaim though, son, much bigger. Like ah sais, much bigger.

Vet   A real back gairdin, John!

John   Aye. Full ay wildlife n aw, eh Roy?

Roy   Wi'll be able tae go tae a safari park, Dad?

John   Ah've telt ye! Ah'm gaunnae git a joab as a park ranger. Wi'll be practically livin in a safari park.

Roy   Barry! (*Suddenly the grown-up* **Roy**, *to audience:*) I was still at the age when, despite being embarrassed at their weirdness, I essentially believed in the omnipotence of my parents.

John   Gordon'll fix us up, Vet. Like ah sais, park ranger.

Roy   My confidence in them was at an all-time high as we circled above South Africa in the sky; as far as I was concerned, we were about to enter paradise. Then we landed . . . and came down to earth.

Gordon *enters, dapper.*

John   Gordon!

Gordon   John. Verity. I'll git you fixed up yere, John, no trubble. But I won't hev you workin with me. I'm a gret believer in keeping buzznes and femily apart.

John   Ay . . . but –

Gordon (*handing a chit*)   You can start as a security guard.

John   Whit?

Gordon   Not a dangerous job, John. Top-notch supermarket. Whites only. Just down the road. Good money – compared to the blecks.

Verity can go downtown, do a spot of filing and typing for a friend of mine. Property management agency, Vet. Whites only. And luncheon vouchers.

John   Luncheon vouchers?

Gordon   This must be Bernard. (*Grin.*)

Bernard (*aside*)   The words 'prick and 'fascist' spring to mind.

Gordon   And this must be little Roy. (*Wink.*) OK?

Roy   Barry!

Gordon   Barry? I thought it was R – O yis! (*Laugh.*) (*Scots*) Barry! (*Laugh.*) That's a small pair of binoculars. Want to try mine?

Roy   Aye . . .

John   Lunchun fuckin vouchers?! (*Stomps off.*)

Vet *runs after him.*

Gordon   What can you see?

Roy   Flamingos!

Gordon   You like birds, do you?

Roy   I like books about birds. Big books wi big pictures.

Gordon   Well. I'll see what I can do. Have to get some sun on these legs. Could do with a bit of meat on you, boy. (*He feels* **Roy**'s *thigh.*) Birds, eh? (*He gets* **Roy** *to take his top off and rubs suntan oil on him.*)

African village music . . .

Boy *watches.*

Bernard *enters as a young man, visiting* **Roy** *in hospital.*

Bernard   Mind South Africa, Roy? Johannesfuckinburg!
I fuckin hated it there. Mind you, there was bags of talent.
Ah hudnae really come oot then but. That was the wan
waste, these boys of all races. (*Regards* **Boy**. *Watches* **Gordon**
fondling **Roy** *and masturbating himself* . . .) But of course you
scored more than me in that department, you mercenary
wee closet rent boy you. Oh aye, ah kent aw aboot you and
Gordon. 'S practically a family tradition, what wi grandad's
extra coaching sessions with the laddies' fitba team. Sorry,
that was outay order. That was outay order.

Night falls . . . distant thunder, cicadas . . .

Vet *and* **John** *enter the sitting room . . .*

Gordon *has an orgasm.*

TV light.

John   Fuckin thirty-six rand a year fir this shite! It's no
that, it's no that I grudge it. It's jist that we dinnae want tae
become slaves tae the telly aw the time.

Vet   Switch it oaf well.

John   Naw, naw, that's no the point ah'm tryin tae make,
Vet. Yir misunderstandin the point ah'm tryin tae make.
Like ah sais, it's no the telly that's wrong; it's jist that thir's
nowt else tae dae. Ye cannae git oot fir a fuckin pint, ken
whit ah mean? There's no like a local; nae fuckin pub fir
miles. Even Muirhoose had a fuckin pub. Likesay in the
toon though but, Vet, thir's tons ay pubs doon in the city.
Ah wis thinking ah might jist go doon git a couplay pints in
the city likes. Like ah sais –

Vet   Go oot fir a pint well.

A bar-room door opens up. **John** *goes off through it. Door closes.*

Roy   On my first day at the school I was introduced as a
new boy from Scotland. It was all right because the school
uniform had long trousers that hid the scars on my legs, the
skin grafts where Winston had mauled me. The kids were

much more docile than in Scotland. Actually doing school work was acceptable. My interest in nature and wildlife was positively encouraged. They were nice to me. So was Uncle Gordon . . .

Gordon *enters and gives* **Roy** *a boxed present.*

Gordon   Roy . . .

Roy *takes it and opens it: a small good-quality telescope.* **Vet** *and* **Bernard** *gather to watch.*

Vet   Aw, Gordon, you shouldnae. Ye'll spoil the laddie.

Gordon   What did you see today, Roy?

Roy   Ah saw some lions stalking wildebeests and zebras. Some cheetahs had goat hold of a baby wildebeest. But two lions chased them oaf. And then they ate it.

Vet   O Christ.

Gordon   It's the law of the wild, Vet, the law of the wild. Eh, Roy?

Vet   Ay, well, it's no ma cup ay tea.

Bernard *examines the telescope.*

Roy   N ah saw flamingos, Ma. Beautiful pink creatures. Standing along the shores of a lake. Thoosands of them. N then . . . these other birds, big ugly birds . . . waddled intae them, and scattered them. I hud nivir seen anything as horrible-looking as those ugly birds. Bent over like beggars wi huge grinnin beaks and dead eyes.

Vet   Aw, tell yir faither whin he comes in. 'S no mah cup ay tea. (*Exiting*) Law ay the wild . . .

Gordon   That's the marabou stork, Roy. Bad bastards.

Bernard, *knowing, returns the telescope to* **Roy** *and leaves.*

Gordon   But it's nature, Roy. It's just the law of the wild. (*He masturbates* **Roy** . . .)

Roy   I saw one of them tryin to swallow a flamingo's head.
The severed head of one bird lolling in the jaws of another.
I saw –

Gordon   Shh, shh. It's all right, Roy. It's all right.

Roy *has an orgasm.*

Roy   That night I had my first marabou stork nightmare.

Gordon   Marabou Stork Nightmare . . . (*Climbs on* **Roy**.)

Meanwhile in downtown Johannesburg, **John** *is chucked out of a bar,
reeling drunk. He is picked up by a* **Cabbie** *in a taxi . . .*

Back in the hospital, a **Nurse** *sits on* **Roy**'s *bed . . .*

Nurse   Well, once he got what he wanted, he was off, like
a shot into the night, and there I was, left alone again. I
should have known. I should have known. You always think
that the next one will be different and I suppose I let my
emotions get the better of me, got all carried away and read
what I wanted to read between the lines. He was so
charming, so wonderful, so understanding but, yes, that was
before he got me into bed. Why am I telling you this? Why
not? It's not as if you can hear, it's not as if you'll ever wake
up.
Oh God, I'm so sorry I said that. I'm just upset. I mean
some people do wake up, they do get better. I'm just not
myself just now, Roy. You see, I let this one get right into
my head as well as into my pants. Letting them into your
pants is bad enough, but when they get into your head . . .
I can see the good in you. When I shine the torch into your
eyes, I know I can see something and I know it's good. (*She
kisses him.*) I know you felt that, Roy. My little sleeping
beauty. I'll bet you felt that. You know what I think, Roy
Strang? I think all you need is to feel wanted, to feel loved.
Let me in, Roy. Let us all in. You're surrounded by love!
Your family. Your friends. Let us in!
You're very bony, Roy. I'll bet you've always been nice and
slim. But you could do with some meat on these bones, Roy
Strang. (*She gropes under the sheet.*) I'm doing this for you, Roy.

I know you can feel. Why should you be denied sexual contact? I know what you're feeling. I was on a course on sexuality and the disabled. I want to make you feel, Roy. (*Her head goes down under the sheet.*)

Roy   Aa . . . aaahh . . . aargh!

Nurse (*surfacing as* **Vet**)   Awright, son?

Roy   A . . .!

Vet   Aw, 'sno ma fuckin cup ay tea anywey . . .

Roy   Naw!

Vet   Argh! Japs! (*Running off*) Japs! Japs!

Roy (*tossing and turning*)   Nae Japs! Nae japs! Sandy, Sandy!

Campfire light.

Sandy   I say, Roy old chap, steady.

Roy   Nae Japs . . .

Sandy   Steady.

Roy   Sandy?

Sandy   Nightmare?

Roy   Nae Japs?

Sandy   No Japs in Africa, Roy. Only chaps. Decent chaps.

Roy   I saw a group of ugly birds waddling into a flamingo colony and scattering the beautiful pink creatures across the waters of a lake. I saw one of them tryin to swallow a flamingo's head. The severed head of one bird lolling in the jaws of another. Uh . . .

Sandy   Ah. (*He puts an arm round his shoulder.*)

Roy (*abreacting*)   Ah!

Sandy (*desisting*)   There, there.

Both   Marabou stork nightmare.

Sandy   I know what you need. (*He fishes out a spliff.*)

Roy   For as long as I can remember, I have been engaged in a quest. For some reason I am driven to eradicate the scavanger-predator bird known as the marabou stork.

Sandy   The marabou stork has a huge sharp-pointed beak which hangs heavily down the front of its body. Behind the beak hangs a throat in the form of a pendulous bag of wrinkled skin. What does this put you in mind of?

Roy   I can't keep my eyes off Sandy Jamieson. He extends his long, tanned muscular legs in the firelight.

Sandy   A giant penis and scrotum. A dick on legs, Roy. To dream of such a creature, to hunt it, yet to feel driven to eradicate it, is to be a man haunted by a sexuality he does not understand, a sexuality which is naturally his own, but which has been alienated from him by forces beyond his control. Such a man may find himself engaged on a lifelong quest, driven by nature to be a sexual animal, yet driven by fear and disgust to destroy sexuality as such. Thus the act of creation may also be an act of destruction; the act of love, an act of hate. (*Tokes heavily.*)

Roy   I remember . . . that night . . . naked legs . . . It was a girl . . . she was . . . we . . .

Ozzy   Ach, the fuckin hoor asked fir it. She'd've goat it fae some cunts anywey, the wey she fuckin well carried oan and the fuckin fuss she made. Aye, she goat slapped aroond a bit, but we wir fuckin vindicated, British justice and that. She wis jist in the wrong place at the wrong fuckin time.

Roy   Anywey, it wis aw Lexo's fault.

Ozzy   Whit? Dinnae you play mister fuckin innocent.

Roy   Eh? Whit you oan aboot?

Ozzy   You were thair!

Roy   Naw man, ah couldnae git a hard-oan!

Car horn jammed down.

Enter a taxi containing **John** *and* **Cabbie** *(***Bernard***).*

Ozzy *(tussle)* You were fuckin thair! *(Etc., ad lib)*

Roy Ah never . . . ah didnae . . . naw! *(Etc., ad lib)*

John *(dragging* **Cabbie** *out)* Fuckin poof! Queer-faced cunt!

Slow motion in smoke and strobe: **Ozzy** *slaps* **Roy** *around.* **John** *slaps* **Cabbie** *around.*

Police sirens.

Policeman *enters.*

Vet *(slow)* John! Fucksake John no! The polis! W'll be sent hame! W'll lose everything!

John *(slow)* JOHN STRANG'S MA NAME. FUCK YIS AW! YA CUNTS!

Ozzy *and* **John** *deck* **Roy** *and* **Cabbie**.

John ANY BASTARD IN THIS FUCKIN COUNTRY'S GOAT ANYTHING TAE SAY TAE ME –

Policeman *swipes* **John** *with his baton.* **Roy** *takes a fit.*

Ambulance sirens.

A **Nurse** *runs to* **Roy**.

Policeman *marches* **John** *away.*

John YA CUNTS! YA CUNTS!

Vet Aw Christ!

Bernard Back to Scotland!

Distant burglar alarms.

Ozzy In Muirhouse, nae cunt can hear ye scream!

Silence.

Distant football crowd Hi-bees! Hi-bees! Hi-bees! . . .

Ozzy Well, they can. They jist dinnae gie a fuck.
Nurse *(shining a torch in his eyes)*   Roy? Roy? Roy?
Football match atmosphere . . .
Interval.

Part Two

Kim   Hiya Raw-oy. Big brother. It's Kim. Can ye hear me? The nurse telt us ye could mebbe likesay hear us. Awright! Ah'm seein this new felly. Eh's a wee bit aulder. N it's likesay eh's mairried n eh's goat two bairns bit it's likesay eh's gaunnae leave hur cause it's likesay eh disnae really love hur any mair n it's likesay hard fir him wi him huvin the mortgage n the bairns n wi his responsibilities in a position in the civil service n aw eh sais. Bit ah'm like still sortay seein Kevin n aw, well no really seein um bit we met at the Edge n ah wis a bit drink n a really only went back tae his place tae see this leather jaykit eh goat bit wan thing jist led tae another n ah jist sortay ended up steyin the night ken wi Kevin likes, it wis jist like ah kinday felt sorry for um, bit ah sais dinnae think this is us gaun back oot thegithir coz it's no, coz ah've goat a new felly now, bit the thing is, Roy, ken it's like ah've sortay missed another period again n ah dinnae ken if ah'm, well, ken, that wey, n if ah am whaes it is ken, Roy: coz ah've been wi Kevin n the new felly, bit thair wis this other laddie ah met wan night it Buster's n we went back tae his fir a perty so ah'm no really sure, but that's jist sayin like, that's jist supposin ah am.

It's Setirdy the day, Roy. Yull miss the fitba. Roy? O Roy!

Roy   The things Gordon wanted to do to me were getting heavier. He said if I told anyone I would get the blame: my dad would believe him not me. I know that that was true. I knew I mattered less than a dog.

'Dinnae you tell nae cunt . . .'

But see, being abused . . . I mean, I felt a sense of power, I felt a sense of attractiveness that I hadn't ever felt before. I used that power by extorting gifts from Gordon – like the telescope. I saw a black and white colobus, a side-striped jackal, a clawless otter, a black-tipped mongoose, a porcupine and an African hare, a grey wagtail, African marsh owl, olive thrush, doves of the pink-breasted and red-eyed variety, African snipe (which might have been a Jack

snipe, I couldn't be one hundred per cent sure) and a
golden-rumped tinkerbird.

To me, everything in South Africa was ten times, naw, one
hundred times better than anything in Scotland. I felt at
home there. When I thought back to Edinburgh I
recollected it as a dirty cold wet slum; a city of blackened
tenements and run-down concrete housing schemes
populated by scruffs but run by snobs for snobs. And when
people asked me what I wanted to be, I said a soldier, cause
it seemed good fun shooting at people – like bees. But in
South Africa I could see a future; I wanted to be a zoologist!
The old man's piss-up blew all that away. Ma dad assaulted
that taxi driver with such force that several of the man's
teeth were produced in court in a plastic bag. They
deported us back to Scotland. In Muirhouse the council
shoved us back in the same block we'd escaped from, only
higher up in the sky, among the poorest.

I'd been a daft cunt to ever have dreams.

Ah came down to earth and walked into the dark . . . like,
doon to the chippie tae get a fish supper for ma ma n da.

Hammy   Hi pal, gi'es a chip!

Roy   I cannae, it's fir ma faither.

Skelly   Leave um, ehs jist a fuckin bairn.

Gilly   Ken whae this cunt is? Eh chibbed Davie Matthews'
brar. Thinks he's a fuckin wide-o.

Hammy   So ye cairry a blade eh?

Roy   Nup.

Hammy   Heard ye hud yin at the school but, eh?

Gilly   Ye a wide-o, aye?

Roy   Nup.

Hammy *laughs and does strange birdlike dance.*

Skelly   Leave um, Hammy. Ah'm no fuckin jokin.

Hammy   Git um in the fuckin stair.

Caroline   Goat a girlfriend, son?

Roy   Nup.

Hammy   Ivir hud yir hole?

Skelly   Hu-hu-hu-hu-huh.

Gilly   Leave the perr wee cunt.

Hammy   This is ma wee girlfriend. Caroline. Eh hen?

Caroline   Dinnae Doogie.

Hammy (*slaps* **Roy**)   Gie's a fuckin chip!

They stare each other out. The others edge back sensing a fight.

Hammy (*knife out*)   Fuckin wide cunt!

Skelly (*ad lib*) *talks* **Hammy** *down.*

Hammy   Whit team dae ye support?

Roy (*lightly*)   Hibs.

Hammy (*mocking*)   Hebs! Hebs! (*Tears into chips.*) H.M.F.C. ya cunt! (*Grabs his hair, boots his face.*)

Skelly   Fuck oaf, Hammy, ya Jambo cunt!

Gilly *gives* **Roy** *a kick too.*

Kids *go off.*

Roy, *mouth bleeding, reaches his front door.*

John *comes out to him.*

John   Ye'll huv tae learn tae fuckin stick up fir yirself, son. (*Takes chips.*) Yir a Strang. Or supposed tae be. (*Exits.*)

Roy   I can take pain. Physical pain I can take. If you can stand pain, you're gaunnae give any cunt proablems. If you can stand pain and you arenae feart and you're angry. At school in Muirhouse ah worked out this simple formula: if you hurt them, they don't laugh. Simple. I'll take nae shite

from any cunt who brands me as a freak. Back in primary
I'd stabbed a laddie wi a compass. Now I bought a small
hunting knife fae Boston's of Leith Walk. Tam Matthews
spat on the back of ma neck. Ah stabbed um. Did ah dae
that? How? Ah'm university material. Wid ah dae that? I
became a cunt.

Alan Moncur (Bernard) *enters in a duffle coat.*

Roy   In the laddies' toilets I captured this baby-faced cunt
called Alan or Alec Moncur. Neat tidy cunt as if his ma still
dressed him. Dressed-By-His-Ma-Cunt. He was quite pally
though. He'd sort ay befriended us for a bit. Once I
pretended to hypnotise him. Hyp-i-not-ise. Hyp-i-not-ise.
You could tell he was shitein it but. His eyes! Lot goin on
heind they lassie-like eyes. Hyp-i-not-eyes! (*Blow to groin.*)
Now you're balls are paralysed!
Tony had done that to me. One time in the hoose. But
Tony was awright. Never battered me much. Mainly
Bernard he battered, and that was barry, seein that fuckin
poof get battered. So one day, in the laddies' bogs:
'Captured!' I bundled him into one of the cubicles.

Brian (*head*)   Strangy! Whit ye daein in thair, ya cunt?

Roy   Keep fuckin shoatie, Bri . . . keep fuckin shoatie. (*He
forces* **Alan** *to wank him off.*) Slowly . . . ah'll fuckin kill ye . . .
slowly . . . (*He comes.*) Castrate all poofs!

Alan *scurries away.*

Caroline *returns.*

Roy   Caroline. Every cunt fancied hur. But she always
acted as if her shite didnae smell. Must huv thought her
looks bought her immunity, like she could dae what she
wanted. One time in the class she flicked the back o ma
fuckin ear. Every cunt laughed. I purchased a Swiss army
knife fae Boston's of Leith Walk. Nae cunt laughs at Roy
Strang. (*Knife out, he shoves* **Caroline** *up against the wall.*)

Caroline   What ur ye daein? What ur ye daein, Roy?

Roy   You fuckin flicked ma ears! Whit dae ye say?

Caroline   Sorry . . .

Roy   Roy Strang is ma fuckin name. Nae cunt fucks aboot wi me. Lift up yir skirt. Higher! (*He tugs her pants down.*) I wanted tae see if ye hud ginger pubes like.

Caroline *emits a forced laughed.*

Roy   What's fuckin funny? Eh? Think ah'm fuckin funny?

Caroline   Naw . . .

Roy (*dry-rides her*)   Slut . . . slut . . . dirty fuckin slag . . . ya fuckin love it ya dirty wee cunt. (*He soon comes.*)
Ma hot wallpaper paste filled ma pants. That was it. Ma first ride. Dry ride, they call it, when ye dinnae git it up the lassie's fanny, ye jist rub up against them till ye come. Right. You say anything aboot this ya fuckin ginger-pubed wee cunt n you are fuckin well deid! Right?

Caroline   Ah'll no say nowt.

Roy   Fuck off.

Caroline *runs off.*

Roy   Sorted. (*Wry smile.*) 'Dinnae you tell nae cunt . . .'
I always felt a bit shite eftir I did something like that. It made me feel sad and low. So I'd try to make it up by doing a good deed, like giving up my seat oan the bus tae some auld cunt or daein the dishes for ma ma.
I used tae see ma brother Tony. Tony wis driven by hormones, without logic or conscience. He told me all about burds.

Tony (*entering*)   If thir slags ye jist grab a hud ay the cunts. If it's a decent bird ye stey cool fir a bit and chat them up, then ye grab a hud ay them. (*Exits.*)

Roy   Soon eftir that ah goat ma hole. To my surprise, the actual hole was a lot further down the slit than ah'd thought it wid be. It took a while to get it up: It actually does go up,

not straight *in* likes. Lesley Thomson. Her fanny was wet
and slimy. I had to bend ma knees. Wasnae *that* much better
than a dry ride. She wore these manky white socks. Fucked
her a few times that summer. She tried to take my airm. I
slapped her pus. Still goat ma hole but.

Passed all six O grades. Goat a joab as a systems analyst
with Scottish Spinsters Assurance Company.

John   Computers. Thing ay the future.

Roy   Work. It was jist a place ye went tae during the day
because they paid ye tae. My social life was a bit ay a drag. I
found it harder to get ma hole. I wanted a class burd, no just
knee-trembling some schemie trash in a rubbish room.
Then I met the cashies.

Lexo   Nay cunt better shite out. A cunt that messes is a
cunt that dies. We're the hardest crew in Europe. We
dinnae fuckin run. Mind. We dinnae fuckin run.

Roy   Lexo.

Lexo   Alex James McKay Setterington ya cunt. Not
Guilty!

Roy   Demps!

Demps   Nay cunt better shite out. A cunt that messes is a
cunt that dies. We're the hardest crew in Europe. We
dinnae fuckin run. Mind. We dinnae fuckin run. Allan
Edgar Dempsey.

Demps/Lexo   Not Guilty!

Roy   Ozzy!

Ozzy   Nay cunt better shite out. A cunt that messes is a
cunt that dies. We're the hardest crew in Europe. We
dinnae fuckin run. Mind. We dinnae fuckin run. Ian George
Osmotherly.

Ozzy/Demps/Lexo   Not Guilty!

Roy   Nay cunt better shite out. A cunt that messes is a cunt that dies. We're the hardest crew in Europe. We dinnae fuckin run. Mind. We dinnae fuckin run. Roy Irvine Strang.

All   Not Guilty! (*Arms-round-shoulders tableau.*)

Flashbulb.

Demps   The Motherwell boys were oan us at the station and I was shit-scared. This cunt I was hittin was hittin me back: I couldnae feel a thing but I knew he could coz his eyes were filling up with fear. It was –

Demps/Lexo   – the best feeling on earth!

All   Adrenalin!

Roy   Then he was on his arse.

Ozzy   Next thing I knew was that I was being pulled off one cunt by some of our boys and dragged away down the road as polis sirens filled the air.

All make siren noises.

Lexo   I was snarlin like a demented animal, wantin only tae get back and waste the cunt on the ground for good.

Demps/Ozzy   They ran into a pub but thir wis nae escape, we just steamed in and wrecked the fuckin boozer.

Roy   Ghostie hud a Weedgie ower the pool table n wis tryin tae sever his meaty Hun heid oaf wi a broken gless.

All   Ah'll take your fuckin face off, ya fuckin Weedgie cunt!

Demps   Ozzy wis tryin tae cram a bar ay soap intae the ratshagger's face.

All   Get a fuckin wash ya smelly soap-dodgin Weedgie cunt! Dae yous cunts nivir fuckin wash?

Ozzy   Lexo had taken a couple ay thum oot, one Hun's face burst like a ripe tomato shot by an air pistol as his chunky fist made contact with it.

All   Pow!

Lexo   Whair's all the fuckin Glasgey hard men now, eh?

Lexo/Ozzy   FUCKIN QUEERS!

Roy   Ah opened up one skinny Hun's coupon with a sharpened carpet-tile knife.

Demps   Purchased from Boston's of Leith Walk!

Roy   Aye!

All   HIBS BOYS, YA FUCKIN CUNTS! EUROPE'S NUMERO UNO! FUCKIN RATSHAGGIN BASTARDS!

Lexo   LET'S HIT THE FUCKIN ROAD.

Demps, **Lexo** and **Ozzy** *withdraw, doing the Hi-bees chant.*

Roy   ROY STRANG'S THE FUCKIN NAME! REMEMBER THAT FUCKIN NAME! ROY STRANG! HIBS BOYS YA FUCKIN CUNTS!

The boys return to **Roy**.

Ozzy   Whit's yer name, pal?

Roy   Roy. Roy Strang.

Ozzy   Strang. Got a brar?

Roy   Aye, Tony Strang.

Lexo   Tony Strang. Shag artist.

Ozzy   Whair ye fi?

Roy   Muirhoose.

Ozzy   Schemie, eh? Hu-hu. Me n aw. Fi Niddrie. Stey in toon now, though. Cannae be bothered with the fuckin scheme any mair. Ye ken satellite dishes?

Roy   Aye.

Ozzy   Whit dae they call the wee boax oan the back ay the satellite dish?

Roy   Eh, dunno likes.

Ozzy   The cooncil's. [*OR 'A cooncil hoose.'*]

All laugh . . .

A **Barman** *hands out beers.*

Ozzy   The marabou stork is one of the major dangers to the greater and lesser flamingo. The stork walks along the shore causing flamingo flocks to panic. It then makes a short flight and stabs a selected flamingo in the back. Once disabled the flamingo is drowned and then torn to pieces and eaten by one or several marabous in three to four minutes. Bad bastards.

Kirsty *arrives, in a flamingo-pink dress.*

The boys watch her arrival . . . and then get up and dance.

Kirsty *and* **Roy** *smile at each other.* **Lexo** *spits beer across the floor.* **Kirsty** *moves away, wary of* **Lexo** *and co.* **Roy** *senses a come-on and follows.* **Kirsty** *gives a backward glance and runs off.* **Roy** *returns, feeling knocked back.*

Lexo   Fuckin total ride that wee cow.

Roy   Legged it?

Lexo   Like fuck. Nae cunt's been up that sow, so far as ah ken. KB'd every cunt. Tell ye one thing, see if she comes up tae Buster's next week n comes back to Dempsey's perty, she's gittin her fuckin erse shagged. Even if she is a virgin, her fanny'll be no tight enough once ah've fuckin gied it a few strokes.

Roy   The boys are entitled tae a line-up.

Ozzy   If yir up fir gang-bangin that wee sow, mind n cut ays in oan the action.

Lexo   A sow's goat tae reliase that if they hing aroon wi top boys, they huv tae dae the biz. Examples must be made.

They rise. **Demps**, **Lexo** *and* **Ozzy** *move upstage . . .*

Roy   It wis jist a half-pished wind-up in the pub. Ah didnae ken the cunts were serious. 'Please don't kill me,' she said, quietly. Please don't kill me . . .

Kirsty *has returned, meeting* **Demps**, **Lexo** *and* **Ozzy***.*

Roy   Lexo spiked her drink with a tab of acid and she was out of her nut. Ah don't think she really knew what was happening. I remember – she was giggling . . .

Kirsty *giggles.*

Demps *and* **Ozzy** *shove her against the side of a van.*

Lexo *puts a knife to her throat.*

Roy   Please don't kill me.

Lexo   Open yir mooth n yir fuckin deid. (*Slowly pulls up her skirt.*)

Kirsty   Please don't, please don't, please don't . . .

Roy (*joining in*)   . . . please don't . . . (*Runs over to them.*) C'moan, Lexo, we've put the shits up her enough, man.

Lexo   Gaunny pit a wee bit mair up her thin the shits, eh.

Demps (*to* **Roy**)   Nay cunt better shite out.

Ozzy (*to* **Kirsty**)   Think ay this as yir initiation.

Lexo (*to* **Kirsty**)   Aye, yuv no been done yit.

Demps (*to* **Roy**)   The boys are entitled to a line-up.

Ozzy   Top boys' perks. Hu-hu-huh. Cannae say fairer thin that, eh?

Kirsty *struggles.*

Lexo *hits her across the face.*

Kirsty *goes passive.*

Ozzy and **Demps** *raise her arms up . . .*

Lexo (*carefully removing her dress*)   Dinnae want any signs ay a struggle.

Kirsty *cries.*

Lexo *pulls her bra down and scoops her tits out.*

Kirsty *tries one huge scream for help.*

Lexo *hits her again and grabs her round the neck.*

Lexo (*possessed*)   Ah'll cut yir fuckin tongue out the next time you make a fuckin sound. Git a handful ay they titties, boys, no bad.

Ozzy (*tweaking her nipple*)   She's a fucking lovely piece ay meat.

Demps   Only the choicest cuts for the top boys.

Lexo (*gesturing to* **Roy**)   Shoes.

Roy *pulls her shoes off and stands hugging them.*

Lexo (*slowly slides off her panties*)   Ivir hud yir fanny licked oot? (*Puts his hand roughly between her legs.*)

Kirsty *closes her legs on his hand.*

Ozzy and **Demps** *pull her legs apart.*

Kirsty   Dinnae . . . please Lexo . . . Alex . . . dinnae . . . please . . . ah'll tell the polis . . . ah'll get the polis . . . please . . . don't hurt me . . . don't kill me . . .

Lexo   Get hir in the back. Thir's gaunny be a whole loat ay shaggin the night!

Lexo, **Demps** and **Ozzy** *bundle her into the open back of the van.* **Lexo** *pulls down his jeans and shorts and goes in with her.* **Ozzy** *and* **Demps** *crowd at the back of the van.* **Kirsty** *screams.*

Roy   She scramed as he forced his cock into her. But still he was slow and deliberate: he knew what he was doing. The expression on her face . . . I remember seeing a documentary about an animal being eaten from behind while its face seemed to register disbelief, fear and self-hate at its own impotence. That was what she reminded me of . . .

Kirsty *shouts.*

Roy   Wildebeest . . . (*He puts the shoes down.*)

Ozzy (*seeking a beer*)   Nay sign ay her gittin turned oan yet.

Roy   Some cheetahs had got hold of a baby wildebeest . . .

Lexo   Yo! Ah'm needin a wee bit ay back-up here, boys! Thir's three holes here n only one ay thum in use.

Ozzy *laughs, tosses beer to* **Roy** *and shambles back, unzipping.*

Roy   Bent over like baggars wi huge grinnin beaks and dead eyes . . .

Demps *drops his trousers and he and* **Ozzy** *pile in.*

Roy *opens the beer bottle, but he is shaking.*

Van creaks . . .

Lexo   Phoah, ya fucker!

Roy (*like desperate praying*)   You blessed ones who shall inherit the future age of which we can only dream, you pure and radiant beings who shall succeed us on this earth, when you turn back your eyes on us poor savages grubbing in the ground for our daily bread, eating flesh and blood, dwelling in vile bodies, tortured by pains, when you think of what we are and compare us with yourselves, remember that it is to us you owe the foundation of your happiness . . .

Sound: car horn pressed down for several seconds.

It wisnae as if ah wis intae daein anythin.

The boys now emerge from the car for a beer. **Ozzy** *first . . .*

Roy   Ah couldnae even git a hard-oan . . .

Ozzy *comes down to him.*

Roy   Wisnae me . . . it wisnae me . . . remember . . .

Ozzy   Nice n lubricated fir ye, Strangy. (*Swigs beer.*)

Demps (*comes down*)   Cmoan. (*Gets a beer.*)

Roy   Ah'm fucked if ah'm gaun in thair eftir youse cunts.

Lexo (*coming down*)   Nae cunt shites oot.

Ozzy   Dinnae go aw fuckin poofy oan ays, Strangy. It's an education fir the sow.

Roy   Ye dinnae ken that, though. It might fuck her up. She might never be able tae go wi a guy again, like.

Lexo   The only fuckin reason it'll no be able tae dae it again is cause it's hud the best n the rest jist dinnae fuckin measure up.

Demps *and* **Ozzy** *laugh.*

Ozzy (*flare of anger*)   Dinnae go aw fuckin poofy oan us!

Demps   Like a fuckin soapy sponge in thair man, ah'm tellin ye.

Demps *and* **Ozzy** *laugh. They watch* **Roy** *go to the car.*

Lexo   Last ay the rid-hoat lovers! (*Gets beer.*)

Demps *points a TV remote.*

Projection: film of Hibs–Rangers football match.

Demps   Fuckin barry!

The boys do some coke.

Lexo (*toast*)   Tae slags thit huv tae fuckin learn lessons!

All   Slags!

Kirsty *shouts.*

The boys move about, coked up.

Roy *emerges from the van.*

Lexo (*possessed*)   That wis jist a wee bit ay foreplay. Git us aw in the mood fir the slag's erse, eh? (*Going up to the van*) Eh? Eh? C'moan! (*In van again.*)

Demps *and* **Ozzy** *join him.*

Roy   We jist kept her with us, having her over and over again. I managed one more – pretend likes. The others were up all night. Up her all night. Dempsey and Lexo together. In her together. 'Ah kin feel your cock, Lexo.' Demps gasped. 'Aye, ah kin feel yours n aw,' Lexo said.

Lexo (*in van*)   Woah!! A fuckin cracker fi Beastie thair!

Roy   Ozzy had put on a tape of Hibs goals on the video and we watched George McCluskey smash home a beauty against Rangers. 'A fuckin cracker fi Beastie thair,' Lexo growled as he blurted . . . his load . . . into her rectum . . . for the umpteenth time – that – night.

Projection stops.

Then we got bored and watched cartoons on breakfast telly. *Superboy* and his loyal friend Krypto were flying through the air, dedicated to what the commentator described as 'the pursuit of truth'.

Kirsty *crawls from the car and curls up on the ground.*

Roy   I remember . . . Winston: looking down at Winston who sat curled up in front of the electric fire. I stared at the soft-breathing beast and thought of how his ribcage could be so easily shattered by simply jumping on it with a pair of heavy boots. (*He picks up* **Kirsty**'s *shoes and looks round at the car.*)

Roy   So easy . . . You – are – going – to – die.

John *enters in shirtsleeves; he covers* **Kirsty** *with his fur coat.*

Neighbours *and* **Vet** *stand in doorways.*

John   Daein this tae a defenceless animal. What kind ay sick mind does this tae a dug? Fuckin disgrace. Six-inch nails. The sick cunt goat a bone fae the butcher's and he hammered six-inch nails through the bone and the meat, and he left it oan the wasteland wi all they stray dugs. But it was Winston that goat it, Winston. And it – the nails – O! And the strays set upon him, savaging his bleeding jaws to get the meat which hung fae them. Bichrist. But he didnae die. The vet stitched Winston's face together and gave um one of they cone things aroond his head, to stop um scratching his wounds like. Whit happened then? How did it come tae this? Fireworks?

John *carries Winston's body to a shallow grave . . .*

Sea . . . mist. . .

Roy   Fireworks. I took the dog out to Crammond Island. You can walk out to it at certain times before the tide comes in and cuts it off from the mainland. There's nothing ower there, just a few pillboxes from World War Two, full ay beer cans n used condoms. And birds. So I took my bucket n spade, and Winston with his cone. I tied him to a rusty hook at the side ay a pillbox, removed his cone n taped an assortment of fireworks round his head wi plastic masking tape. I then put back the cone. I heard him make those almost-empty-Squeezy-bottle noises dugs make when they're shitein it.

Then I saw a small bird on top ay the pillbox – a robin. For a second or two I thought about Christian forgiveness. Nae cunt believes in that shite any mair. It's you against the world. N you matter less than a dug. 'Dinnae tell nae cunt it wis Winston.'

I looked at um straight in the eye. The funny thing was, he was just lying down on his side, panting softly. He seemed almost contented. Almost at peace. I lit a couple of fireworks where the blue touchpaper was exposed around his face and stood well back.

Firework exploding . . .

I buried his remains in the sand.

John   Well that's it now, ma ain laddie, sick. A sick person. Like ah sais, a common criminal.

Roy   It was her but, Dad. Likesay Lexo wis a wee bit over the top, but it wis her . . . she wanted it . . .

Vet (*helping* **Roy** *into a suit*)   Eh's no that kind ay laddie, John! Eh's no that kind ay laddie!

John   Vet! Fuckin shut it! Like a sais just fuckin shut it! Ah'm gaunnae ask ye this once, and jist once. Did you touch that wee lassie? Did you hurt that wee lassie?

Roy   Da . . . it wisnae like that . . . ah nivir touched her, ah wis jist thair whin she pointed the finger at everybody. It wis a perty . . . everybody wis huvin a good time. This lassie, she wis crazy, high oan drugs n that, she jist wanted tae screw everybody thair. Then in the mornin a couple at the boys started callin her a slag. Ah ken it wis a bit ootay order, but she goes aw spiteful n starts takin it oot oan ivray cunt. Ah nivir did nowt!

Vet   That's whit it wis! A slag! A fuckin slag's gaunnay ruin ma laddie's life. N you're gaunnay jist stand thair n take that slag's word against yir ain flesh n blood!

John   Ah'm no sayin that, Vet, like ah sais, ah'm no sayin that . . . it's no meant tae be like that . . .

Vet   Eh's a good laddie, John! Eh's got a joab in computers – thing ay the future. Wi eywis brought um up right!

Roy   AH WIS THE WAN THIT TRIED TAE GIT THUM TAE STOAP!

John   Ah jist hud tae ask, son, ah jist hud tae ask. An nivir doubted ye, though, son, nivir fir a minute.

Vet   Eh's a good laddie . . .

John   Ah hud tae ask though, son, tae hear it fae yir ain lips, like ah sais, fae yir ain lips.

Vet   Wi eywis brought um up right!

John   Ye understand that, son?

Roy (*aside*)   Git thum tae stoap . . .

John   Ah ken ah've been hard oan ye, son. That's cause yir the one wi brains. Ah hud brains n ah didnae use them. Ye dinnae want tae end up like me.

Roy   Fucksake . . .

John   Ah ken what they cunts think ay us. Ah ken aw they cunts. Ken what they are? Ah'll fuckin tell ye what they are. Rubbish. No fuckin quoted.

Vet *calms him, leads him off.*

John   Computers.

Vet   Thing ay the future.

John   Like ah sais. Meant fir better things.

Vet   O son . . .

Ozzy, **Demps** and **Lexo** *enter wearing smart suits.*

Ozzy   Allan Edgar Dempsey.

Demps *looks up.*

Lexo   Not guilty.

Demps *looks relieved.*

Lexo   Ian George Osmotherly

Ozzy   It was as if she was daring us to see how far we'd go. She was very drunk and I think she'd taken some . . . stuff. I don't really know that much about drugs, but it was like she'd taken something.

Lexo   Not guilty.

Ozzy *smiles.*

Ozzy   Alex James McKay Setterington

Lexo *looks up.*

Lexo   I don't think 'consent' puts it strongly enough, Your Honour. The term I would use would be insistence.

Ozzy   Not guilty.

Lexo   Roy Irvine Strang

Roy   I thought the whole thing was just . . . sick. It was horrible. If it had just been me and her together, but it was like she wanted everyone. I could've been anybody. She just laughed at me.

All   Not guilty.

Flashbulb.

Waiter *brings drinks.*

Ozzy   The fuckin hoor asked fir it. She'd've goat it fae some other cunts anywey, the wey she fuckin cairried oan and the fuckin fuss she made. Ay she got slapped aroond a bit but –

Lexo   But we wir fuckin vindicated. British justice!

Music . . .

Dorrie (*Warrington*)   Hiya. Hiya. It's about time I introduced myself. I've seen you at work. I'm Dorrie.

Roy   Dorrie . . .

Dorrie   Dorothy!

Roy   Dorothy from Pensions?

Dorrie   Oh bloody hell, that makes me sound ancient. It's Dorothy from Warrington really. I hate it when people say what do you do, and people talk about their sodding jobs all the time. What do you do? I eat, sleep, shit, pee, make love, get out of it, go to clubs, that's what I flamin do. Sorry, I'm rabbitin here. What's your name?

Roy   Eh, Roy.

Dorrie   Look, Roy, I'm sorry about this but I'm E'd out of my face. I just want to talk to everyone.

Roy   What do they do for you?

Dorrie   Ain't you done E before? I thought you were all big ravers in Scotland. This gear's brilliant.

Roy *takes an E.*

Music: 'Born Slippy'.

Dorrie   You're really rushing, really riding the crest of a wave; the music is inside you, the music is coming from you; you're lost in it, you're lost in music, lost in movement, your body is singing; you're all right, we're all right, everything is all right; people, strangers, come up and hug you and you want to hug them all, we're all in this together; you let them in, you let them find you, you let them love you: you love them!

They dance and go off.

Bernard *and* **Another Boy** *snog and grope in a doorway . . .*

Roy *and* **Dorrie** *return.*

Roy   I loved them. I couldn't stop hugging them, like I'd always wanted to hug pals, but it was too sappy, too poofy. But it was fuckin awesome, beyond anything I'd ever known. It was something that everyone should experience before they die, in their offices, in their suburbs, in their schemes, their dole queues, their bookies shops, their yacht clubs; I was one with them and myself and we were the world.
Outside, the street lights were brilliant. When the music ended I got dead sad, my eyes were watering; didnae matter, I wisnae embarrassed at being sappy. I saw what a

silly, sad, pathetic cowardly cunt I was, ever to be
embarrassed at having feelings.

They reach home.

Roy   I told them about my fears and hang-ups and they
told me about theirs. Not in a smarmy false-intimacy
middle-class counselling way, or in a big, weird, space-out
hippie bullshit trip. It was just punters saying how they felt
about life. I loved listening, listening to all the punters,
hearing about their lives, getting up to all sorts of mischief
with each other. And I loved just blethering away. I could
talk about anything.
Almost anything . . .
Dorrie and I started sleeping together. When I was eckied
like. Then she said, 'You don't –'

Dorrie   Y'don't have to be E'd up to make love to me
y'know.

Roy   I was scared of exposing myself.

Dorrie   We kissed for a bit and you stopped shaking.
Then we played with each for a long time . . . and after we
had joined . . .

Roy   . . . you and me became the one thing.

Dorrie   The one thing.

Roy   Then it seemed to vanish as we took off on a big
psychic trip together. It was our souls and minds that were
doing it all; our genitals, our bodies, they were just the
launch pads and soon fell away as we went around the
universe together, moving in and out of each other's heads
and finding nothing in them but good things, nothing in
them but love. Afterwards, she told me I was beautiful.

Dorrie *sleeps.*

Roy   I held her as if I could force her love into me, drive
the shit out of me, but what I was doing was infecting her
with my hurt, my pain. I could feel the sickness and doubt

transmit in our embrace, while my chin rested on the top of
her head and my nostrils filled with the scent of her
shampoo.
I remember that night . . . naked legs . . . it was a girl . . .
I lost it completely. And then I lost Dorrie.

He sits gazing at the flickering TV . . .

Music: Nat King Cole singing 'Nature Boy'.

Dorrie *wakes.* **Roy** *rejects her. She leaves, defeated.*

Roy   See ya.

Dorrie   Sorry . . .

Roy *takes an E and wanders out by the riverside.*

Bernard *is also wandering . . .*

Music ends.

Roy   Bernard?

Bernard   Roy! All right?

Roy   Bernard! (*He hugs him.*)

Bernard   Are you oan somethin?

Roy   Ecstasy.

Bernard   Nivir thoat ah'd see you Eckied up, Roy.

Roy   Oan it non-stoap fir the last six months, man.

Bernard   Well, it agrees wi ye.

Roy   Bernard. Listen. You're all right, man, ken?

Bernard   Roy –

Roy   Naw, you hud the whole thing sussed way back. I
was a fuckin wanker, I couldnae handle anything. I'm no
just talkin aboot you being a buftie . . . eh being gay, I jist
mean everything . . . I mean . . . aw fuck, Bernard, I'm
really sorry man . . . it's not the E talkin, ah've just fucked
things up, Bernard.

Bernard   We aw fuck things up, Roy.

Roy   Ah nivir goat tae know ye, Bernard. Ah acted like a cunt tae you . . .

Bernard   It worked both ways.

They hug.

Roy   But ah've changed, Bernard. I've allowed myself to feel. That means that ah huv tae dae somethin, like tae sort ay prove tae myself that I've changed.

Bernard   It's okay, Roy . . .

Roy   Try tae understand. Ah mean . . . likesay . . . Fuck, ah sound like the auld man. Meant fir better things!

Bernard   Aye . . .

They are back at Roy's.

Roy   You all right?

Bernard   No bad.

Roy *looks at* **Bernard**'s *clothes, face . . .*

Bernard   Roy . . .
I've got the virus. I tested positive. I'm HIV.

Roy   Bernard . . . naw . . . fuck . . . how . . .

Bernard   A couple ay months ago. It's cool though . . . aw mean it's no cool, but that's the wey it goes eh. But it's the quality thing in life, Roy. Life's good. Hang on to life. Hang on to it.

Roy *cries.*

Bernard   C'moan, Roy, stoap acting like a big poof!
(*Laughs.*) It's awright, man. It's okay.
(*Cries.*) See y'around. Ah'll – (*Exits.*)

Roy   Bernard!
Time tae go eh?

(*Takes thirty paracetamol* . . .) It's not running away. That's
what I've been doing all my fucking life, running away from
feelings. Running away because a fucking schemie, a
naebody, shouldnae have these feelings because there's
naewhere for them tae be expressed; and if you open up,
every cunt will tear you apart. So you become a fucking
animal. Or you run. But sometimes you can't run, can't
sidestep, duck and weave, because it just all travels along
with you, inside your fucking skull.
This isn't opting out. This is the way forward.

He puts a plastic bag over his head and tapes it round his neck.

Ambulance siren.

Dorrie   Roy! (*Tears bag off* **Roy**'s *face* . . .)

Paramedics *arrive.*

Paramedic 1 *tests for breathing and applies air bag.*
Paramedic 2 *breaks out defibrillator.* **Paramedic 3** *tests for
pulse.*

Paramedic 1 (*to* **Dorrie**)   Stand clear, please.

Paramedic 3   No pulse. (*Starts heart massage.*)

Paramedic 2 *applies paddles.*

Paramedic 3   VF!

Paramedic 2   Two-hundred-joule shock.

Paramedic 3   Charged.

Paramedic 2   Stand clear! (*Gives shock.*)

Shock slap.

Paramedic 3   No.

Paramedic 2   Two-hundred-joule shock.

Paramedic 3   Charged.

Paramedic 2   Stand clear. (*Gives shock.*)

Shock slap.

Paramedic 3   Sinus rhythm!

Paramedic 2   Okay.

Paramedics *carry* **Roy** *to a bed, between heaven and earth.*

Kirsty   The crazy thing is, I actually fancied you. I thought you were a bit different. Remember that night, in the club? I thought you were a nice-looking felly. But I was scared to talk to you. Scared. Now I just hate you. For what you did to me. I hate you . . . for what you did to me: my hate is understandable. But what about yours? I'd really love you to explain to me how you hated me so much, to do what you did. We know what you did, Roy; what you actually did. What happened to you? What was your fucking problem, you sad, sad cabbage, you sick, brutalised, fucked-up bastard? Why did *you* hate *me* so much?

Roy   I didnae hate ye. I wanted you.

Kirsty   O!
You buggered me.
When the others had done with me, you came to me with a mirror –

Roy   Naw, dinnae tell –

Kirsty   You pushed the mirror under my face and held my head back so you could see my pain while you buggered me, violently, roaring like like an animal. And when they cried enough, fucksake enough, she's had enough, you shouted, you shouted AH'M RUNNIN THIS FUCKIN GIG! AH SAY WHIN THE SLAG'S HUD ENOUGH!

Roy *buries his head in the bed, moaning.*

Kirsty   Why? WHY? WHAT HAPPENED TO YOU?

Gordon   Roy? Roy? Are you sleeping, Roy? You're not sleeping. It won't hurt, Roy. Your Uncle Gordon would never hurt you. Just lie perfectly still now, Roy, or there will be big trouble when your dad hears about this.

Roy *screams . . .*

Gordon   Shut up you little bastard, I'm warning you,
shut the fuck up!

Gordon *buggers* **Roy** *violently . . .*

Roy *cries for his mother.*

Gordon *quiets him . . . lays him down on the bed, and leaves.*

Kirsty   I understand.
Pain gets passed from body to body, life to life. It has a life
of its own. Like a virus.
Maybe there are exceptionally strong people who can just
say 'no more' and stop the pain passing on. Maybe there are
nice people who bottle it up and let it tear them apart
without ever hurting anyone else.
But we're not exceptionally strong people, are we, Roy? Or
particularly nice people. We're ordinary. And when we
hurt, we have to pass the pain on to others. We have to
hate.
There is no justification; no one has the right to do what you
had to do to me . . . or what I have to do to you now. All
that matters is, we have to do it.
Her fingers are holding his eyes open, one eyelid at a time,
and her surgical scissors are snipping his eyelids neatly off.
Look up, see! See, she is cutting his penis off now. And she is
letting him taste it, as she once had to – in his mouth. Don't
speak. There's nothing more to say. It's all been said. It's
over now, and the scissors are pushed into his neck. And the
blood flows all around his shoulders, like a girl's long hair
spread out on the bed.
She walks out of the hospital. It is snowing.

It snows . . .

End.

Irvine Welsh's

Ecstasy

Adapted by Keith Wyatt

Love the life you live. Live the life you love.

Sound Advice

'We're just pulling it out of our asses.'

Ecstasy Tour Slogan

To Victoria

Adapted for the stage by Keith Wyatt, based on the story 'The Undefeated' from the novel *Ecstasy* by Irvine Welsh.

Ecstasy was first performed in Edmonton, Alberta, Canada, at the Rev nightclub, during the Fringe Festival in August 1998. The cast was as follows:

Lloyd	Keith Wyatt
Heather	Shannon Quinn
Hugh	Troy O'Donnell
Ally	Garett Ross
Marie	Sarah Wells
Hazel	Victoria Stusiak
Amber	Clarice Eckford
DJ	Cory Payne

Dancers
Ben/Mandy/Chad/Carmen/Iain/Celina/Cam/Steve/Shannon/Tabitha/Jordan

Bar-tender	Jordan Stewart/Jay Hanley

Visuals by Ryu Tono
Sound production and spinning by Cory Payne
Direction and dramaturgy by Sandra Nicholls
Produced by Raven Productions and Oliver Friedmann from the Rev

Ecstasy Tour 1999 performed at the Rev nightclub in Edmonton and the Republik in Calgary with the following cast:

Lloyd	Keith Wyatt
Heather	Shannon Quinn
Hugh	Troy O'Donnell
Ally	Garett Ross
Marie	Pru McEvoy
Hazel	Victoria Stusiak
Amber	Celina Stachow
DJ	Cory Payne

Lighting design by Tanya Lampey
Visuals by Cody Wan Kenobi
Sound production and spinning by Cory Payne
Direction and dramaturgy by Sandra Nicholls
Produced by Raven Productions and Oliver Friedmann from the Rev

For the performance at the System Soundbar in Toronto, the part of **Heather** was played by Erin Malin, and **Marie** was played by Jennifer Goodhue.

The Canadian company Raven Productions returned *Ecstasy* to its Edinburgh origins by performing at the Venue during the Edinburgh Fringe Festival in August 2000. The Edinburgh performance was accomplished only through the cooperative support and encouragement of Brian McCallum and Norman Evans with Raven Productions.

The majority of the characters were recast with Scottish actors for the Edinburgh performance.

Characters

Lloyd
Heather
Hugh (Woodsy/Nukes/Mr
Moir/Eric/Restaurateur)
Ally (Drewsy/Mrs Mckenzie/Vaughan/
Mr Case/Bill/Reverend Brian/Robert)
Marie (Veronica/Moll)
Hazel
Amber (Victim/Polis)
DJ

Act One

Scene One

Nightclub. Dancers are moving in slow motion, while **Lloyd** *is getting a backrub from* **Amber**.

Lloyd   Ah am fuckin well fed up cause there's nothing happening and ah've probably done a paracetamol but fuck it you need to have positive vibes and wee Amber, she's rubbing away at the back ay ma neck saying –

Amber   It'll happen, Lloyd, it'll happen.

Lloyd   When this operatic slab of syth seems to be 3D and ah realise that I'm coming up in a big way as that invisible hand grabs a hud ay me and sticks me on to the roof because the music is in me around me and everywhere, it's just leaking from my body.

Music intensifies as does dancing. Music comes down and dancing slows.

Lloyd   This is the game this is the game and ah look around and we're all going phoah and our eyes are just big black pools of love and energy and my guts are doing a big turn as the quease zooms through my body and ah think I'm going tae need tae shit but ah hold on and it passes and I'm riding this rocket to Russia . . .

Music and dancing intensifies again, it eases.

Lloyd (*to* **Amber**)   No bad gear, eh.

Amber   Aye, sound.

Ally   Awright eh.

Lloyd   Then it's ma main man on the decks, and he's on the form tonight, just pulling away at our collective psychic sex organs as they lay splayed out before us and ah get a big rosy smile off this goddess in a sexy top, and this big

boneheided cunt falls into me and gives me a hug and
apologises and I'm slapping his hard wall of a stomach
thanking my lucky stars we're E'd and at this club and not
pished at the Edge or somewhere braindead no that ah
would touch that fucking rubbish . . . whoa rockets . . . whoa
it's still coming and I'm thinking now is the time to fall in
love now now now but not with the world with that one
special her, just do it, just do it now, just change your whole
fucking life in the space of a heartbeat, do it now . . . but
nah . . . this is just entertainment . . .

Music and dancing up, then:

DJ*'s speeches are said to the audience and should build with the same
energy as a hard-hitting track, drawing the audience in and providing it
with a means to understand.*

DJ (*ecstatic exhale*)   It's kicking in. (*Breathe and feel.*) The music
is, surging, defining. Before it was pushing and pulling. Now
ah'm going wi it, my body bubbling – flowing with the
roaring bass lines and the tearing dub plates. Aw fuck, ah'd
love to give the world an E! Man, all the joy of love for
everything good is in me, even though ah can see all the
bad. Ah can see what needs to be done!
You have to party!
You have to party harder than ever!!
It's your duty to show that you are still alive!!!
Ah know this isn't the complete answer, because it will all
still be here when we stop tonight, but right now it's the best
show in town.

Music and dancing swell. Sound levels drop.

Lloyd (*to* **Amber**)   Listen, fancy hitting a bedroom for a
meeting of minds and other bits?

Amber   No, ah'm no into sex with you. Ah fancy firing
right intae Ally later on, he looks so fucking gorgeous.

Lloyd   Yeah. Yeah he does.

Amber *moves away and is replaced by* **Hazel**.

Hazel   Ah'm up for it.

Lloyd   Eh?

Hazel   A shag, like. That's what you were talking to Ambs aboot, eh? You and me, then. The bedroom.

Lloyd   Ah, was going to get round to asking you before ah goat diverted by . . . let's just see . . . before ah was diverted by Amber's KB . . . whoa ahm ah in touch with mae feelings or what. (*Walking past* **Ally**) Amber's saying she's intae firing intae ye.

Ally   The important thing, man, is that ah love Amber, whatever happens sexually . . . that's just detail. The important thing, man, is that ah love everybody I know in this room. And ah know everybody! Except these boys, but ah'd love these cunts as well if ah knew them. Ninety per cent of people are lovable, man, once ye get tae ken them . . . if they believe in themselves enough . . . if they love and respect themselves, ye ken what ah'm saying . . .

Lloyd (*to* **Hazel**)   Let's go for it . . .

Lloyd *and* **Hazel** *move to a platform that serves as a bed. Music and dancing intensify then give way to music for the next scene, dancers exit.*

Scene Two

Lloyd (*undressing, to audience*)   We're all back at Hazel's gaff, and in the bedroom Hazel struggles out of her kit and ah get out of mine. We jump under the duvet. It's too hot to be under the duvet but this is in case any cunt comes in, which they will. We've got the tongues working hard and ah probably taste very salty and sweaty cause she does. It takes me yonks tae get an erection, but that doesnae bother ays because ahm mair intae the touching oan E than the penetration. She's gaun pretty radge though and ah manage to bring her off using my fingers. Ah'm just lying there

watching her orgasm like ah was watching her score for
Hibs. We'll just play that one back again, Archie . . . I want
it tae happen for her seven times. (*Ecstatic exhale.*) This is so
good cause ah'm still rushing and the tactile sensitivity has
been increased a mere tenfold by the Ecky. Our skins are so
sensitive it's like we can just reach inside each other and
caress all those internal bits and pieces. We work ourselves
round into the sixty-nine and as ah start licking and she does
there's no way that ah, at any rate, am no going to come
quickly so we break off and ah get on top and inside her and
then she's on top of me and then ah'm on top of her and
then she's on top of me. It's a bit too much theatrics from
her, ah suspect; could be wrong, perhaps she's just
inexperienced because she must only be about eighteen or
something when I'm thirty-fucking-one which is possibly too
old to be carrying on like this when ah could be married to a
nice fat lady in a nice suburban house with children and a
steady job where ah have urgent reports to write informing
senior management that unless certain action is taken the
organisation could suffer, but it's me and Purple Haze here
together, fuck sake. And now it's getting better, more
relaxed, it's getting soulful, it's getting good . . .

. . . It's fine fine fine and Hazel and ah spill fluids in and
over each other and ah'm sticking the amyl nitrate up her
nose and mines and we're holding on to that high crashing
wave of an orgasm together.

WHOA HO HO

HO HO

HO

OOOOOOOHHHHHOOOOOHHHHHHOOOOOO
OHHHHH!!!!!!!!

Ah like the after-feeling with my heart pumping from
orgasm and nitrate. It's barry feeling mae body readjust my
heartbeats slow doon.

Hazel   That was brilliant.

Lloyd   It was . . . fruity. A full fruit-flavoured one.

Scene Three

Bits from Lorraine Goes To Livingston *can be mixed by the DJ as a voice-over or they may be read as a voiced scene.*

Heather *stands holding a book and an umbrella. She reads.*

Heather   'It was not until the end of March that Lorraine and Miss May set out to accomplish the long trek to London. To a young girl from the Scottish borders, who had only once been as far as Edinburgh, every new sighting on the road was viewed with eager interest.
They travelled by an old coach pulled by two sturdy beasts and driven by Tam Greig, who cursed the rain that had been falling heavily for most of the day; for the sodden Lincolnshire landscape greatly slowed thier approach to the Gonerby Moor.'

Scene Four

Music: soft ambient track.

Lloyd   It's really weird how you can be so intimate with someone you dinnae really ken on E. It takes a long time to get that intimate oan straight street. Ye huv tae build uptae it, eh.

Ally   That wee Hazel's a total wee doll. Dirty cunt man, you, eh. Fuck sake, Lloyd, ah wish as wis sixteen now and had aw this. Punk and that, that was shite compared to this . . .

Lloyd   But ye have got it, ya daft cunt, just like you had punk, just like ye'll have the next thing that comes along, cause you refuse tae grow up. Ye just like tae have yir cake and eat it. It's the only fucking way, man.

Ally   Nae point in huving yir cake if ye cannae fucking well scran it back, eh no?

Lloyd   This is brilliant . . . how wis Tenerife by the way?
Ye never really telt ays.

Ally   Ace, man. Better than Ibiza. Ah'm no joking. Ye
should've come, Lloyd. You'd have lapped it up.

Lloyd   Ah really wanted tae. Cannae save, that's mae
problem.

Amber *enters with two pieces of orange, she gives them to the boys,
kisses* **Lloyd** *on the cheek and leaves.*

Lloyd   You should fire intae Amber. She's up fir ye, man.

Ally   Fuck, Lloyd, man, ah cannae be bothered shagging
Amber. Ah've started tae feel bad aboot chasing wee dolls,
filling thir heads wi shite and knobbing them, then running
like fuck until the weekend. Ah feel like ah'm between
fourteen and sixteen years auld again, when it was just a
shag tae try and get it over wi as soon as possible. Heading
straight back tae the first stage ay sexual development, me,
eh, man.

Lloyd   Aw aye, what's the next stage?

Ally   Ye take yer time, gie the lassies a good feel, try to get
her tae come, find clitoris, try oral sex . . . that wis me fae
aboot sixteen tae aboot eighteen. Then eftir that it wis eywis
positions wi me. Dae it different weys, try different
approaches like doggie style, on chairs, up the arse, and aw
that sort of shite, sort ay sexual gymnastics. The next stage
was tae find a lassie and try tae tune intae each other's
internal rhythms. Make music thegither. The thing is,
Lloyd, I think ah've passed that stage and ah'm headin back
in the full circle when ah want tae go forward.

Lloyd   Maybe yuv jist covered everything.

Ally   Naw. No way, man. Ah want that kind ay psychic
communion, gittin right inside each other's nut, like astral
flight and that. And that period is now until I find it. Never
had it, man. Had the internal rhythms, but no the joining of
the souls. Never even came close. The Eckies help, but the

only way you can get the joining ay the souls is if you let her into your head and she lets you into hers, at the same time. It's communication, man. You can't get that with any Party Chick, even when your both E'd up. It has to be love. That's what ah'm really looking for, Lloyd: Love.

Lloyd   Yir a fuckin sexual philosopher, Mister Boyle.

Ally   Naw, ah'm no joking. Ah'm looking for love.

Lloyd   Maybe that's what we're all really looking for, eh, Ally?

Ally   The thing is, Lloyd, man, mibbe ye cannae look fir it. Mibbe it hus tae find you.

Lloyd   Aye, but until ye do, ye want a fucking good ride but, eh. (*To audience*) Ah thought about crashin with Hazel, but ah could feel masel growin distant with the MDMA runnin down in ma body. So ah headed home where ah necked two eggs and washed them down with a bottle of Beck's. (*Exits.*)

Scene Five

Bar sounds – radio-quality sound on music.

Heather   It seems like it's all men here in the bar this dinner time. One prick looks at me like I'm soliciting. Here! (*Sits, opens romance novel* Lorraine Goes To Livingston.)

'Lorraine's attention was caught by the flirtatious eye of a handsome young man. He seemed strangely familiar, and she fancied that she might have seen him before; upon recollection she felt herself blush – Colonel Cox! You are . . .'

Marie *enters carrying two gin and tonics. She approaches* **Heather** *and completes Lady Huntingdon's line:*

Marie   'You are so scandalous . . . drinking alone.'

Heather   Marie! (*Gets up to give* **Marie** *a hug.*) Marie is the same age as me. She parties and sleeps with loads of guys. I – I live with Hugh in a house.

They greet each other until **Marie** *sees they are being watched by the same guy who was staring at* **Heather** *earlier* (could be an audience member).

Marie   What the fuck are you looking at?

Heather   He's been staring like that since I got here.

The first part of the following speech can, in part, be delivered for the benefit of the 'voyeur'.

Marie   You know, Heather, men can be divided into three categories like, they're either: gay, married, or pricks!

Heather   Do you think so?

Marie   Aye. Fortunately the pricks can be subdivided into two different classifications – the tolerable and the intolerable; though it seems it's always a woman's sense of pity that allows her to tolerate him. But you must be careful. Don't think just because a man is married or gay he cannae be a prick.

Heather   Don't be daft, Marie . . . you can't think all men are pricks.

Marie   Aw hen, I don't think all men are pricks. Just the ones I date. (*They both laugh.*) Let's get out of here.

Scene Six

Woodsy *with headphones at the decks. Music comes up. Levels come down.*

Lloyd   A coupla days later ah woke up on Woodsy's couch feeling shitey. The night before some of us went off to the pish and in preparation we had taken a coupla jellies each to save money. Now ah'm sick with a dentist-drill headache and my lip is burst and swollen and have like a nasty smudged bit of purple-black mascara under my right eye. This reminded me why ah took class As instead of alcohol. Ah mind ay Nukes and me paggering. Fuck knows whether it was wi each other or some other fucker. Given the slightness of my wounds it was probably some other fucker cause Nukes is a hard cunt and would have done me a lot more damage.

Woodsy (*comes out from behind the decks*)   You fucked it up good-style last night, eh?

Lloyd   Aye, Nukes an me hit the satellite tellies and went for it. Ended up in some brawl.

Woodsy   Youse cunts are fuckin crazy. Alcohol's Satan's instrument, man. As fir jellies . . . well, it's no often that ah agree wi that poofy wee Tory cunt on the telly . . . but fuckin hell, man, ah expect such behaviour fae Nukes, him being a cashie n that, but I thought you'd have a wee bit mair savvy, Lloyd.

Lloyd   Ah Woodsy, man. (*To audience*) That cunt Woodsy was on this religion kick. He'd kept at it mind you, it was last summer when it began. The cunt had claimed to see God after two Supermarios and two Snowballs at the outdoor Rezurrection. We dumped him in the Garage Room tae chill, he seemed tae be overheating badly. Ah stuck a Volvic in his hand and left him to the pink elephants. Wrong really, but ah was so fuckin up, and the light show was so phenomenal in the main tent that ah wanted tae get back to the action. The care-plan fucked up though when Woodsy's queasy attack necessitated him heading for the putrid chemical bogs to converse with God on the big aluminium telephone.

Woodsy (*as if he is vomiting*)   Oh God! Oh Jesus!

Lloyd   There he met the Big Chief.

Woodsy   Oh Christ!

Lloyd   The worst thing was that God apparently told him that Ecstasy was His gift to those in the know, who then had the duty to spread the word. He apparently instructed Woodsy to set up a Rave Gospel Club.

Woodsy   Listen, Lloyd, you still goat they Technics decks at yours?

Lloyd   Aye, bit thir Shaun's like. Jist till eh comes back fae Thailand, eh.

Woodsy   Ye must be gitting quite good oan them, eh?

Lloyd   Awright.

Woodsy   Look, Lloyd, ah've goat this gig organised at the East Pilton Parish Church. Ah want you oan the bill. You first, then me. What dae ye think?

Lloyd   When's this?

Woodsy   Next month. The fourteenth. It's a while likes.

Lloyd   Sound. Count ays in.

Woodsy (*exiting*)   Eh ye fancy some eggs?

Lloyd   Yeah awright. (*To audience*) Actually, ah was shite on the decks but ah reasoned that a deadline would force ays tae get my act thegither. Ay wisnae so chuffed when Woodsy telt me he wanted samplings of hymns and gospel music mixed intae techno, house, garage and ambient stuff, but ah was still up for it. Anyway, ah decided tae spend a lot of time at home with the decks.

Scene Seven

Lloyd's.

Lloyd   One afternoon ah was settling down to a bit of Richard Nixon when the door went. The music was low,

but ah still thought it was the yuppie cunts across the
landing who complained about anything and everything.

Ah went for the door and before me stood auld Mrs
Mckenzie from upstairs.

Mrs Mckenzie (*she spits out, face screwed up:*)   Soup.

Lloyd (*to audience*)   Ah remembered. Ah had forgotten to
go to the supermarket to get ingredients for a pot of soup.
Ah always make a big pot on a Thursday before the
weekend ay abuse starts so ah know I've got something
nutritious in if I'm too fucked or skint tae dae anything else.
Ah take auld Mrs Mckenzie some up in a Tupperware bowl.
She's a nice auld cunt, but what started off as a one-off
gesture of goodwill has now evolved into custom and
practice and it's starting tae fracture ma tits tae pieces.
(*To Mrs Mckenzie*) Sorry, Mrs Mack, no had a chance tae
make it yit eh no.

Mrs Mckenzie   Aye . . . ah jist thought . . . soup . . . the
laddie doonstairs always brings up a bowl ay soup oan
Thursday . . . ah wis jist tellin Hector. Soup . . . ah wis jist
sayin tae Hector the other day. Soup. The laddie doon the
stairs. Soup.

Lloyd   Aye, ah'll be makin it in a bit.

Mrs Mckenzie   Soup soup soup . . . ah thought we'd be
gittin some soup.

Lloyd   It's aw in hand, Mrs Mack, ah kin assure ye ay
that.

Mrs Mckenzie   Soup . . .

Lloyd   THE SOUP ISN'T READY YET, MISSUS
MCKENZIE. WHEN I'VE MADE IT, WHICH WILL BE
LATER ON TODAY, I SHALL BRING SOME UP TO
YOU. OKAY?

Mrs Mckenzie   Soup. Later on.

Lloyd   THAT'S IT, MISSUS MCKENZIE. SOUP.
LATER ON.

Mrs Mckenzie   The soup's comin.

Lloyd (*to audience*)   Ah went back inside, wrapped it on the
Richard and headed oot tae the shops tae get the
ingredients for the soup. As ah left there was a message on
the answer machine. It was a long rambling statement fae
mae pal Nukes that actually said nothing except that his
hoose had been raided by the polis . . .

Scene Eight

Hugh *and* **Heather**'s. *No music.* **Heather** *filing her nails* . . .
Hugh *enters whistling/singing Dire Straits' 'Money for Nothing'.*

Hugh   Good day?

Heather   Yeah, no bad. What do you want for tea? I
should of got something ready before this. I just couldn't be
bothered.

Hugh   Whatever there is. (*Sits down in front of TV, picks up
remote control.*)

Heather   Eh, scrambled eggs on toast okay?

Hugh   Great.

Heather   How was your day?

Hugh   Not bad, Jenny and I did a presentation for the
area management team on zoning. It seemed to be well
received, I think we'll persuade them.

Heather   Nice one. (*Pause.*) I'm going out tonight.

Hugh   Oh.

Heather   With Marie. Now that we work in different
offices we never get a chance to see each other. I'm just

going round to hers. Probably get takeaway and a bottle of wine.

Hugh   There's a good film on Two tonight.

Heather   Oh aye?

Hugh   *Wall Street.* Michael Douglas.

Heather   Oh right. I said to Marie but.

Hugh   Oh yeah. I see.

Heather   Fine then.

Hugh   Fine.

Scene Nine

Lloyd*'s.*

Lloyd (*walks in with bag of groceries. To audience*)   Soup ingredients.

He puts down the groceries and turns on the portable stereo. Music on (volume low). He pulls a small plastic bag of pills out of his crotch. He holds them up to the light.

These are shite, ah'll never fuckin well sell these!

Picks up phone and starts dialling. Phone starts to ring as **Lloyd** *takes a seat.* **Nukes** *enters another part of the stage, answers phone.*

Lloyd (*to* **Nukes** *on phone*)   Nukes, what's the story?

Nukes   That's me finished wi the cashies and the collies. Ah'm a marked man now, Lloyd. Polis doon here the other night accusing ays ay aw sorts ay things, man. Well oot ay fuckin order.

Lloyd   Ye git charged?

Nukes   Naw, but it shit ays up a bit. Some ay the boys say no tae worry, but fuck that, man. Ah'm daein a bit ah dealing and that could be three fucking years oot my life jist for a bit ay swedging at the fitba.

Lloyd   Ah wis gaunnae ask if you could punt some stuff fir ays n aw . . .

Nukes   No way. Low profile for a while, that's me.

Lloyd   Awright then. Come doon fir a blow next week but, eh.

Nukes   Awright.

Lloyd   Cheers, Nukes . . . eh, ye mind ay what happened the other night? Did we git intae some bother?

Nukes   Ye dinnae want tae ken, Lloyd.

Lloyd   Nukes . . . (*Hangs up phone, the doorbell sounds.*) Fuck!

Veronica (*Poisonous Cunt*) *enters with the* **Victim**, *they are carrying overnight bags and their hands are full of personal items – it appears as though they will be staying for a while.* **Lloyd** *speaks to the audience.*

Lloyd   It was the Poisonous Cunt; she'd got her nickname because some bastard fucked her once and either wouldn't do it again, or did do it but not to her satisfaction so she'd got her old man Solo to trash his coupon. She was in tow with the Victim whose eyes were fixed in a nervous, tense stare which even my most open smile couldnae break down. The Victim was a chronic fuck-up. People like her always seemed to hang out with the Poisonous Cunt. In turn, she kept their self-esteem low and made sure that they stayed in psychic immiseration. She was a curator of dead souls. It concerned me that ah seemed tae be spending more time with the Poisonous Cunt: we just turned each other on to suppliers of drugs and good deals. (*To the girls:*) Diddly dit dit dee, two ladies, and I'm ze only man. Yah.

Veronica   She's fucked up.

Lloyd   What's new?

Veronica   She's deluding herself, ah told that tae her, 'You're fucking well living in a fool's paradise, hen,' ah said to her, Lloyd. But she would not listen. Now she's getting it aw back. And who's the first one she comes runnin tae?

Lloyd   Right . . . right . . .

Veronica   She misses fucking periods aw the time and goes through this 'I'm up the stick' shite. Ah felt like saying to her: you cannae get up the stick when he's shagging you up the arse, but I dinnae. Ah felt like saying to her: the reason you always miss periods is because you're fucked up in the heid, hen: your life's a mess and if you're that fucked in the heid it's bound tae tell on yir body. But ah bit my tongue.

Lloyd   Her and Bobby again, eh . . .

Veronica   Aye, fuckin Bobby, but that's no all, Lloyd, we wouldnae have come here if the problem wis jist Bobby. Mind that Firm, Davey, that she used to go with?

Lloyd   Aye. Him that started fuckin around with that girl whae had no arms?

Veronica   Aye . . . well he's oot ay jail, and after four years she's still no so chuffed to see him.

Lloyd   Sounds sensible after what he and his girl did to that executive-type.

Veronica   Lloyd, it isnae that she thinks they're gonnae tape her to some motor-yard workbench and saw her arms off? She jist disnae want to be near him. The thing is, Lloyd, he belled Solo earlier and said he was gonnae come roond for some blow. Ah telt Soho that it'd be best if the fuck didnae come over, but Solo just started fuckin laughin, so we had tae get oot. We just want tae sit here and chill for a bit until that horror-show Davey leaves.

Lloyd   Look, that's sound by me, but ye'll huv tae dae it alaine, eh. Aw fuck! (*Moves to get soccer ball.*) Today is Thursday?

Victim   Nae – it's Doomsday.

Lloyd *is moving to exit and is stopped by the* **Victim**'s *words.*

Veronica   Aw hen, listen, it's not the end of the world . . .

Victim   Nae, today is Doomsday, that is the only reasonable explanation. The stars and planets have aligned themselves, moved out of their random formation to become one long shaft that has been rammed up my arse on the last day of the world, the last day of my miserable existence.

Veronica (*seeing the decks*)   These your decks, Lloyd? You any good?

Lloyd   Naw . . . yeah . . . ah mean ah'm awright. Look ah've goat tae go. Ah'm meeting this boy whaes supposed tae have some ay they pink champagnes, the speedballs, ken?

Veronica (*digs in her pockets for some money*)   Give me five . . . naw, six . . .

Lloyd   That's if ehs goat thum likes. (*Takes money.*) Ah goat tae go, ah shouldnae be late meeting this cunt. (*Exits.*)

Scene Ten

Street.

Lloyd (*to audience*)   Ah wisnae gaunnae try and score, ah was just going to meet my brother Vaughan. It was pretty glorious summer's evening when ah got out on the street and ah found myself with a strange spring in my step. Of course, it was a Thursday. Last weekend's drugs had been well and truly processed by now (*the rest of the speech is said while* **Lloyd** *juggles and kicks the soccer ball*), the toxins discharged: sweated, shat and pished out; the hangover finito; the psychological self-loathing waning as the chemistry of the brain defucks itself and the fatigue sinking into the past as the old adrenalin pump starts slowly getting back into gear in preparation for the next round ay abuse. (*Stops playing with the ball.*) This feeling when you've cracked the depressive hangover and the body and mind is starting to fire up again, is second only to coming up on good E.

Vaughan *and* **Eric** *enter in slow motion. They are playing bools in slow motion as* **Lloyd** *finishes the above speech.* **Lloyd** *moves to join them.*

Lloyd   At the club Vaughan's playing bools with this old cunt. He nods at me, and the auld cunt looks up with a slightly tetchy stare and ah realise that I've broken his concentration by casting my shadow over his line of vision. Steeling himself, the auld codger lets the bool roll, roll, roll, and I'm thinking he's gone too far out, by naw, the wily auld cunt kens the score because the bool does a Brazilian spin, that's what it does, a fuckin Brazilian spin, and it comes back like a fuckin boomerang and slips like a surreptitious queue-jumper in behind Vaughan's massed lines of defence, rolling up the jack and sneaking it away. Ah cheer the auld gadge for that shot. Vaughan has his last one but ah decided not tae watch but to go in and get some drinks. Ah discover I've a wrap of speed in my pocket, left over from fuck knows when. Ah take it to the bog, and chop it out into some lines on the cistern. (*Snorts a line.*) If I'm gaunnae have to talk bools ah might as well go for it in a big fuckin way . . . (*Snorts a second line.*) Ah come out, charged up to fuck. Ah remember this gear, dabbing away at it the other week. It's much better to snort though, this stuff.

Vaughan *and* **Eric** *enter the booling club bar. Ambient bar sounds and music.*

Vaughan   Didnae stay for the climax, could have done wi yir support fir that last shot thair.

Lloyd   Sorry, Vaughan, ah wis burstin fir a tropical fish, eh. Did ye git it?

Eric   Naw, eh wis miles oot!

Lloyd   Nice one there, mate! Brilliant shot by the way, that wee spinner that nicked it in the end. Ah'm Lloyd, Vaughan's brother. That's L-L-OH-Y-D.

Eric   Aye, Lloyd, ah'm Eric. That's E-R-I-C. Ye play the bools yersel?

Lloyd   Naw, Eric, naw ah dinnae, mate; it's no really ma scene, ken. Ah mean ah'm no knockin the game n that, a great game . . . ah mean ah wis chillin oot the other day watchin that Richard Corsie gadge oan the box . . . he used to be wi the post did eh no? That boy kens how to fling a fuckin bool . . .

Vaughan   Eh, what yis wanting?

Lloyd   Naw naw naw, ah'll git them. Three lager, is it no?

Eric   Poof's pish, make mine Special.

Lloyd   A special drink for a special victory, eh Eric. (*Returns with drinks.*) Cheers, boys! Tell ye what, Eric, ah knew that you had the bools after seeing ye in action there. This gadge has bools, ah telt maself. That Brazilian spin, man! Whoa, ya cunt that ye fuckin well are!

Eric   Aye, it wis jist a wee thing ah thought ah'd try. Ah said tae masel, Vaughan's marshalled his defences well but, ah thought, try a wee sneaky one roond the back door and it just might come off.

Vaughan   Aye, it wis a good shot.

Lloyd   It wis fuckin ace. You've heard of total fitba, the Dutch invented it, right? Well this man here is total bools. You could have went for the blast there, Eric, tried that Premier League-style huffing and puffing but naw, ay bit ay class ay bit ay art. Fuckin hell! Expect the unexpected wi this man, eh?

Vaughan   Aye, too right. (*Takes a drink.*) Ye should go up and see Ma n Dad.

Lloyd   Aye . . . (*Pause.*) ah've been meanin tae drop by this tape ah made up for them. Motown, eh.

Vaughan   Good, they'll appreciate that.

Lloyd   Aye, Marvin, Smokie, Aretha n aw that. Listen, Eric, that stunt you pulled wi the bools . . .

Eric   Aye, fair took the wind oot ay Vaughan here's sails, that's if ye dinnae mind ays sayin like, Vaughan! Expect the unexpected!

Lloyd   (Twilight Zone *theme:*) Do-do-do-do, do-do-do-do, listen, Eric, your second name isnae Cantona, by any chance, is it?

Eric   Eh naw, Stewart.

Lloyd   It's just that there wis a Cantonaesque quality about that final shot thair. It fair blew fuckin Vaughan Buist's Express right out the fuckin water . . .

Lloyd *moves to* **Eric** *singing the cancan. The two begin to cancan.*

Vaughan   Aye . . . awright then. C'moan, Eric, Lloyd's no a member here!

Eric   Aye, well, the laddie's been signed in. Signed in as a guest. It's aw bona fide.

Lloyd   Ah think a certain Monsieur Vaughan Buist may be smarting over a recent sporting setback, n'est pas, Monsieur Cantona? He ees, ow you say, ay leetal peesed off.

Eric   Je suis une booler. Ha ha ha. (*The cancan stops. Laughing,* **Eric** *is taken by a coughing fit and moves back to his seat and his beer.*)

Vaughan   It's no that, Lloyd, aw ah'm tryin tae say is thit yir no a member here. Yir a guest. Yir the responsibility ay the people that bring ye. That's aw ah'm tryin tae say. It's jist like that club you go tae, Lloyd. That place up at the Venue. What's that club called?

Lloyd   The Pure.

Vaughan   Aye, right. It's like if you're at the Pure n ah wis tae come up n you were tae sign ays in.

Lloyd   As ma guest.

Vaughan   As yir guest . . . as the guest of one's brother Lloyd at the exclusive club in town he frequents . . .

They are interrupted by a choking sound as **Eric** *boaks thin beer-sick over the table.* **Eric** *begins laughing again.* **Lloyd** *moves to* **Eric**.

Lloyd   Aye, Eric, yir awright, man. Nae danger.

Laughing, **Lloyd** *and* **Eric** *move to exit together.* **Vaughan** *leaves alone.*

Lloyd   Aw fuck ah forgot ma ball.

Lloyd *returns for his ball. Then walks into the street scene.*

Scene Eleven

Lloyd *meets* **Veronica** *in the street. Street sound.*

Veronica   Eh Lloyd. Ah wis jist pickin up some stuff for Solo. You're pished!

Lloyd   A bit, aye.

Veronica   Did ye git the speedballs?

Lloyd   Naw . . . Ah didnae see the boy, eh. Eh . . . whaire's the Victim?

Veronica   Still at yours.

Lloyd   Fuck!

Veronica   What is it?

Lloyd   The Victim's bulimic! She'll clean out all the fuckin shoppin! (*He races back to his flat. Finds the grocery bag. To audience*) She had eaten and vomited up three raw cauliflowers. (*To* **Veronica**) There's only one left!

Cooking-show music. Replacing the grocery bag **Lloyd** *grabs a pot, cutting board and knife and starts chopping a cauliflower for the soup. Music level comes down.*)

Lloyd (*to audience*)   It took me ages, half pished, tae make the soup while the Victim sat and sobbed in front of the TV.

Veronica *moves to* **Lloyd**.

Veronica   Lloyd, about that money ah owe ye. Ah cannae afford tae pay ye, but ah dae have these. (*Pulls a tiny wrap of blotted paper from her pocket and hands it to Lloyd.*) Go light wi these trips, Lloyd, they're the fucking business.

Lloyd *pockets the tabs as* **Veronica** *moves over to the* **Victim**.

Cooking-show music comes up again and **Lloyd** *goes on preparing the soup.*

Lloyd (*to audience*)   After what seemed like an eternity, I finally finished making the soup. (*Pulls a Tupperware bowl and two spoons out of the pot. He gives the spoons to the two girls. To audience*) Ah took a tupperware bowl up to Mrs McKenzie. (*Exits flat.*)

Scene Twelve

Lloyd *enters street.*

Lloyd   That evening ah was heading through to Glasgow for the weekend to see some mates there. The thing was that ah had said tae my mate Drewsy that I'd help him out the morn's morning which ah wisnae really up for, but it wid be cash in hand for the weekend. (*Enters young lassie's bedroom. Observes his surroundings.*) Drewsy and me are in this Gumleyland ghetto.

Drewsy   It's just a skirtin job, Lloyd. That and new doors. Take nae time at aw.

Mr Moir *enters, gives* **Lloyd** *and* **Drewsy** *each a cup of tea and watches them work. Aware that they are being watched the two look up from their work.*

Mr Moir   Anything you need, lads, just give ays a shout. I'll be in the garden. (*Exits.*)

Lloyd (*to audience*)   Anywey, wir knockin oaf the rooms finestyle, and I'm starting tae recover from last night's pish, looking ahead tae the night oot wi the Weedgie cunts. Drewsy and me are in this room which is like a young lassie's bedroom. There's a poster ay the boy fae Oasis oan one waw, and one fae the dude oot ay Blur oan the other. (*At the portable stereo*) There's a few tapes thair n aw. Ah pit oan Blur's *Parklife*, cause ah quite like the title track where ye hear the boy that wis in *Quadrophenia* spraffin away.

Music comes up while **Lloyd** *goes back to work.*

Drewsy   Hey! Phoah . . . (*Music level is lowered.*) Look at this! (*Holds a pair of panties out reverently.*) Wish tae fuck ah could find the *dirty* laundry basket. Still, some nice wee panties here, eh?

Lloyd   Fuckin hell, man, ah'm totally in love wi this wee chick. Eh, how auld dae ye reckon she is?

Drewsy (*sniffing the underwear*)   Ah'd say beteeen fourteen and sixteen.

Lloyd   What a fuckin ice-cool wee bird.

Music comes up, **Drewsy** *dances around wi ay pair ay the lassie's knickers stretched ower his head and his glasses on top.* **Mr Moir** *catches him unawares.*

Mr Moir (*enters with a pair of garden shears*)   What's going on! What are you doing? That's . . . that's . . .

Drewsy   Eh, sorry, Mr Moir . . . just huvin a week joke, eh. Ha ha ha.

Mr Moir   Is that your idea of humour? Going through someone's personal belongings? Acting like an animal in my daughter's underpants!

Lloyd (*laughs*)   Heagh heagh heagh heagh . . .

Mr Moir   And what are you sniggering at? You think that's fuckin funny?

Lloyd   Aye.

Mr Moir   This . . . fuckin sick imbecile rummaging through my daughter's personal items!

Drewsy (*removes the panties from his head*)   Sorry.

Mr Moir   Sorry? Fuckin sorry are ye? Have you got children? Eh?

Drewsy   Aye, ah've got two laddies.

Mr Moir   And you think that's the way a father should behave?

Drewsy   Look, I've said I'm sorry. It was a stupid thing tae dae.

Drewsy *picks up his hammer.* **Lloyd** *is still holding his. They advance on* **Mr Moir**. **Mr Moir** *holds up his garden shears in defence.*

Drewsy   Now we can stand here and discuss how faithers should behave or me and my mate can get on and finish the job. Either way, you get billed. What's it to be?

Mr Moir   Take your tools and leave. I'll pay ye for the work that you've done, but you should think yourselves lucky you aren't getting reported!

Lloyd (*while they tidy up*)   Sorry ah couldnae tip ye oaf in time, Drewsy. It wis the music. Ah never heard the sneaky cunt. One minute nae sign, the next the cunt wis standing over ays watchin you daein yir wee dance.

Drewsy   One ay they things, Lloyd. Good fuckin laugh though, eh. Did ye see the cunt's face?

Lloyd   Did ye see yours?

Drewsy   Right enough! (*Laughter, exits.*)

Lloyd (*to audience*)   Drewsy peyed ays and ah got a taxi up tae Haymarket and got oan the train tae Soapdodge City. When ah got off the train at Queen Street ah took a taxi up tae Stevo's flat in the West End. Ah dropped a tab of the Poisonous Cunt's 'business' acids on the proviso that if her Eckies were shite then her acids wouldnae be too hot either. The acid wasnae up to much at first. Then it kicked up. Then it kicked up some mair.

Scene Thirteen

Amanda, **Claire** and **Stevo** *exist as voice-overs during* **Lloyd**'s *trip.* **Lloyd** *moves to a working surface with a cutting board, knife, stawberries and cream cheese.*

Lloyd   There is a ringing in my ears and ah hear some cunt say something which sounds a little like . . .

Stevo   Perhaps they'll understand the truth some day of why things remain different.

Lloyd (*to audience*)   Who was that?! Ah start to panic because it's goat nae context and because nobody could have said it. To calm down ah start on the masterchef preparation of the stawberries which becomes something of an urgent mission in my head. This is not because I'm para or fuck-all like that, but because there is a vacuum, a space in my head, which will be filled with bad thoughts if ah don't busy busy busy chop chop chop these strawbs and the trick is to daintily use this sharp knife to stab some cunt. (*Pause.*) Eh? No no no fuck off the trick is to why did ah say that no no no bad thoughts cannae be explained, that makes them worse, they just have to be ignored because what you do with the knife is to remove the white bit of strawberry and fill the resulting hole with cream cheese with a knob of cream cheese of what . . . Fuck . . . Ah don't know if I'm thinking this or saying it or both at the same time. (*Breathes.*) Phfoo phfoo . . . it takes more than a wee tab ay LSD to knock auld Lloyd Buist here out of his fuckin stride.

Amanda   Fine by us you eatin aw the strawberries by the by, Lloyd.

Lloyd   Ah look and sure tae fuck the remnants of strawberries are in evidence, husks n that, but examples of the fruit in its complete state are conspicuous by their absence. Greedy guts, Lloyd, I think to myself.

Claire   Greedy guts, Lloyd.

Lloyd   Fuckin hell, Claire, ah wis jist thinkin they words . . . it's like telepathy . . . or did ah say thum . . . this acid is really fuckin mad n the strawberries, ah've eaten aw the fuckin strawberries!! Ah start to panic a little bit. You see, the strawberries were my means of transportation from this dimension or state into another. Without strawberries I'm condemned to live in their fucking world which is no good at all. (*To the gang*) Ah'm away doon tae the deli fir mair ay they strawberries.

Claire   You mind yirsel, trippin like that.

Amanda   Aye, watch it.

Stevo   Mad gaun oot like that.

Lloyd   Naw, man, it's sound, ah feel great.

He moves on to the street.

Scene Fourteen

*[**Lloyd** *has to piss, he pisses – pissing sound – time passes.*

* *Indicates portion of the script that was cut from the last performance.*

Lloyd (*to audience*)   Ah hate pishing on acid because the distortion of time makes you think you've been pishing longer than you actually have and before ah know it ah'm getting bored with this pish and I'm putting my cock away before it's actually finished, well, it's finished but I've not really shaken it out. Fuck. I'll have a map of South America or South Africa on my groin unless ah take some positive fuckin action. Accusations fly, you know? J'accuse.]

What? Fuck off. It's Lloyd Buist. Lloyd Buist is my name, no Lloyd Beattie! B-U-I-S-T! People get me, Lloyd Buist, confused with the cunt Lloyd Beattie who was rumoured to have shagged his wee sister. Ah huvnae even got a fuckin wee sister. I rest ma fuckin case, Your Honour; your judge, jury and executioner psychopath who begins every Leith pub conversation with: Ach ah mind ah you. You wir the dirty cunt that . . . BUT AH AM FUCK-ALL LIKE THAT FREAK, WE SHARE A NAME . . . THAT'S AW . . . take it easy, mate, it's just this fuckin acid. (*To audience*) Ah never shagged my wee sister.

Stevo   You've no got a wee sister tae shag – if you did you probably would have though. Ha ha . . .

Lloyd *on the street.* **Robert** *and* **Richard** *come running through the scene looking back for their pursuer.* **Richard** *exits.* **Robert** *collides with* **Lloyd** *then exits while back-pedalling. He explains matters on the fly.*

Robert   Sorry, big man, cannae stop, we did a wee dine and dash . . . Yuv goat tae fir fuck sake, know what I mean, big man . . . ah mean ye cannae gie up the clubbin n that jist tae eat . . . (*Turns in a hurry to follow* **Richard**.) Catch you in chill-oot. (*Exits.*)

Lloyd   That's fuckin right! Good skills, Roberto! Good skills, Roberto my son! (*To audience*) Ah turn around and this bloated alcoholic is bearing down on me. We both know he will never capture the younger fitter men because their bodies are honed by dance and Ecstasy, and the more weighty, beefy fellow realises this and makes a grab for ays.

(**Restaurateur** *grabs* **Lloyd**.) Violence in the form of blows ah can take, but the idea of being constrained, no fuckin way.

Slow motion, **Lloyd** *hits the* **Restaurateur**. **Restaurateur** *goes down.* **Lloyd** *goes down.* **Restaurateur** *grabs* **Lloyd**. **Lloyd** *yells for help.*

Lloyd   Let go ye cunt it wisnae me. Help! Help polis! Polis help!

Polis *enters.*

Lloyd   Ah turn around and a polis officer is beside ays. Ah! Ah've got four trips in my poakits. I'm fishing out those wee squares of impregnated paper. Ah get the trips between my forefinger and thumb and ah swallow the lot, silly fucking cunt . . . ah swallowed the fuckin lot when ah could've even fuckin flung them away. No thinkin straight . . .

Polis   Was this man in your restaurant? (*Indicating* **Lloyd**.)

Restaurateur   No.

Polis   Well you're oot ay order, pal.

Lloyd (*to audience*)   Lloyd Buist from Leith, who is a waster and who has set himself up in opposition to the fascist British state, now to his extreme embarrassment finds one of its law-enforcement officers taking his side and ticking off the capitalist businessman who tried to apprehend said Leith man. I must have presented quite a compelling case in my defence cause –

Polis   And you – you're out of your face. Ah dunnae what the fuck you're on, and right now ah've goat far too much on tae be bothered. Any mair fuckin lip fae you and ah will be bothered. So shut it! Now you two shake hands and go about your business. (*Exits.*)

Restaurateur   Embarrassment that, eh! (**Lloyd** *shrugs.*) Sorry, mate . . . ah mean, ye could've goat me intae some bother thair. If ye pressed charges like. Ah appreciate it.

Lloyd   Listen, ya daft bastad, ah wis tripping oot ay ma face when the polis wanker came, n ah hud tae swallow some mair trips ah wis haudin. In aboot one minute ah'm gaunne be totally fuckin cunted here!

Restaurateur   Fuck . . . acid . . . ah've no done acid for years . . . Listen, mate, come along the road wi me. Tae the restaurant. Sit doon for a bit.

Lloyd   If ye goat drink thair, aye. Ye see, it's the only way ye can control a trip: force doon as much alcohol as possible. It's a depressant, ken.

Restaurateur   Aye, awright. Ah've goat drink in the restaurant. I'd take ye for a beer in a boozer, but ah've goat tae get back and prepare for the night. Seturday night, the busiest time n that.

Lloyd   Ah'm in nae position tae refuse.

Lloyd *sees the audience, he panics. Restaurateur calms him down and helps him to the restaurant.*

Restaurateur   'Sawright, mate, ah've goat ye here . . .

Lloyd   Ah love to boogie on a Saturday night . . . mind that cunt T-Rex?

Restaurateur   'Sawright, mate, wir jist alang the road . . . wir jist alang here . . .

They enter the restaurant. **Restaurateur** *dumps* **Lloyd** *on to a table, and goes to work behind the bar.*

Restaurateur   Jist cause ah've goat a restaurant though, pal, it disnae mean tae say that ah'm some big rich bastard who's hud it aw handed tae them oan a silver plate. Ah, jist like they boys, they pals of yours. Stealin fae thir ain kind! That's what that wis. That's the thing that disgusts me the maist. Ah mean tae say. Ah'm fae Yoker, ye know Yoker? Ah'm a red sandstone boy, me.

Lloyd   He's fuckin rabbiting oan a load ay shite and I'm fuckin blind and my breathing is fucked oh no don't think about the breathing no no no bad trip hopeless when ye think aboot the fuckin breathing most bad trips happen when you think about the fuckin breathing, but, but, we're different from say dolphins, because these daft cunts have tae think consciously about each and every breath they take when they come up for air and that. Fuck that fir a game ay sodgirs the poor wee cunts. No me but, no Lloyd Buist. A human being with a superior breathing mechanism, safe from the acid. You didnae have to think aboot the breathing, it just happened. Yes! (*Looking back to the* **Restaurateur**) What if . . . no no no, but what if, me now flying off to space seeing the Buist body: a deserted shell being dragged along to the mass-murderer pervert restaurateur's lair, this body being folded over a table with lubricants applied to the arsehole and penetration achieved just as the victim's carotid artery is severed with a kitchen knife.

Restaurateur   Take it easy. Ah've known hard times n aw, that's aw ah'm sayin.

Lloyd   Ah seem to be just breathing oot. There's nea sense of breathing in and if the breathing mechanism is part of the subconscious which it has to be, is that no precisely what the acid fucks up? Precisely, Holmes. Ha ha ha ha ha ha Flight Lieutenant Biggles reporting for duty, sir. Biggles, old man, don't stand so bloody close to me and put away that weapon while I'm talking to you. Did ah tell ye that your breathing is rather laboured, it's aw fuck fuck fuck fuck – (*Turns to* **Restaurateur** *who is wearing a ridiculous sombrero, screams.*)

Restaurateur   Take it easy there, yir hyperventilatin . . . I'll get ye a wee bevvy.

Lloyd   Whair the fuck is this?

Restaurateur   Stay cool, mate, it's ma restaurant. Gringo's. (*Cheesy music up, Mexican flavour.*) Gringo's Mexican Cantina. Now, what is it ye want?

Lloyd   A Long Island iced tea would be nice.

Restaurateur (*prepares drink*)   It's no that ah'm a money grabber and ah know that there are plenty people are starvin and homeless in Glasgow, bit that's the fuckin government's fault, no mine. Ah'm tryin tae make a fuckin livin. Ah cannae feed aw the poor, this isnae a soup kitchen. Ye know how much they fuckin criminals at the council charge in rates for this place?

Lloyd   Naw . . .

Restaurateur   It's no that ah'm a Tory, far fuckin from it. Mind you, that council's jist a fuckin Tory council under another name; that's what that is. Is it the same in Edinburgh?

Lloyd   Eh, aye, Edinburgh. Leith. Lloyd. (*He turns to see the* **Restaurateur** *serving him his drink with an arm that is six feet long. Panics.*) Ah nivir, ah mean, no the one that shagged ehs sister, that wis a different Lloyd . . . (**Restaurateur** *holds cocktail out for* **Lloyd**. *He takes the drink.*) Gracias.

Restaurateur   Cheers. Aye, see if ah wis votin fir any cunt, which ah'm no, ah'd vote SNP . . . naw, ah widnae, ah tell ye what ah wid vote for if ah wis votin fir anybody now; mind that boy that got sent tae jail for no peying his poll tax? What wis the boy's name?

Lloyd   Strawberry daiquiri.

Restaurateur   Naw . . . the boy that got sent tae jail for no peyin his poll tax. The militant boy.

Lloyd   Naw . . . ah need strawberries . . . A strawberry daiquiri, mate . . . that would dae me fine.

Restaurateur   Sorry, ma man, nae strawberries. It'll huv tae be lime daiquiri.

Lloyd   Nae strawberries . . . nae fuckin strawberries what a load ay shite, man . . . (*Cools down.*) That's sound, man. And thanks fir lookin eftir ays, eh.

Restaurateur   Naw, ah sortay feel bad about it, you takin aw they trips n that. How ye feeling?

Lloyd Sound.

Restaurateur Cause as ah say, ah'm jist trying to make a livin. But these guys, they're jist rubbish. They've goat the money tae go oot tae fuckin clubs aw night, but they steal food fae the likes of me. That's fuckin out of order.

Lloyd Naw, man, naw; ah admire they boys . . . they know that the game isnae fuckin straight. They know that there's a government fill ay dull, boring bastards who gie the likes ay us fuck all and they expect ye tae be as dull and miserable as they are. What they hate is when yir no, in spite ay aw thair fuckin efforts. What these government cunts fail tae understand is that drug and club money is not a fuckin luxury. It's a fuckin essential.

Restaurateur Ye cannae admire people like that. That's jist rubbish, then.

Lloyd Ah do admire the guys. Massive respect from Lloyd here; Leith's Lloyd, the one that never shagged his wee sister: massive respect tae they boys Richard and Robert fae Glesgie . . . dear auld Glesca toon . . .

Restaurateur Thought you said ye didnae know them?

Lloyd Ah know them as Richard and Robert; that's it, mate. I've blethered wi the boys, in chill-oot zones n that. That's as far as it goes . . . listen, ah'm fucked. Ah could be dying. Ah need tae get ma heid doon or something . . .

Restaurateur *exits.* **Lloyd** *sees that he is alone.*

Lloyd The boy went up to the front room to fix up some tables for the evening. Ah crawled across the bar and slid through an open window, fell on to the street down below. Ah goat up and started to run. Ah had tae keep movin. Then ah saw it. The sun rising above the tenements and ah knew ah had tae get into it. Ah had tae get right up intae it. Ah ran and ran as fast as ah could right up intae that big golden bastard in sky. (*Exits.*)

Scene Fifteen

Heather   I suppose what attracted me to Hugh in the first place was his sense of commitment. He was what I thought a rebel was: working class; into student politics; committed to the liberation of working people from the horrors of capitalism. What a lot of nonsense. Over the years Student Hugh has mutated into Private Sector Manager Hugh; committed to maximising profit through cost efficiency, resource effectiveness and market expansion. Hugh's ready.

Hugh *stands by the bed wearing nothing but a kilt. Sound: race-track starter's horn*

Heather   He's got the wife, the job, the house, the car. There's something missing. He thinks it's a baby. He doesn't have a great deal of imagination.

Hugh *drops the kilt. Sound of car ignition and revving motor.* **Hugh** *is bare-arsed. A sporin covers his genitals. He bumps his pelvis as the engines rev and then gets under the blankets with* **Heather**.

Heather   We don't really communicate so I can't actually tell him that I don't want a baby. We talk all right, talk in that strange language we've evolved for the purpose of avoiding communication. That non-language we've created. Perhaps it's a sign that civilisation is regressing. Something is anyway. Now his fingers have gone to my cunt. It's like a child trying to get into a jar of sweets. There's no sensuality to it, it's just a ritual. Now he's trying to get his prick inside me, forcing his way through my dry, tight, tense walls. (**Hugh** *starts to grunt.*) He's grunting. He always grunts. I remember when I first slept with him at university. Marie asked – What's he like? – Not bad, I said – bit of a grunter. I was sassy, in my own quiet way. I'm not like that now. My mother always said that I was lucky to have found someone like Hugh. 'He'll be a provider that one – just like your father.'

If Hugh provides everything, what do I have left?

Nurture Hughey-woowey. Nurture Baby-waby of Hughey-woowey.

Nurture resentment.

Hugh   . . . Ohh . . . you sexy fuck . . . (*Grunts.*)

Heather   Sexy Fuck. (*Pulls* Cosmo *out from under the pillow and browses while* **Hugh** *bumps her from behind.*) I habitually leave *Cosmo* open strategically on the coffee table and watch Hugh squint at and then recoil from its headlines: the vaginal and clitoral orgasm; is your partner good in bed?; how's your sex life?; does size really matter? A degree in English literature, a worthless qualification, but worth more than a browse through *Cosmo*.

Hugh (*part contempt, part patronising approval*)   Why do you read that muck, honey?

Heather   Does this captain of local industry in Dunfermline realise that he's sailing the ship of our relationship on to the rocks of oblivion? (**Hugh** *comes to a raucous of grunts while* **Heather** *speaks over him.*) Does he realise the effect he's having on his esteemed wife, Heather Thomson, also known in some select circles as Sexy Fuck? (**Hugh** *rolls over.*) No, he's looking the other way. His toxic sperm is inside me, trying to batter through my egg. Sexy Fuck. For four years he's fired his wallpaper paste into me. Sexy Fuck. I'm twenty-seven nearly, and I haven't had a fuckin orgasm in four years!

Scene Sixteen

Lloyd'*s.*

Veronica   Where you been?

Lloyd (*collapses*)   Glasgow.

Act Two

Scene One

Nightclub. **Dancers** *in chill-out. Music.*

Lloyd (*to audience*)   Later on that night ah went up tae Tribal wi Ally. Ah was just wanted tae crash but the cunt insisted that ah come along. Ah even had tae take a couple of my ain Es which was bad news. This batch were different again, like ketamine or something. (*Crashes out and calls:*) Ah'm pure cunted, ah cannae dance. Help! Ah'm trapped in chill-out.

Ally *enters.*

Ally   How you feelin, Lloyd?

Lloyd   Fucked.

Ally (*pulls out a wrap of meth and snorts it off* **Lloyd**'s *belly*) You should try some ay this crystal meth. Didnae even fuckin well blink eftir ah'd snorted this. Ah've hud a fuckin hard-on for three fuckin days, eh. Ah wis gaunnae abandon this quest fir love, break ma vows and bell Amber tae come roond n sit oan ma face. Didnae want tae fuck wi her heid even mair though, eh.

Lloyd   She in here the night?

Ally   Aye, here she comes, her and that Hazel. (*Gets up, leaving the meth, tempted by* **Amber** *he runs off.*)

Amber *takes his place.*

Lloyd   Ye dinnae huv tae sit wi ays, ah'm awright. Jist a bit cunted . . .

Hazel   'Sawright. (*Moves to* **Lloyd**'s *head.*)

Amber (*gets close to* **Lloyd**)   Aw aye, that Veronica wis looking for you.

Lloyd   Veronica? . . . The Poisonous Cunt! Is she in here the night?

Amber   Naw, this wis earlier at the City Café, eh . . . How you doin, Lloyd?

Hazel   Are ye feelin okay?

Lloyd   Fine.

Amber   Dinnae look fine tae me.

Lloyd   It's good ay ye tae say so.

Amber (*to* **Hazel**)   Keep an eye on him awright. (*Exits after* **Ally**. **Hazel** *raises* **Lloyd***'s head, he sees the meth that* **Ally** *has left.*)

Lloyd (*picking up the wrap of meth*)   Eh . . . Ye want a snort ay this? (*Snorts.*)

Hazel   Nup, widnae touch it.

Lloyd   That's sensible. (*Snorts again.*)

Hazel   You're mental, Lloyd. What dae ye dae that fir?

Lloyd (*puts the wrap in his pocket*)   Dinnae ken. There's something missing in ma life. Ah'm an auld cunt now, compared tae you at any rate, and I've never really been in love. That's fuckin sad.

Hazel   Aw Lloyd . . . (*They hug.*)

Lloyd   Ah wish ah could be in love with you, but there's nae sense in kiddin oan about it, aw ah'd get is a good ride oot ay it, and a good ride is never worth a good friendship.

Scene Two

Heather   He's going to say something. Brian Case. Something like he says every other morning. He's going to say something creepy. Mister Case. What am I going to do?

I'm going to smile like I do every morning. Like I have a spoon stuck in my mouth. Smile. Smile, when you feel like you're being stripped naked, exposed, held up for ridicule. No. I'm overreacting. I have to take responsibility for how I react. I have to train myself to not physically react that way, to not cringe inside. To not do that. It's my fault. I must control how I react. I can't . . .

Mr Case   How's the light of my life today?

Heather (*turns on* **Mr Case**)   For fuck sake! . . . what makes you think I'm the light of your life?

Mr Case   Well . . . seeing you every day brightens up my life.

Heather *walks towards* **Mr Case**; *he backs away from her.*

Heather   Look, your behaviour towards me has been based on an assumption you've made that I actually care about how you think I look. It's nothing to do with anything. You're my manager in the organisation, an organisation which is concerned with getting the job done rather than aesthetics or sexuality or whatever. It's none of my business and I don't intend to make it my business (*backs* **Mr Case** *up against a wall and grabs him by the balls*), but if how I look brightens up your life in the manner you suggest, I'd take a long hard look at myself and ask how much of a life I really had.

Mr Case   Oh, well thanks for putting me in the picture, I was just trying to be friendly.

Heather (*lets go of* **Mr Case**)   Yeah, well it's me who is apologising. This is nothing to do with you. By acquiescing to your childish and boring behaviour I gave you the tacit impression I approved of it, which was wrong of me. I'm sorry for that, I really am.

Mr Case (*nods and smiles*)   Right . . . I'll just be getting on then. (*Exits.*)

Scene Three

Heather (*to audience*)   My rebellion has moved from inside my head to into my world . . . and as a result, the doctor has given me Prozac.

Enter **Hugh**.

Hugh   You've been a bit down in the dumps. This will help to tide you over. (*Hands* **Heather** *a glass of water and a couple of pills. Gathers his golf clubs.*)

Heather   I don't like the idea of taking drugs like this, becoming dependent on them. You hear so much about it.

Hugh (*returns to* **Heather**'s *side and watches her take her pills, then takes the pill bottle and the glass, and pats her on the head*) Hu-neh-eh . . . the doctors are professionals. They know what they're doing. (*Looks at watch*) God, I'd better go. Billy-boy'll be wondering where I've got to. We're on tee at Pitreavie today, just cause I slaughtered him last week at Canmore. That's Bill. Maybe we'll nip round to his and Moll's later, eh? Bye, honey. (*Exits singing Dire Straits 'Money for Nothing'.*)

Scene Four

Heather (*to audience*)   My pal Marie and I take the day off work sick and go around the shops and then back to her place. We sit and drink tea, smoke a coupla joints and blether all afternoon.

Marie   Stay here tonight. Let's go out. There's a club on in town. Let's get E'd up and go out, you and me.

Heather   I can't . . . I have to get back . . . Hugh . . .

Marie   He's old enough to look after himself for one night. C'mon. Let's do it. You've got Prozac, that's brilliant. We can take them after the Es. They prolong the effects of the Ecstasy while destroying the toxins in the MDMA which may or may not cause brain damage in later life. Therefore Prozac makes E completely safe.

Heather   I don't know . . . I've never taken drugs in years. I've heard a lot about Ecstasy . . .

Marie   Ninety per cent of it'll be bullshit. It kills you, but so does everything, every piece of food you ingest, every breath of air you take. It does you a lot less damage than the drink.

Heather   Okay . . . but I don't want to hallucinate . . .

Marie   It's no like acid, Heather. You'll just feel good about yourself and the rest of the world for a while. There's nothing wrong with that.

Heather   Okay. But I don't really have anything to wear to the club.

Marie   Not to worry, try this on. (*Holds a dress out for* **Heather**.)

Music rises – a canticle (solo female vocal). **Heather** *is bathed in a bright coloured light. She undresses slowly to her underwear.* **Marie** *helps* **Heather** *put on the dress. The entire procedure should resemble a ceremonial transformation. Once she has finished changing she turns in a circle with her arms in the air.*

Heather   Whoa!

Music and lights change to nightclub. Female **Dancers** *take the dance floor. Along with* **Heather** *and the female* **Dancers**, *also present are* **Marie**, **Amber** *and* **Hazel**.

Scene Five

DJ   Dunnae worry about me (*takes a drink of bottled water –* *Volvic*), ah'm still up here, thank fuck.

Ah'll be up here all night and all morning, ah will not give in. It is my job to move, to spin a vibe and outmanoeuvre the icy sensation. Ah will resist being brought down by the aches and pains of my shivering body until every last one of you has had enough. Ah will ride my river of sweat through the quease, fatigue and dizziness and ah will bring anyone who wants to come with me.

Fuck money, fuck television, fuck food, fuck ignorant control; ah don't need anything ah don't have.

(*Puts on sunglasses, rushy sigh.*) Whoa fuck – ah love each and every one of you. (*Breath.*) This is the only way to be . . . and this (*beat*) is the only place to be. (*Music breaks into a very danceable beat.*)

Heather (*to audience*)   When we got to the club I craved a gin for my nerves but Marie told me not to drink; she said that it would spoil the effects of the E. It came on strong at first and I felt a bit sick in the stomach. Then I felt it in my arms, through my body, up my back: a tingling, rushy sensation. I looked at Marie and she was beautiful. It was like I'd died and was moving through heaven. All those beautiful people were smiling and looking like I was feeling. The thing was, they didn't look any different, you just saw the joy in them. I looked at myself in the mirror. I did not see the stupid fucking wife of Hugh Thomson. She was gone.

Hazel   Hiya . . . Havin a good one?

Heather   It was like I knew everybody, all those strangers. We shared an insight and an intimacy that nobody who hadn't done this in this environment could ever know about. It was like we were all together in our own world, a world far away from hate and fear. I had let go of fear, that was all that had happened. I was taking the next day off work as well.

Music level rises. Everyone dances.

Scene Six

Lloyd   Whoa fuck!

Lloyd *enters.* **Dancers** *from previous scene exit. High-energy music blasts (e.g. drum 'n' bass).* **Lloyd** *runs about wildly. Music stops.*

Lloyd (*to audience*)   Ally was right about this stuff. It was true. (*Music up. He runs about wildly. Music stops.*) Ah couldnae blink. (*Music up. He runs about wildly. Music stops.*) Ah tried, tried tae force a blink as ah sat oan the lavvy daein a shite. Then something happened: ah couldnae stop blinking. (*Music up. He runs about wildly. Music stops.*) Ah wis phonin every cunt up and spraffin shite. (*Music up. He runs about wildly. Music stops.*) Ah kept thinking about how ah got involved with the Poisonous Cunt. It was a while back, basically for reasons of finance. Ah should have suspected the worse when ah belled her to dae some business and she wouldnae come to the phone. Ah had nae choice! (*Music up. He runs about wildly. Music stops.*) When ah goat there ah discovered that she got off her tits last night . . . freebasing coke and she was oan a brutal bastard of a comedown. She was lying on her bed. Ah remember once when ah was Eckied ah got an erection when ah saw her unshaved armpits visible in a white, sleeveless cotton top. Ah once had a wank about fucking her armpits, ah don't know why this should be, but sexuality's a weird cunt tae try and fathom oot. It was Ally had started me off about them. We were on acid a Glastonbury and Ally said 'Phoah . . . that lassie Veronica: an awfay abundance ay hair that lashie . . .' After that we couldnae keep our eyes off her armpits.

Veronica *stirs.*

Veronica   Well?!

Lloyd   Goat it likes. (*Hands over a bag of coke; she tears into it like a desperate predator – chopping and snorting.*) How ye feeling?

Veronica   Shite!

Lloyd   Dae some rocks, eh?

Veronica   Aye . . .

Lloyd (*to audience*)   Her face was drained of colour, but her hair looked well washed, had a kind of sheen to it. Her face, though, looked rough, scabby and dehydrated and its contrast with the health of her hair made her look like an old hag wearing a wig. Looking at her now ah understood just why it should really be totally impossible to fancy her. The Poisonous Cunt shagging: what a thought right enough.

Veronica   Ah'm feelin fuckin crap. Ah've goat bad PMT. The only thing that helps me whin ah'm like this is a good fuck. That's aw ah want. A good fuck.

Lloyd   Ah'm fuckin well up fir that . . .

Lloyd *rushes over and pulls her track bottoms off to reveal her grotesquely over-exaggerated body hair.*

Veronica   Lloyd!

Lloyd *runs about swinging the end of an exaggerated prop penis (five to six feet) that extends from his crotch, while the **Poisonous Cunt** howls and roars like a caged animal.*

Lloyd   Ah was licking her craggy face like a demented dug wi a dry, chipped auld bone as ah pumped mechanically. Numbed by the crystal meth ah showed nae signs of coming, but the Poisonous Cunt had orgasm after orgasm. (*She screams like a banshee.*)

Veronica   That's it . . . that's enough.

Lloyd   Ah tried to bend my stiff cock into a semi-comfy position in my jeans.

Veronica   That was fuckin mad.

Lloyd   She fell into a deep sleep. Ah sat rigid, looking up at the ceiling wonderin what the fuck ah was daein wi ma life. Ah reflected that ah should've fucked the Poisonous Cunt's armpits while ah hud the chance. If ye huv tae dae something unsavoury that yir gaunnae regret as soon as you've done it, then at least realising a sexual fantasy would make it mair acceptable. (*They exit.*)

Scene Seven

Heather   I got a wee bit out of control. I took four Es. Marie said it was too much. This morning I picked up a book of Shelley's poems, then Blake, then Yeats . . . I looked around an art shop. I wanted to paint. I wanted to buy every CD I saw; anything would be all right after Hugh's Dire Straits, U2 and Runrig. (*Puts on a CD. Music: beats.*) There was a message on the machine:

Hugh (*voice-over*)   Honey, it's Hugh. Phone me at work –

Heather   I then came across a scribbled note:

Hugh (*voice-over*)   'You gave me a bit of a fright. I think you've been a bit selfish. Call me when you're home. Hugh.'

Heather   I crumpled up the note and put the *Brothers in Arms* CD in the microwave just to prove that what people say about CDs being indestructible is a lot of rubbish.

Music levels are raised. **Heather** *appears to place CD in microwave. Sounds of microwave door closing, microwave set and running. Sound of explosion.* **Heather** *wraps herself in a blanket and takes a seat.*

Hugh *enters, sees* **Heather**. *He sets his things down, turns music off, searching round the stereo, he whistles a bar from 'Money for Nothing'.*

Hugh   Seen the *Brothers in Arms* CD, honey? Can't find it anywhere . . .

Heather *is experiencing the comedown of a four-E high. She is depressed, it all seems hopeless.*

Heather   No. (*Slight shiver, pulls blanket around herself.*)

Hugh   Too much to drink at Marie's? What a pair! Seriously though, Heather, if you're going to take days off work, well, that I can't condone. I'd be a hypocrite if, after underlining the importance of a good attendance record to my own employees, word was to get around; if people were to say that my own wife was a slacker and that I was turning a blind eye to it . . .

Heather   I'm really tired. I did drink a wee bit too much . . . I might go upstairs for a lie-down. (*Doesn't move.*)

Hugh   Cribbage? (*Holding up a crib board and a deck of cards, waving them*) I thought that some cards might cheer us up a wee bit.

Heather (*small voice*)   I'm ugly. (*Staring at one spot, not moving although she feels sick, dizzy and tired – she puts on sunglasses.*)

Hugh   You're tired. It's the strain of being in an organisation that's rationalising. I know; it's the very same at our place. They're bound to feel it at your level of the organisation too. There's always a human cost, unfortunately. Can't make an omelette without breaking a few eggs, eh?

Knock at the door. **Hugh** *moves.*

Hugh   I told Bill and Moll it was hunky-dory to pop round for a drink.

Heather   I . . . eh . . . I . . .

Hugh   Bill's been on about his office extension so I thought I'd show him mine.

Heather   I think I should . . . (*Gets up.*)

Hugh (*turns to* **Heather**)   That's the spirit, honey! That's my girl! (*Opens the door.*)

Heather (*in a tired voice*)   No. I think I should go. Just go. For good. Go away from you, Hugh.

Bill *and* **Moll** *enter.*

Bill   It's the Thomson Twins! How's the fair Heather? Looking gorgeous, as per usual! (*Goes to* **Heather**.)

Heather   Hugh's jealous, he says that your extension is bigger than his. Is it?

Moll *laughs*.

Bill (*nervously*)   Ha ha ha . . . We brought some of Moll's world-famous garlic dip.

Heather *does not respond*.

Hugh   You shouldn't have gone through such trouble.

Bill   It's no trouble at all.

They come in and get as comfy as they can, **Hugh** *gets something to dip.* **Heather** *is the only one who doesn't eat, but becomes fixated with* **Bill**'s *crotch*.

Heather (*voice-over*)   I'm looking at Bill's fly. I decide that opening it and looking for his prick would be like opening a bin liner and rummaging through its contents. That fetid stench in your face as you grasp the limp rotting banana.

Bill *is smiling, unaware.* **Moll** *is smiling ridiculously*.

Bill   Oh by the by I got the seasons. (*Heather lifts her stare.*)

Hugh   Excellent!

Heather   The seasons? (*Pulls blanket around her.*)

Bill   I've got a couple of season tickets for myself and your true-blue hubby at Ibrox, in the old stand.

Heather   What?

Bill   The football. Glasgow Rangers FC.

Heather   Eh?

Hugh (*sheepishly*)   It's a good day out.

Heather   But you support Dunfermline. You always supported Dunfermline. You used to take me to East End Park . . . when we were –

Hugh   Yeah, honey . . . but Dunfermline . . . I mean, I never really supported them as such; they were just the local team. You have to get behind Scotland in Europe, a real Scottish success story. Besides, I've a lot of respect for David Murray and they know how to put a good corporate hospitality package together at Ibrox. Besides, I've always been a bit true-blue deep down.

Heather   You supported Dunfermline. You and I went. I remember when they lost that cup final to Hibs at Hampden. You were heartbroken. You cried like a wee boy!

Moll *smiles.*

Hugh   Darling, I don't really think Bill and Moll want to hear us arguing about football . . . besides, you've never really taken an interest in the game before . . .

Heather *covers herself with the blanket.*

Heather (*voice-over*)   That's it! A man who changes his woman you can forgive, but a man who changes his team . . . that shows a lack of character.

Hugh   What's all this about?

Heather (*concedes*)   Oh, nothing . . .

Silence.

Hugh   This is lovely garlic dip!

Moll (*mouthful of food*)   It was no trouble.

Heather (*sweating and shaking*)   I'm really sorry, Moll, I've just no appetite.

Bill   Hugh, I don't think Heather's doing too well. She's sweating and shaking.

Moll   Have you got a touch of the flu, Heather?

Hugh Maybe we should call it a night – another time, eh? (*Everyone gets up politely.*) She's been under a lot of stress at work. (*They exit.*)

Heather *gathers her things, leaves a note, and exits.* **Hugh** *re-enters, tidies up, sees the note and reads. The note is heard as a voice-over.*

Heather 'Dear Hugh, Things haven't been right between us for a while. This is my fault, I put up with changes in you and our life over the years. No blaming, no regrets, it's just over. Take all the money, the house, the goods. I don't want to keep in touch with you as we've nothing in common so nothing but falseness or nastiness would be served by that, but no hard feelings on my part.
P.S. When we fucked over the last four years it was like rape for me.

Hugh *exits.*

Scene Eight

Lloyd (*to audience*)   The mair ah thought about Woodsy's gig, the mair uncool it was. A rave at the East Pilton Parish Church; on a Tuesday afternoon! Pretty fuckin weird. Nae cunt was around except the hall caretaker, but Woodsy had the gear set up, so I gave it a spin. (*Music comes up as he starts spinning.*)

Woodsy This is the Very Reverend Brian McCarthy. He's supporting the gig.

Lloyd *shakes the reverend's hand.* **Woodsy** *approaches the rev. holding a bag of pills.*

Woodsy Hey, ah've got some fuckin good Es here. (*Pushes one into the reverend's face.*) Neck it, Bri.

Brian I'm afraid I can't take . . . drugs . . .

Woodsy Neck it, man, neck it and find the Lord.

Brian   Mr Woods, I can't condone drug taking in my parish . . .

Woodsy   Aye, well, whair's aw your parishioners then, eh? Yir church wisnae exactly stowed oot when ah wis doon last Sunday. Mine wis! (*The minister walks away.*) Fuckin hypocrite! You've nae spirituality! Dinnae fuckin tell ays otherwise! Thirs nae church except the church ay the self! Thir's nae medium between man and God except MDMA! Fuckin scam artist!

A lone **Dancer** *has entered by the end of* **Woodsy***'s speech.* **Dancer** *waves at* **Lloyd** *and starts to dance.*

Lloyd   Shut it, Woodsy, c'moan, let's git started. A crowd's formin.

Woodsy   Yah, awright.

(**Dancers** *enter and fill the space.*)

Lloyd (*to audience*)   Plenty of young cunts were coming in, and ah started really gaun for it, trying oot one or two things. It was shite but ah wis so intae it, every cunt was getting intae it tae. Within an hour the place was filled tae the brim. Woodsy's Es were all snapped up and Amber and Hazel even managed to flog a few ay mae Doves. Ah necked a couple myself and swallowed a wee wrap ay that crystal meth. East Pilton Parish Church went off! (*Music explodes.* **Dancers** *go off, then music and* **Dancers** *slow as if their batteries have died.*) At first ah dinnae see the polis come in (*yells and screams as everyone scatters*), but the guy pulled the plug oan us before perr auld Woodsy got to dae anything. (*Exits.*)

Scene Nine

Heather   I had anticipated a reaction from the world which was nothing like the way it really responded. It wasn't going to condemn. It just didn't give a fuck. But there could be no going back. It just wasn't an option. (**Hugh** *enters.*)

I don't know how he got my address but he found me. I trembled when I first saw him at the door. He had never been physically violent towards me, but all I could sense were his size and strength compared to me. That and the rage in his eyes. I only stopped trembling when he started talking. Thank God he started talking. This sad prick, he had learned nothing. As soon as he opened his mouth I could feel him shrink and me grow.

Hugh   I thought that you might have got this silly wee game out of your system by now, Heather. Then I got to thinking that you might be worried about the hurt that you've caused everyone and be too ashamed to come home. I admit that there's a lot that I can't quite fathom about this at the moment, but you've made your little statement, so you should be happy now. I think it would be better if you just came home. What about it, honey?

Heather   Hugh . . . ha ha ha look ha ha ha . . . I think you should go home before you . . . ha ha ha . . . before you make an even bigger prick of yourself than you already have . . . ha ha ha . . . What a fucking wanker . . .

Hugh   Are you on something?

Heather   Ha ha ha . . . Am I on something? Am I on something? I should be on something! I should be E'd off my tits with Marie, shagging the first guy I set eyes on! Getting fucked properly!

Hugh   I'm going! You're off your head! You and your junky pal. That fucking Marie bitch! Well, it's over! It's over!

Heather   YOU FUCKING WELL CATCH ON QUICK DON'T YE, YAH STUPID FUCK! GET A FUCKING LIFE FOR YOURSELF! AND LEARN HOW TO SHAG PROPERLY!

Hugh   YOU'RE FUCKING WELL FRIGID! THAT'S YOUR PROBLEM!

Heather   NO IT WAS YOUR FUCKING PROBLEM!
YOU HAVEN'T GOT FINGERS! YOU HAVEN'T GOT
A TONGUE! YOU HAVEN'T GOT A SOUL! YOU
HAVEN'T GOT AN INTEREST IN ANYTHING BUT
YOUR STUPID FUCKIN BUILDING SOCIETY YOU
POMPOUS LITTLE PRICK! FOREPLAY! LOOK IT
UP IN THE FUCKING DICTIONARY!
FOREFUCKINGPLAY!

Hugh   FUCKING LESBO! STICK WITH MARIE,
YOU FUCKING DYKE! (*Exits.*)

Heather   GET SHAGGED UP THE ARSE BY THAT
OTHER BORING PRICK BILL! THAT'S WHAT YOU
FUCKING WELL WANT! (*To audience*) I am going to take
every drug known to the human race and shag anything
that fuckin well moves.

Scene Ten

Nightclub, scene explodes. **Dancers** *yell and hoot as they pour on to
stage. Music: pounding bass. Nightclub lights. Music level comes
down.*

Heather (*to audience*)   That night I went to the club with
Marie and in the time it takes for that first Ecstasy to flow
through your body and for you to dance and hug and cry
about how you fucked everything up for the last few years,
you learn that we are all basically the same and that all we
have is each other. (*To Marie*) The politics of the last twenty
years are liars' politics, we are ruled by the weak and the
small-minded, who are too stupid to know that they are
weak and small-minded . . .

Music comes up. **Lloyd** *dances into the scene and sees* **Marie**. *He
stops dancing and moves close to her.*

Lloyd   Wasted.

Marie   Yeah, us as well.

Lloyd   Ah'm Lloyd.

Marie   Marie. (*Sees* **Lloyd** *has been clocking* **Heather**; *informs* **Lloyd**:) Heather.

Lloyd (*crosses to* **Heather**; *small pause*)   Listen, Heather, is it cool for me tae gie ye a hug, eh? Ah'd just like tae hold ye for a bit.

Heather   Okay.

They hug, and an angelic light encircles them while a solo bagpipe plays 'Amazing Grace'.

Ally   Pardon me, miss . . .

Lloyd *and* **Heather** *separate. Club music fades in. 'Amazing Grace' fades out. They do not take their eyes off of each other.*)

Ally   Lloyd, we've got to go, our ride's leaving.

Lloyd   Give us a minute, Ally. (**Ally**, *moves to exit, leaving* **Lloyd** *with* **Heather**. *To* **Heather**) That was mair than just brilliant. I'll gie ye a phone. There's a lot ah want tae talk tae ye aboot, cause ah really enjoyed that. Gave me loads to think about, in aw ways.

Heather   Me too.

Lloyd   Well, ah'll phone ye.

They kiss.

Lloyd   Fuckin hell . . . (*Exits.*)

Marie   Whoah!

Scene Eleven

Scenes Eleven and Twelve exist simultaneously as two separate pub/bar scenes. While Scene Eleven is happening **Heather** *and* **Marie** *are at their own table. Their light is dim and they move slowly so as not to draw focus. At the end of Scene Eleven the light* *dims on the boys, they slow their actions, and the light level comes up on the* **Heather** *and* **Marie** *scene (Scene Twelve).*

Pub. Sounds of football on the television and ambient pub noise.

Lloyd   See, Nukes, ah'm no used tae this game, eh no? Ah mean ah've never really been in love before so ah dinnae ken whether or not it's real love, the chemicals or just some kind ay infatuation. There seems to be something thair though, man, something deep, something spiritual . . .

Nukes   Cowped it yet?

Lloyd   Naw, naw. Listen the now . . . sex is nae the issue here. We are talking aboot love. But I dinnae ken what love is, man, likesay being in love.

Nukes   You wir married wir ye no?

Lloyd   Aye donkey's years ago. But I didnae have a clue then. Ah wis only seventeen. Aw ah wanted was my hole every night, that wis the reason tae git married.

Nukes   Good enough reason. Nowt wrong wi yir hole every night, eh.

Lloyd   Aye, aw right, but ah soon discovered that, aye, sure, ah wanted it every night awright, but no offay the same lassie. That wis when the trouble started.

Nukes   Well that's mibbe it but, Lloyd. Mibbe you've just found the definition ay true love: love is when you want yir hole every night, but offay the same lassie. There ye go. So did ye git yir hole offay this bird then?

Lloyd   Listen, Nukes, thir's some lassies that ye git yir hole offay, and there are others that ye make love tae. Ken what I mean?

Nukes   Ah ken that, ah ken that. I fucking well make love tae them aw, ya cunt, ah just use the expression 'git yir hole' cause it's shorthand and sounds a bit less poofy, eh. So where did ye meet this bird?

Lloyd   Up the Pure, eh. It wis her first time there. Fuck, man, she's aboot twenty-six or some shite. She wis married, tae this straight peg, and she just fucked off and left him. She was oot with her pal, jist her first or second time Eckied like.

Nukes   Whoa . . . slow down there, gadgie . . . what ye fuckin well sayin tae ays here? Ye meet this bird whaes oot fir the first time since she escaped this straight peg, she's taken her first ever Ecky, you're E'd up and yir talking love? Sounds a wee bit like the chemical love tae me. Nowt wrong wi that, but see if it lasts the comedoon before ye start thinking aboot churches, limos and receptions. See if the feelings transfer tae yir everyday life, then call it love. Love's no jist for weekenders.

Lloyd   The thing is, Nukes, ah'm changing the keks every day and cleaning under the helmet . . . my personal behaviour's starting tae change.

Nukes (*shrugs*)   Must be love then, oan your side, right enough. What's gaun oan with her though, mate?

Lights dim, football sounds cut. **Heather** *and* **Marie**'s *light level rises.*

Scene Twelve

Bar. Ambient bar sounds and music. **Heather** *and* **Marie** *laugh.*

Heather   Lloyd. You never really think that you'll be going out with someone with a name like that.

Marie   Yeah, it's funny how it all works out.

Heather   The thing about Lloyd is . . . is that he doesn't seem to want anything.

Marie   Everybody wants something. Does he want you?

Heather   I think so.

Marie   When are you going to shag him? It's about time you fucked properly.

Heather   I don't know. I feel pretty strange around him. Very inexperienced and nervous.

Marie   Well, that's exactly what you are.

Heather   I've been married for five years.

Marie   Exactly! If you've been with the same guy for five years who hasn't even been fucking you satisfactorily, then it's like being totally inexperienced. If the sex is just a meaningless ritual, if it means nothing and feels nothing, then it is nothing, and it's like never having had it. A lot of men are wankers cause they don't mind bad sex, but for a woman bad sex is far worse than no sex at all. You're free, you're attracted to this guy who sounds a bit of a waster. Nae job, deals drugs, no ambition to do anything else. That must seem a very tempting world after the one you've been in, Heather, but I wouldn't get too carried away by it all. It's one thing winning freedom, it's another thing holding on to it.

Heather   You're a cynical fucking cow, hen.

Marie   I'm trying to be realistic.

Heather   Yeah, you're right. That's the big fucking problem. You're right.

Scene Thirteen

Nukes *and* **Marie** *exit. Light level comes up on* **Lloyd**. *Dovetail lines.*

Lloyd   It was just so beautiful, beyond anything ah could have imagined ah'd ever feel. It was love no sex.

Heather   It was a nightmare.

Lloyd   It was pure love action. Ah felt her essence ah know ah did.

Heather   Our first fucking time and it was a nightmare. (*Exits.*)

Scene Fourteen

Outside. Night.

Lloyd   Ah fucked up big style the first time. She telt me how it felt for her. It was a bit ay a shock. Ah think it's because you always want to get the first one over, there's too much at stake when it's someone you really care for . . . really love. It's funny how there's nae embarrassment stickin your cock into a strange lassie, but things like likin and caressin her are a bit dodgy the first time. Ah should of got E'd up. The barriers come down so that sex with a stranger on E is magnificent. See wi someone you love though, the barriers should be down anyway, so the chemicals shouldn't make any difference. Ah've never been sae scared in ma puff, Ally. Mibbe huv tae chill on this relationship thing a bit. It's getting too heavy.

Ally   If you run fae this, Lloyd, make sure it's fir the right reasons. Ah see ye when yir wi her. Ah know how ye are.

Lloyd   Aye but . . .

Ally   Dinnae deny it!

Lloyd   Aye but Ally!

Ally   Aye but nowt! Dinnae be feared ah love, man, that's what they want. That's the wey they divide. Dinnae ever be feared ah love.

Lloyd   Mibbe yir right, eh ye fancy some eggs? (*They exit.*)

Scene Fifteen

Marie's.

Marie   How was it then?

Heather (*smiling*)   Let me get my coat off first.

Marie   Fuck the coat, how was it?

Heather   He's a total shag.

Marie   Mizz chessy grin herself.

Heather   Well, darling, if you'd been sucking on a cheesy cock you'd have a chessy grin too.

Marie   C'mon then, I want all the details.

Heather   Well he's hot on fingers and tongue stuff, once he relaxed and stopped trying to please me, stopped being so . . .

Marie   Performative?

Heather   Yeah, that's the word I was looking for.

Marie   He didn't give you head . . . (**Heather** *nods*.) Heather! The second date!

Heather   It wasn't the second date, it was the sixth date. It was the second shag, remember.

Marie   Go on.

Heather   I came bucketloads, woke up the whole of Leith. It was fucking marvellous. So good, in fact, I did it again. I could feel him right up in my stomach. It was weird, I thought it was because he was bigger than Hugh, but they looked about the same size. Then I realised that it was because Hugh had only been fucking me with half his cock, the poor bastard. I was just so tense with him I'd never open up properly. With Lloyd, though, he just opens me up like he's peeling a fucking orange. What a wide-on I got . . . you could have got a convoy of lorries up there.

Marie   Lucky cow . . . no, you deserve it, hen, you really do. I'm just jealous, I fucked a cokehead last night. It was good for him and shite for me. So fucking cold.

Heather (*goes to hug her*)   It's awright . . . it's just one of those things . . .

Marie   Yeah, next time . . .

Scene Sixteen

Lloyd *enters his place. He is shirtless and appears as though he is on a comedown. Music: something hopeful.*

Heather   The thing about Lloyd, though, was that he was never around during the week. The weekends, it was great, we were E'd up and we made love a lot. It was a big party. But he used to avoid seeing me during the week. I went over tae his. I did not call first.

Lloyd*'s.*

Lloyd   Ah'm not avoiding you . . . it's jist thit ah'm intae a different scene during the week, Heather. Ah know myself. Ah'm just no good company.

Heather   I see, you come out with all that bullshit about how you love me but you only want to be with me when you're high at the weekend. Great.

Lloyd   It isnae like that.

Heather   It is like that, you just sit here during the day all depressed and bored. We only make love at the weekend, only when you're E'd up. You're a fake, Lloyd. An emotional and sexual fake. Don't touch what you can't emotionally afford. Don't lay claims to emotions you can't feel without drugs!

Lloyd   It's not fucking false. When ah'm E'd up it's like I want to be. It's no like anything's been added to me, it's like it's been taken away; aw the shite in the world that gets intae yir heid. When ah'm E'd up. I'm my real self.

Heather   So what are you just now then?

Lloyd   Ah'm an emotional wreckage, the waste product of a shitey world a bunch of cunts have set up for themselves at our expense, and the saddest fuckin thing is that they can't even fuckin well enjoy it.

Heather   And you are enjoying it?

Lloyd   Ah have my moments . . . weekends. Why the fuck shouldn't ah be able to have that?

Heather   You should be able to have it. I want to give you it! I need you to give it to me! Listen, just dinnae phone me for a bit. You can't do without drugs, Lloyd. If you want to see me, do it without drugs. (*To audience*) I waited for the phone to ring, jumping out of my skin every time I heard it. But he never called and I couldn't bring myself to call him. Not then and not later, not after what I'd heard at the party. Marie and I at a party, and my blood running cold in the kitchen as I hear some guys talking about a certain Lloyd from Leith and what he was supposed to have done and who with. I couldn't call him.

Scene Seventeen

Music starts slow build. **Dancers** *entering.* **DJ** *speaks with the music. At the end of the* **DJ** *speech music explodes. Everyone goes mental on the dance floor. This scene has the highest dance energy in the play.*

DJ (*takes a deep breath from an inhaler*)   Whoa fuck . . . number two's kickin in finestyle, rushin me right tae the edge, and ah can feel my heart, the solid bass beat, pumping the Ecstasy to every cell in my body and ah know right now ah'm ready, ready to open my heart and mind to anything and anyone. Right now. Now, as my soul shoots through every pore in my body and blends itself into the brilliant lovevibe we have created. Love. Love, love is the thing. True love. Real love, open and unconditional. That is the complete answer. That is what everyone needs. That is what the world needs and ah want tae give it, ah want everyone tae feel it at least once in their life, and right now, tonight, ah can dae something about it.

Music explodes. Everyone dances for a bit then the music levels come down and the **Dancers** *slow down, except for* **Lloyd**.

Heather (*to audience*)   The DJ's moved up seamlessly from ambient to a hard-edged techno beat and the lasers have started and everybody is going crazy and through it all I can see him, jerking and twitching under the strobes and he sees me and he comes over. (*To* **Lloyd**) What do you want?

Lloyd   Ah want you, ah'm in love with you.

Heather   Yeah, well tell me that on Monday morning.

Lloyd   Ah'll be round.

Heather   I'll believe it when I see it.

Lloyd   Believe it. (*He moves back to the dance floor.*)

Heather (*calling across dance floor as* **Lloyd** *moves away*)   Easy to say when you're E'd up.

Music up. **Heather** *dances like mad. Everyone on the dance floor goes crazy. Music levels come down.*

Heather (*to audience*)   He's a freak – a sad sister-shagging freak.

Music up. Everyone is going insane on the dance floor. **Heather** *is dancing very hard. Music levels come down.*

Heather   I was thrashing to the music, trying to forget about Lloyd, trying to dance him out of my mind . . . but he looked so fuckin good to me.

Music up. Hoots and yells from the dance floor. **Dancers** *pull out their best moves.* **Heather** *takes a wee break, gets her bottle of water and joins* **Ally**. *Act Two Scene One. Music levels come down.*

Heather   What's Lloyd on tonight, then?

Ally   Nowt, he's just had a couple ay drinks. Didnae want a pill. Sais eh wis gaunnae take six months oaf n aw that shite. Didnae want ehs perspective damaged, that was what the daft fucker sais. Listen, Heather, man – ah hope yir no gaunnae make him intae a straight peg, eh.

Heather   Lloyd is not E'd up?

Ally   No.

Heather   Listen, Ally, I want to ask ye something. Something about Lloyd. I was at a party with some friends last week and these two guys were talking about how a couple of years ago a certain Lloyd from Leith was found shagging his wee sister in a launderette . . .

Ally (*laughing*)   Ah Heather! You're speaking of Lloyd Beattie. Lloyd Buist hasn't even got a sister, and ah don't think he ever stepped intae a launderette before he met ye.

They laugh and hug. **Ally** *is high.*

Heather   How ye feeling, Ally?

Ally   Phoah . . . Brilliant!

Heather   Listen, Ally, ah want you to have this. (*Pulls a pill out of her bra.*)

Ally   Ye dinnae want your second?

Heather (*looking to* **Lloyd**)   Naw, I thought I might ride this one out.

Ally   Cheers, Heather. (*Takes the pill.*)

Heather *sees* **Lloyd** *is talking to* **Hazel** *on the dance floor. She calls out to him:*

Heather   You talking to anybody special?

Lloyd   Ah am now.

Heather   Want to go?

Lloyd   Yeah.

Heather *jumps into his arms, they dance their way off the stage.*

End.

Ecstatic love and deepest thanks to the people whose
support and belief in the *Ecstasy Project* has changed my life.
Cheers to Breanna Johnson, Linda Wyatt, Ben and Cody
Petruk, Victoria Stusiak, Mindy Cooper, Troy O'Donnell,
Oliver Friedmann, Garett Ross, Celina Stachow, Cory
Payne, Sandra M. Nicholls, Jim and Nelle, Sheila Cleasby,
Tarek Sherif, Mr and Mrs Petruk, Tara Hughs, Raymond
Theriault, the Briscoes, Sean Hay, Deborah Arnott,
Norman Evans, Brian McCallum, and to all my family and
friends.
To anyone who has ever danced in the show, 'Keep kickin!',
and to the *Ecstasy* cast members (past and present) 'Are you
ready for something *completely* different?'
Thanks to Irvine for *Ecstasy*, and for his warm support.
Again thanks to Irvine, also to Debs, and Paul, Shannon,
Aiden, Levi, Kaidi Tatham and Dave Lilico for their
unforgettable enthusiasm in the audience.
Cheers to Greg and Tony @ Snug Industries and Marcus @
Fiction Design Co. 416 in Toronto for their continued
support.

Irvine Welsh's

Filth

Adapted by Harry Gibson

Characters

One actor plays

DS Bruce Robertson

and his wife Carole and her sister Shirley; his father and brother; his girlfriend Chrissie; freemasons Hector the Farmer and Cliff Blades, and Cliff's wife Bunty; police Gus Bain, Andy Clelland, Amanda Drummond, Dougie Gillman, Peter Inglis, James Niddrie, Ray Lennox, Robert Toal, Marrianne San Yung and old Ina in the cannie; Leith casuals Lexo Setterington, Ghostie Gorman, Ocky Ockendon and girlfriend Stephanie; Mrs Colin Sim; Dr Patel, reporter Brian Scullion, rent boy Sinky, John Lewis staffer; a Lassie with a broken leg, a Paramedic and an intestinal Worm.

Other voices do Bunty, Chrissie, Gus, Ray, Shirley and Toal.

Filth premiered at the Citizens Theatre, Glasgow, on 14 September 1999.

Performed by Tam Dean Burn
Directed and designed by Harry Gibson
Lighting by Paul Sorley

Music

Pre-show:
Felt – 'Dance of Deliverance'

Part One:
Michael Shenker Group – 'Into the Arena'
Led Zeppelin – 'Black Dog'
Frank Sidebottom – 'Christmas Medley'
Miles Davis – 'Round Midnight'
Michael Bolton – 'How Am I Supposed to Live Without You?'

Interval:
Bachman Turner Overdrive – 'Looking Out for Number 1'
Foreigner – 'I Want to know What Love Is'
Darlene Love [Phil Spector] – 'Christmas (Baby Please Come Home)'
Ozzy Osbourne – 'Ultimate Sin'

Part Two:
Pramod Kumar – 'Raga Deepavali'
The Tamperer and Maya – 'Feel It'
Curtis Stigers – 'Keep Me from the Cold'
The Flaming Lips – 'The Observer'
Pink Floyd – 'Echoes'
Michael Bolton – 'Georgia on my Mind'
Regular Fries – 'The Pink Room'
Sweetbox – 'Everything's Gonna Be Alright'

Christmas carols played by the Salvation Army Staff Band

Songs quoted in the show

'Whatever happened to all . . .' – 'No More Heroes', The Stranglers; 'I'll be there . . .' – 'Reach Out I'll Be There', The Four Tops; 'I am the Antichrist . . .' – 'Anarchy in the UK', The Sex Pistols; 'We three kings . . .' – traditional Christmas carol; 'I'm the king of the castle . . .' – traditional children's chant; 'What's she gonna look like . . .' – 'Feel it', The Tamperer.

One

He farts . . .

Bruce The technique is to let it ooze out a bit before heading off, or you just take it with you in your troosers. It's like the fitba: you have to time your runs. Fart silently. Pause . . . Then move swiftly to the other side of the room. Crime briefing. Nine a.m. I've a bad nut. I've been fuckin busy. And he's told me to be here, not asked mind, told. Toal, T-O-A-L Detective Inspector Robert Toal.

He grabs a police magazine, finds a photo of **Toal** *. . .*

Aye . . .

. . . cuts it out and pins it to the board.

Thinks he's a fuckin intellectual, Inspector fuckin Morse type. Pacing up and down at his briefings is the closest to action the spastic ever gets.

Toal Our victim is a young black male in his early thirties. He was found on Playfair Steps at around five o'clock this morning by council refuse workers. We suspect that he lives in the London area but there is at present no positive identification.

He farts.

Bruce Good timing. Talking of timing, Gus Bain is the last to arrive, red-faced old fart, with the sausage rolls fae Crawford's. He's passing them around as Toal drones on.

Toal The man was wearing blue jeans, red T-shirt and a black tracksuit top with orange strips on the arms. His hair was cut short. Amanda –

Bruce He gestures to Amanda Drummond, bulldyke Drummond, a silly wee lassie doing all that she's good for, dishing oot copies of the dead coon's description. Her hair is cut short too, making her look even more ay a carpet muncher.

He finds a Polaroid of her and pins it up . . .

She's wearing a long brown skirt too thick to see the pant line, with a checked blouse and a fawn striped cardigan. I've seen mair meet on a butcher's knife. I bite into my sausage roll.

He produces one and bites into it.

Toal   His assailants kicked him down to a recess in the stairs where a savage beating took place. One of them went further than the others and struck the victim with an implement. Forensics say that the injuries sustained are consistent with those that would be made by a hammer wielded with force. This was done repeatedly, caving in the man's skull and driving the implement into his brain.

He spits out his mouthful of sausage roll.

Bruce   The pepper 'n' ketchup I normally have with my sausage roll are up the stairs and it tastes bland without them. Toal is trying to wreck my fuckin day. I've got paperwork to dae, overtime to claim. I've goat my winter week's holly-bags comin up. He'd better not be thinking of cancelling my leave: he's done it before, the cunt. See Drummond sucking up to the old bastard, going on aboot racial fuckin motivation and building bridges wi the wog community. The future ay police work? I think not. Ma fartgas escapes via the air vent and I am not far behind. I team up with Ray Lennox fae drug squad n we shoot off in my Volvo. Ray Lennox is a good young guy. (*Displays photo.*) About six foot tall, brown hair in a side parting, a mustache that's a tiny bit too long and unkempt and makes him look a wee bit daft, and a large hooked nose and shifty eyes. Sound polisman. And he's now starting tae take a mair active role in the Craft. Under my guidance.

See, Toal resents my pull with the lads, my status as Federation rep, and also the fact that I'm more prominent in the Craft than he'll ever be. That's what cuts the ice with the boys in the canteen, not fucking name, rank and serial number. The basic fact is: *nobody* tells me what to do.

In the car, I go to put on a tape of *Deep Purple in Rock*, but I decide against, because it will only precipitate an argument with Lennox over whether Coverdale is a better vocalist than Gillan, which as any spastic knows is a non-argument. I mean, who could compare Coverdale's Purple or Whitesnake output to the original Deep Purple line-up Gillan graced alongside Blackmore, Lord, Glover and Pace? Only an idiot would try. But I'm not getting into this with Lennox, so I put on Michael Shenker's *Into One Arena*.

He does.

The air feels raw and sharp. Winter's diggin in. Holly-bags! Every cunt kens that I have my three weeks' summer in Thailand and my winter's week in the Dam. Tradition. Custom and fuckin practice! Nae pen-pushing cunts are stopping that. Come the tenth of this month I'll be fuckin well shaggin for Scotland!

Ray *nods thoughtfully as Shenker struts his stuff.*

Ray   Tell ye what though, Robbo, you've got a very understanding wife. If Mhari had found out I was off to Amsterdam with a mate . . .

Bruce   Mhari. Ray's bird. She left him anyway. Probably wasn't giving her enough. The mooth department and the trooser department are well out of sync in the not so superstore that is Ray Lennox, I kid you not. 'It's a question of values, Ray. Give and take. Keeps the spice in a relationship!' We hit Crawford's . . . I get a couple of bacon rolls and Ray gets another sausage roll which we scran back and wash doon with hot milky coffee!

He drinks coffee and rocks happily . . . But it soon becomes an itch . . .

He stops the music.

I have a rash developing on my testies and my arse. Caused by excess sweat and chafing, the quack said. The cream he gave me seems to be making it worse.

I cannae . . .

He scratches . . .

How do they expect me to do my job under these circumstances?
I need a proper fucking laundry service.
I go into the public bogs, whip everything down and remove the dampness from around my arse with toilet paper. Then I scratch like fuck but it stings as the grease from the bacon roll is still under my nails. I claw and claw, feeling a delicious liberation as the wound tears and pulsates. I see the blood on my fingers . . .
My balls are not too bad.

He washes his hands at a sink . . .

Ray   You down the lodge tonight, Bruce?

Bruce   'Nah.'

Ray   Quiet night in with the missus?

Bruce   'Yeah. Carole's making a special meal tonight.'

Ray   I wish I had somebody to make me a special meal.

Bruce   'Huv tae fix ye up wi ma sister-in-law again, eh Ray? Shirley, eh?'

He laughs.

He hates tae be reminded of the time we both rode that cow.

He makes the sign for a small dick.

Every cunt has their achilles heel, and I just make a point of remembering my associates' ones. Something that crushes their self-esteem to a pulp. It's all sorted for future reference.

The new DI post which is coming up in the departmental
reorganisation. Detective Inspector Robertson.
Back at HQ I force myself to look through the file that Toal
has now opened up on the topped silvery.

He does . . .

Positive identification!
A Mr Efan Wurie.
Son of the ambassador for Ghana . . .
Staying at the Kilmuir Hotel. Checked in Friday.
Friday . . .
A journalist!
What sortay a journalist was he?
Only on some commie nigger mag that no cunt reads!

Panic attack: heavy breathing . . .
Panic waves surge under following scenes . . .

Maybe he was up here to meet an Edinburgh darkie.
I decide to knock off early, taking the motor out to my pal
Hector the Farmer, who's got some good videos.

He does a bit of **Hector** *clowning . . .*

Hector crushes my hand in a masonic grip, his alcohol-
flushed face beaming at me.

Hector   Got time to come for a dram?

Bruce   'Sorry, mate, I'm on a murder investigation. Some
daft nigger's only gone and got himself topped. Still, there's
big OT possibilities. Got the goods?'

Hector   Aye . . .

Tesco bag . . . He sits down, clutching the bag.

Bruce   Home alone!

Domestic lighting.

I've got a large slice of gala pie for my tea! I put it in the
microwave. I sit down and watch the video. I make no
apologies for this: the job is one in which it's dangerous to

think too much, so the best thing is to channel your energy into something that's the easiest to think about but which does you no harm! For most of us sex fits the bill nicely. Two hoors are having a licking and frigging session and the black studs are just about to come and join them. No! I don't want any black studs. I put on another tape featuring two lesbians and a milkman.

I bite into my gala pie.

The fuckin thing's still frozen in the middle.

I eat it anyway.

He pulls some pie from the bag and wolfs it down . . .
He grabs a bottle of whisky and drinks . . .
He watches porn . . .
His guts ache . . .
He drinks till he crashes out.
Dawn comes . . .
He wakes, gagging, and retches . . .
The music dies.

Carole . . .

She's away to her ma's. She'll be back soon.

She knows what side her bread's buttered on.

My fuckin guts. That gala pie. Good mind to report they deli spastics to the environmental health. No that they cunts are any use at all.

He tidies himself up, and scratches his arse and balls . . .
A fax comes through . . .

'Internal Memo. From Chief Superintendent Niddrie. Re: Racism Awareness Training Modules.'

He pins up a photo of **Niddrie** *. . .*

Niddrie   As you will be aware, concern has been expressed regarding the handling of racial issues within the Department. Senior Management has been aware of this for some time, but following on from recent criticisms it has been decided that all staff will undertake Racism Awareness Training modules, run by our Personnel and Equal

Opportunities staff . . . Marrianne San Yung and Amanda Drummond.

He snorts . . .

Bruce   'Some silly wee tart goes tae college n gets a degree in fuckin sociology and then does some Daz-coupon certificate in Personnel Management and joins the force on this graduate accelerated programme and she's earning nearly as much fuckin dough as you and me,' ah says tae Gus Bain, red-faced auld fart, over a coffee and a KitKat. 'We've seen fuckin years in service, you 'n' me, and we're pitting ourselves oan the fuckin line tryin to stop schemies killin each other. Then she writes this fuckin stupid Policy Document saying "Be kind to coons and poofs and silly wee lassies like me" and everybody gets the fuckin hots.'

Gus   Aye. Scotland's a white man's country. Always has been, always will be.

Bruce   'Precisely, Gus. Ah mind the time when I took Carole and wee Stacey tae see that *Braveheart*. How many Pakis or spades did ye see in the colours fightin for Scotland? Same wi *Rob Roy*, same wi *The Bruce*.'

Gus   Aye, but that's a long time ago now, Bruce.

Bruce   'Precisely! We built this fuckin country. There was nane ay them at Bannockburn or Culloden when the going was tough. It's our blood, our soil, our history. We were fuckin slaves before these cunts were ever rounded up and shipped tae America!'

He plays **Marrianne**.

Marrianne   Right, I wanna do a free-association brainstorming exercise. Just call out at random any responses you can think of.

She writes up: '*WHAT DOES "RACISM" MEAN TO YOU?*'

Andy   Discrimination!

She writes it up.

Dougie   Conflict!

Bruce   As she's writin this up, Andy says . . .

Andy   Might no be conflict. Might be harmony.

Bruce   N Gus Bain says . . .

Gus   You're thinkin of the hairspray.

Bruce   N ah chip in n say 'That girl's not wearing Harmony hairspray.' Everybody has a wee laugh at that.

Marrianne   I think . . . is it, Andy? I think Andy made a valid point there. We in policework tend to be conditioned into seeing a conflict-based society due to the nature of our jobs, but in fact race relations in Britain are characterised much more by harmony than anything else.

Bruce   'It's the leading brand of hairspray,' I tell her. Nobody laughs this time and I feel like a daft cunt. At least the hoor seems upset, which is what the game is all about. She looks directly at me and says . . .

Marrianne   What does the term 'racism' means to you –

Bruce   She looks at my name tag.

Marrianne   – Bruce?

Bruce   'It doesn't mean anything to me. I just treat everyone the same.'

Marrianne   Okay, very laudable. But do you not recognise racism in others?

Bruce   'Nup. That's their lookout. You take responsibility for your own behaviour, not other people's.' Ha! That was a good one, straight from these cunts' daft interpersonal training jargon. It almost strikes a chord with this Kitchen Sink's fucked-up way of thinking. But then Bulldyke Drummond jumps in.

Amanda   But surely in our professional role as law-enforcement officers, we have to accept responsibility for society's problems. This is implicit, I would have thought.

Bruce (*sotto voce*)   You are a silly wee cunt. That is *ex*plicit, I would have thought.
'I was speaking as an individual. I thought that was what you wanted. No hiding behind professional roles. I think we were told at the pre-course briefing we were to respond as human beings. Of course, as a law enforcement officer I accept that we have these responsibilities.'

Marrianne   Good point, Bruce.

Bruce (*sotto voce*)   Yess!

Marrianne   Anybody else got anything to add?

Silence . . .

Marrianne   Fine

Bruce (*sniggers*)   So much for brainstorming. But of course, if we won't talk, then these fuckers are never shy about filling in the gaps. So we listen to a dull lecture, dozing in the heat from the radiators, before finally adjourning for 'Coffee Break'.
Shitey wee fuckin biscuits, that's all they give us! I usually get a roll from the canteen or something from the baker's for my piece. But naw, that's all forgotten about with this disruption for their coon-loving courses. They think of nay other cunt's routine but their own! They think that you're fuck-all, that they can just use you to clean up their shite, and, in fact, most of the time, they are spot on. What they don't know though, is that you're always lurking in the shadows. The opportunity to pounce usually never comes along but you're always lurking, always ready. Just in case. Lennox is talking to Amanda Drummond. Most likely tryin to slip her a length, the dirty fucker. Although with Lennox it wouldnae be much ay a length. I'd give her one if only to pass the time of day, in the bogs, if I had a bit of time between finishing the crossword and piece break. Lennox's

index finger rubs the side of his beak. Ice-cool cunt, Ray
Lennox's giveaway that he's telling porky pies, that
underneath it all he's a suffering bag of nerves.

My guts feel . . . It's like there's something in me. I can
almost feel it growing. A tumour perhaps, like the one that
did in the auld girl. Prone to it, our family. But she was . . .
(*Sweat* . . .)   A panic attack's coming on . . .

Fuck that! I'm not like one of those long-term sick-through-
stress saplings that can't handle the big time. The cunts
here'll never fuckin know, they'll never fuckin ken, cause
I'm better than that, better than all of them, stronger than
the fuckin lot of those cunts put together. I excuse myself
and go to the bogs. Inside the lavvy I'm shaking and my
teeth are hammering together. My arse is itching really
badly. Fucking cunts! How do they expect me . . .

I give my arse a good clawing till my eyes water. The pain is
something to focus on.

Breathing slows, shaking subsides . . . He comes back.

Marrianne   You don't look very happy, Bruce. Are you
okay?

Bruce   'I'd be a lot more okay if I knew what I was doing
here.

'Like several of my colleagues, I'm involved in a murder
investigation.

'I'm trying to solve the murder of a man from an ethnic
minority group.

'I've been taken off that to spend time here.

'Answer me this if you can. What advances racial harmony
most: this course, or solving that crime?

'Cause we sure ain't gonna solve no crime sittin here, sister.'

Amanda (*weakly*)   It's no a question of one or the other, we
need both. As the strategy paper makes quite clear.

Bruce   'I'm glad you mentioned that because if I could
quote a circular from personnel relating to the strategy
paper: *"There are no sacred cows in a modern organisation like the*

police force. Everything is up for grabs, everything has a priority value.'' '

Marrianne   Exactly! The fact that you're here shows it has priority!

Bruce   'Precisely. Conversely, the fact that we are not out there investigating the murder of a young man shows that *that* does *not* have priority.' (*Triumph!*)

Music: Led Zeppelin, 'Black Dog':
'Hey hey Mam'ah said, the way you move,
Gonna make you sweat, gonna make you groove!'

He grabs a pool cue and plays guitar with it . . .
The phone rings . . .
He stops the music, but doesn't lift the phone.
The caller rings off without leaving a message.
He punches 1471 . . .
Phone: 'You were called today at ten thirty-four hours. The caller withheld their number.'

Bruce   Carole. Seeing the error of her ways. Getting a bit weepy on her own with Christmas approaching. Nothing surer.

Replacing the cue, he gives it a last strum.

White man's soul music.
We came, conquered, and enslaved . . .
I'd a good night at the pool, grinding down young Ray Lennox's resistance. Don't play wi the big boys if your cue action isnae up for it.
It's all sorted for future reference.
Detective Inspector Robertson . . .
(*At member of audience*) I won the fucking tournament! Thank you!

Music: Frank Sidebottom's 'Christmas Medley':

'Thank you. Let's all sing the Christmas medderley, / Switch off the hi-fi, switch off the TV! / And then "Ding-dong merrily" . . .'

Bruce *gleefully produces a Bladesey puppet.*

Music: Frank gives way to a brass band playing 'Ding-dong merrily'
(or similar) in the street . . .

Bruce   I'm out in the frosty streets with ma mate
Bladesey! We are three sheets tae the wind. You ken
Bladesey. Wee cunt fae the Craft. Clifford Blades, Civil
Servant: Registrar General For Scotland's office. Took pity
oan the wee fucker cause he's no goat any mates. [(*Optional:*)
Wee joker wi specs. (*Adds specs to puppet.*) Really thick lenses.]

Vent act! Bladesey speaks with an adenoidal bleat:

Bladesey   My wife . . .

Bruce (*aside*)   English cunt.

Bladesey   My wife, Bunty . . .

Bruce (*aside*)   Bunty is this big piece he married last year.
He worships the big cow!

Bladesey   I've always been a bit of a loner. 'Snot easy
making friends. Getting this job up here I thought I'd
landed on my feet. And meeting Bunty, well . . .

Bruce (*aside*)   Course, she treats him like shite.

Bladesey   I just don't know what she wants, Bruce.

Bruce   'Listen, Bladesey, my auld mucker, do you mind if
I ask you a personal question?'

Bladesey   Um . . .

Bruce   'Are you shagging her?'

Bladesey *hangs his head.*

Bruce   'Eh?'

Bladesey   Well . . . that side of things . . . 'snot been great
lately.

Bruce   'Listen, mate, a bit of advice in the affairs-of-the-
heart department. With women –

He takes a piss . . .

– what you have to do is shag them regularly. Keep them well fucked and they'll do anything for you. Well-shod and well-shagged, that's the auld phrase.'

Bladesey   You actually believe that?

Bruce   'Course I do. The root of a marital problem is always sexual. Women like to get fucked, whatever they make out. If you ain't fucking the woman you're supposed to be with then that creates a vacuum and nature abhors one of thaim. Sure as fuck some cunt'll come along and fill the gap wi several inches ay prime beef. N if she's no daein fur you, you go and get yur hole somewhere else.'

Bladesey   You think it's really that easy?

Bruce   'Course it fuckin well is. There's fanny gantin oan it. I kid you not. In this toon, in every fuckin toon. Right across the big wide world. All you need to know is where to look. Now me, I'm a detective. Ah'm polis. N a good polisman eywis knows where tae look.'

Music: the brass band plays 'Away in a Manger' . . .
Some snow falls on him . . .

It's snowing!
I catch a snowflake and marvel at its perfection through a lager haze, before it disintegrates in the heat of my hand.
Taxi! See a lumbering taxi trying to turn slowly down a side street but sliding on the ice and scraping its bodywork against a lamp-post.
A lassie's getting out.
Or she's tryin tae. The torn-faced cunt ay a taxi-driver isnae helping hur. The lassie's goat wan ay her legs in plaster, tryin tae position her crutches oan that treacherous icy surface. Fucking hell!

'Can you manage? Here, let me!'

Lassie   Thanks . . .

Bruce   We get her oantae the pavement. Ah'm up against her n ah kin feel her soft warmth. The scent ay her perfume fills ma nostrils. I could jist haud hur like this fur ever. Oh, God . . . (*Memories!*) 'Are you goin far? The pavement's very slippy . . .'

Lassie   Naw, I'm just in that stair there.

Bruce   'Ah'll give you a hand over. Can you manage up the stairs?' N ah want hur tae say –

Lassie   Naw, come up with me!

Bruce   Ah've goat a hard-on.

Lassie   'Come up with me and hold me in your arms like you used tae . . .'

Bruce   But . . . It isnae hur. It could never be.

Music dies away . . .

But I wished with all my heart it wis . . .

He mews. It's a gut cry which mixes cat and baby. It will become the voice of the **Worm**.

Bruce   Carole . . .

At home now, he gazes in a mirror . . .
Music: Miles Davis, 'Round Midnight' . . .
He becomes **Carole** . . .

Carole   The problem with Bruce is that he keeps it all in. I know he's seen some terrible things in his job and they've affected him deeply, whatever he says. His hard front fools a lot of people, but I know my man. Complicated person.
If you're a sexy person I think you're always very much aware of the sexuality of others.
I think I'm losing weight.
We play these break-up–make-up games with each other, just a tease.

She wraps her arms around herself . . .

O Bruce . . . !

Blackout.
Music surges.
She groans.
A police siren passes in the night.

Bruce!!

Morning.

Bruce *stands with his trousers round his ankles, immobile . . .*

Bruce   It took me ages to get ready this morning because I couldnae think what to wear. It's Carole's fault. If she was going to shoot off, she could at least have arranged a fuckin laundry service before she went. My trousers are minging. There's a bad Judi Dench [*ie, stench*] rising from me keks. (*Bending over*) Ma rash is worse. Fuckin doctor . . .

Doctor (*Asian*)   Well, Mr Robertson, this looks like eczema.

Bruce   'Eczema! On ma testicles?!'

Doctor   Eczema can occur anywhere. I'm going to prescribe a cream.

Bruce   'What's brought this on?'

Doctor   Well, you may be allergic to certain foodstuffs. It may be part of the stress-related condition you've been experiencing.

Bruce (*aside*)   Aye. Bastards! Fuckin – (*Trousers up.*)

Doctor   Were your parents prone to it?

Bruce   'No.'

Doctor   I can't emphasise strongly enough that you should keep that area clean.

Bruce *zips up. Again comes that mewing sound . . .*

Bruce   Ah'm Hank Marvin. (*ie, starving*) Got to eat . . .

On ma way in, I stop off at Crawford's for a jumbo sausage roll and a vanilla slice. But it doesn't hit the spot, so when I get in, I go down the cannie. I see auld Ina in the kitchen and give her the wink –

Ina   Awright, Bruce darlin?

Bruce   – and she fixes me up with a couple of bacon rolls. When I get to my desk I've still got enough coffee left to wash doon a couple of those wee KitKats. The cunt who invented KitKat ought to be fuckin well knighted.

(*Belch.*) The spicy content of my burps is telling me that a strong curry got into the mix somewhere along the line last night. Last night? Out with Bladesey . . . doon the Lodge . . . intae Jammy Joes . . .

He gazes at the wall map of the city streets . . .

Jammy Joes was where the silvery spoon was last seen alive. A certain Mr Efan Wurie. Huhuh . . . he's a effin worry to me all right!

He laughs . . . and then falls silent.

I'm bored shiteless here. This joab . . . That's why we play the games. The Toal game, the Amanda fuckin Drummond game. The Ray Lennox game. The Bladesey . . . and Bunty game . . .

Idea! He grabs the phone . . .

One . . . Four . . . One . . .

He keys the 141 withholding code, followed by a number.

(*Explains to audience.*)   'The caller withheld their number.'

Bunty   Hello?

Bruce (*aside, sotto voce*)   Buntee!

Bunty   Hello? Who's there?

He holds his nose to produce Frank Sidebottom's Mancunian twang:

'Frank'   Hello.

Bunty   Who's this?

'Frank'   Ai got your noombah from a friend.

Bunty   Who are you? What do you want?

'Frank'   Let's joost say, ai've eard all about yaw, and them services yaw provide.

Bunty   I think you've got the wrong number.

'Frank'   That is 336 9246?

Bunty   Yes.

'Frank'   Then ai haven't got the wrong noombah then, ave ai?

Bunty   Who gave you this number?

'Frank'   Someone who spoke very ighly of yaw. He told me all about yaw. Said yaw were a brilliant fook.

She evidently hangs up. He reaches down and massages his hard-on . . .

'Frank'   Boontay! Coontay Boontay . . .

The internal phone rings . . .

Bruce (*gruff*)   Robertson.

(*aside*)   Toal!

Aye.
Aye, right.
Sure.
What kind of hammer was it?
Any prints?
Well, I'll get some lucky bastard checking sales of hammers from hardware stores –
Probably some young racist thugs out on the town . . .
Schemies! I know these guys –

*But **Toal** is winning . . .*

Right, Brother Toal. *(Hangs up.)*

(Shouts at the phone:)   I know these fuckers! It's time some of these fuckers went down! Whether or not they did this one is immaterial, they are bad bastards and banging some of them up will make the streets safer!

He produces a file and pins up their photos . . .

Setterington . . . Begbie . . . Gorman!

We are the law enforcers of this society. We are paid to do a job we can't fucking well do because of all the snidey little cunts, the politicians, lawyers, judges, journalists, social workers. Poofs, coons and silly wee lassies . . .

Arm me, and I would delve into my little black book and I'd pay a few house calls, leave a little lead, and then you just watch the crime figures drop like a hoor's knickers. It's time to lean on some cunt, I'm bored sitting here shuffling papers. *(Riffles photos.)* Ocky! E-riddled fanny merchant, hangs around with the top boys. *(Photo up.)* Ocky . . .

Five-ten, five-eleven, blond hair, girlish features. O! See the girlfriend! What a cracker! Slim, five-sixish, exact same sortay blonde as him.

Ray   Curvy wee arse.

Bruce   Ray Lennox. Cool young guy.

Ray   She's a fuckin bairn!

Bruce   We're watching thum in the rear mirror as they go into the flat. Ray has trimmed his tache. Lookin a wee bit poofy.

Ray   What dae ye want tae dae, Robbo?

Bruce   'Steam in. Just like these cunts dae. Only nae cunt steams in like the polis. We're the hardest firm in this toon and it's time these scumbags realised it. C'mon. Use the Beast routine, that'll spook the cunt.'

Ray   The Beast! Aw, right. You want a line?

Bruce   'Too fuckin right.' Ray puts some posh on the corner of his credit card n takes a rough hit up the hooter.

He sniffs. Bangs on the door. Grins. Sniffs. Bangs . . .

Ocky   Awright, awright, ah'm comin.

Bruce   Ocky. Brian Ockendon. Soft little twat wi a whingey voice, T-shirt 'n' boxer shorts, eyes wide. 'Mister Ockendon!'

Ocky   You cannae come –

Ray   SHUT THE FUCK UP! YOU FUCKIN WELL SPEAK WHEN YOU ARE SPOKEN TO, DO YOU FUCKIN GET IT?

Ocky   Aye . . .

Bruce   'Cool it, Ray. You are in serious bother, mate. Where's the bedroom?'

Ocky   It's – uh – thir's –

Bruce   'Awright' – Lassie sitting up in bed wi a T-shirt oan.

Steph   What's this?

Bruce   'Polis. Do not attempt to leave this room.'

Steph   I don't have anything to say.

Bruce   Wee honey . . . 'How old are you?'

Steph   Sixteen.

Bruce   I flash a look at the shoulder bag on the bedside table. 'Any ID?' Her cover's blown.

Steph   Fifteen. But I'll be sixteen in September.

Bruce   She doesnae want me in that bag. 'Your boyfriend's broken the law if he's had intercourse with you. Has he?' Oh, barry wee titties . . . The colour drains from her face as I reach over and grab the bag, pouring its contents out on to the bed. Oh! A small plastic bag wi tablets in. Ecstasy!

Steph   I, I, I –

Bruce   'DS LENNOX!' Ray . . . bedroom:

Ray   DS Robertson?

Bruce   'Looks like MDMA to me found on this girl's person, at least six hundred milligrams. Also note this girl is under the legal age of consent.'

Ray   Check.

Bruce   Sitting room, Mr Ockendon, T-shirt, boxer shorts:

Ocky   Ah thoat she wis sixteen!

Ray   Judges are comin doon hard as fuck on stoat-the-baw.

Bruce   'Aye, isnae the time tae be done for stoat, no wi aw that paedophile stuff in the papers, it's fair goat the magistrates on the warpath. You're lookin at six months in Saughton, laddie!'

Ray   Mebbe a year.

Bruce   'Aye, Ray, and thir's a thin dividin line between a stoat-the-baw and a nonce.'

Ray   See, if somebody fae the polis was tae tell a screw like Ronnie McArthur, a strict Freemason n staunch family man, that the lassie was eleven –

Bruce   'Or ten –'

Ray   Or eight . . .

Bruce   'The poor cunt's life wouldnae be worth livin.'

Ray   In Saughton, he'd be taken to the Beast's wing.

Bruce   'You mean, *the* Beast?'

Ray Should be in a fucking mental hoaspital. Things he does tae they boys.

Bruce 'Pretty boys?'

Ray He likes tae see thum struggle. Six foot four ay solid muscle, hung like a fuckin horse. Legendary. Always splits thum first time.

Bruce 'Awww . . .'

Ray They say he prefers blonds . . .

Bruce 'A blond nonce in Saughton? Death sentence, I'd say. For a pretty wee blond . . .'
(*Adjusting his hard-on*) Dominance over another human being is one of the things which makes poliswork such a satisfying career. While Uncle Ray explains to the pissing-himself Mr Ockendon what he needs to do to keep his sweet arse out of the evil clutches of the Beast, I excuse myself and slide back to the bedroom.

Steph Please . . . don't . . . tell . . . my father . . .

He savours the blank cheque this offers him . . .
So . . . he stands there and mugs and gasps his way though an extended blow-job syndrome . . .

Bruce Grip ma baws! Grip ma fuckin baws harder!
Suck, ya wee fuckin hoor or yir auld man'll ken yir a fuckin drug-dealin wee hing-oot!
Yes . . . Yes! YES . . . YES!

He's come.

Merry Christmas.

He puts an overcoat on.

Music: the brass band is playing 'Away in a Manger' again . . .

I decide to head uptown and go for a little stroll. The town is mobbed with Saturday shoppers looking for a Christmas bargain. You can almost breathe in the raw greed which hangs in the air like vapour as the late-afternoon darkness

falls. In the window of a TV shop I try to get a look at the
scores. In England, Man U, Arsenal, Liverpool and Chelsea
all won, so it's as you were. I'm waiting on the Scottish
results coming through when a raucous shriek fills the cold
air, stripping the flesh from my back. I turn and see a crowd
forming across the road. I go over to investigate, pushing
past the stupified ghouls, and see a man, about mid-forties,
well dressed, twitching away on the ground in an ugly
paroxysm, one arm stiff and clutching his side. The boy is
turning blue and a woman is screaming:

Mrs Sim   COLIN! COLIN! PLEASE HELP US!
PLEASE!

Bruce   I'm down on my knees. He's pissed himself, a
black wet patch forming on his groin. 'What's wrong?'

Mrs Sim   It's his heart, it must be his heart, he's got a bad
heart, oh Colin no, OH GOD, COLIN NO!

Bruce   I've got the boy's head back, and I'm giving him
mouth-to-mouth. C'mon you bastard . . . I can feel the life
draining from him, the heat leaving his body and I'm trying
to force it back into him, but there's no response. His face
turns white . . . 'GIT AN AMBULANCE!'
I'm thudding away at his chest.
(*Sotto voce*)   'LIVE! LIVE! LIVE!' There's no pulse.

Music ends.

I don't know how long passed as I sat alongside that
formless thing lying in the stench of its secretions, and I've
got the woman's hand in mine. I hear sirens and I feel the
hand on my shoulder . . . A guy with red hair coming out of
his nostrils, wearing a luminous green waistcoat.

Paramedic   'Sawright, mate. You did more than
anybody could do. He's gone.

Bruce   And they take him away.
The woman grabs me round the waist.

Mrs Sim   He was a good man, he was a good man . . .

Bruce   'Was he? Was he?' N ah've goat tears rolling down
ma cheeks. N the woman is in ma arms, her head in ma
chest, n ah want tae hold hur for ever, tae never let hur go.
But then they're away. They're away . . . And I turn to face
the ghouls. Same faces all the time.
'What youse fucking well lookin at? What dae ye expect tae
see? Go back to yir shoppin! Gaun!'

He flashes his badge.

'Police! Disperse!'

Reporter   Who are you?

Bruce   'Bruce Robertson, DS Bruce Robertson, Lothian
Police.'

Reporter   What happened?

Bruce   'I tried to save the boy. I tried, but he just went. I
tried to save um . . .'

Reporter   How did that make you feel?

Bruce   'Eh?! What the fuck . . .'

Reporter   Brian Scullion, *Evening News*. I was watching.
You did really well, DS Robertson. How did it make you
feel when he didn't make it?

*He turns away in disgust and 'barges through the crowd'. He upsets a
box of trash.*
At home, he sits in his overcoat, shaking . . .

Bruce   Hearts lost five–nil at Rugby Park. I watched one
of Hector the Farmer's videos and had a wank.

He has a wank . . . and wipes himself on **Carole**'s *bathrobe . . .*

There was a time when I slept at night, but now I sit up in
the chair till it gets light, and then nod off. The place is a
fuckin midden. Old plates of food and tinfoil cartons of
curry and Chinky. It stinks. Judi Dench. I don't give give an
Aylesbury [*duck – ie, fuck*].

Music: Michael Bolton, 'How Am I Supposed to Live Without You?'
'Tell me how am I supposed to live without you,
Now that I've been loving you so long?
How am I supposed to live without you,
How am I supposed to carry on,
When all that I've been living for is gone?' Etc.

During this he tans the bottle of whisky and falls asleep as morning comes. He wakes, tidies up a bit and gets newspaper.

Sunday was a quite day. I thought of Carole a lot. I scanned the *Sunday Mail.* (*Shock:*) Aaargh! (*Then laughs . . .*) It's me! It's an old photo of me!
'A Christmas shopper tragically died in the arms of his wife yesterday, despite valiant efforts to save him by a hero off-duty policeman who came to his aid.
'Stunned
'Shoppers in Edinburgh's busy South Bridge were stunned when Retail Manager Colin Smith (41) who has a history of heart trouble collapsed on the city street. "We were shocked. He just keeled over," said Mrs Jessie Newbigging (67). Her daughter June Paton (30) of Hawes Road, Armadale, added: "It's terrible that something like that has to happen, especially at Christmas. It makes you think."
'Hero . . .'

He reads forward quickly and then stows the paper.

Et cetera. How did that make me feel? It made me feel like going out to the Royal Scot for a pint of stout and roast beef, mashed potato, carrots, sprouts and gravy. They had a roasting hot fire going. After a while, the oxygen left my brain and I sat watching the demons in the flames . . .

But they lie too deep for words . . . He mews . . .

I took some sleeping pills when I got home, and slept till Monday morning. There were a few messages on the machine. From people who'd read the bit in the *Mail.*

He goes down to shirtsleeves and gives his hands a good wash and scrub . . .

Woman   Congratulations, Bruce. Phone me.

Bladesey   Well done, Bruce. It must have been . . . harrowing.

Toal   Bruce, Bob Toal. I'm sorry, but well done anyway.

Shirley   I'm proud of you. Call me. Shirley.

Ray (*sings*)   'Whatever happened to all of the heroes?'

He can't seem to get his hands clean . . .

Bruce   I need a fuckin washing done. That slag's abandoned me: trying to fuckin well kill me. She kens I cannae work that fuckin machine. Huvnae hud a proper cooked meal in ages.
And Dr Patel expects me to fuckin starve.

Doctor (*drying his hands*)   Are you avoiding foods with a high fat content? (*He sits to write a prescription . . .*)

Bruce   'Aye.'

Doctor   And I know it's difficult, but do try not to scratch the infected area. I can't stress enough the importance of washing and changing underwear on a regular basis. Cotton briefs. Or better still boxer shorts, let the air (*a delicate gesture*) circulate.

Bruce   Paki fuckin shirt-lifter fuckin brown-bomber.

Doctor   I want a urine sample. And I'd also like a stool.

Bruce   He produces this wee plastic carton – wi a lid. Fuckin perve of the highest order. 'What for?'

Doctor   I think you may have worms. Tapeworms. They are harmless parasites, but they can be hard to get rid of.

Bruce   Ah leave the cunt wi a bottle of lager piss and a carton of curry shite. Cunt wants shite ah'll fuckin well gie'um shite. (*Shit-strains . . .*)
Allergy to fried food? Or cheese!
I never eat fuckin cheese.

I eat all day, but ah'm losing weight.
Maybe I got AIDS off a hoor. Naw, I'm careful. Only
queers n schemies get AIDS.
Worms. Fuckin worms.

Exit.

Two

He farts . . .

Bruce   Worms. I got a book out the library. They picked
one that was forty foot long ootay a boy's arse! Cunts.
In the cannie, I'm sittin there diggin into a plate of auld
Ina's fish pie wi extra chips n baked beans when Toal comes
swaggering in with the air of the wash-hoose bully who's
heard a satisfying piece of malicious gossip. But when he
sees me the cunt goes aw serious and comes over and
squeezes my shoulder.

Toal   Bad luck on Saturday.

Bruce   I'm thinkin he's talking fitba, and I'm just about to
criticise Tom Stronach's performance on the wing when I
realise he's talking about the guy I tried to save. 'Thanks,
Bob.' Then Karen Fulton and Amanda Drumstick spy me
and hurry over with their plates of salad. Fuckin salad at this
time of year. I can see Fulton wantin to lose a few pounds,
but Drummond! That yin would have to move around in
the shower tae get wet.

Amanda   It must've been terrible, Bruce. Are you okay?

Bruce   I feel something moving in my guts . . . Fish?

Amanda   If you need to talk about it . . .

Bruce   Or worms . . . the enemy within . . .
'Not a very pleasant experience, ladies, it has to be said. But
the show must go on.'
As I'm trying to escape, a woman appears.

Mrs Sim   This is the man . . .

Bruce   She's shepherding a wee laddie towards me . . .

Mrs Sim   Sergeant Robertson?

Bruce   What kind of wind-up is this?

Mrs Sim   Sergeant Robertson, I just wanted to thank you personally for everything that you did for Colin . . . Euan, this is the man that tried to help your daddy, son. This is a good man.

Bruce   The wee boy keeps his head bowed but raises his eyes up at me and pushes out a smile.

Mrs Sim   He tried so hard for your dad, son. Thank you . . .

Bruce   'Sorry I couldn't save your husband . . .'

Mrs Sim   This is a good man, son . . . A guid man . . .

Bruce (*grabs a file. It contains Efan Wurie's photograph.*)   A couple of neds in this city have topped a coon who's no business being here in the first place, so fuck it. Who gives a Kate Moss? The answer is me. I'm a detective. I'm going to ferret out the murdering schemie bastard who topped our innocent coloured cousin. It's called, in a word, professionalism.
Crime briefing: two p.m. . . . (*Photo up . . .*)
'We've established that on the night of Efan Wurry's murder, two thugs with a record for violence, Gorman and Setterington, were in the vicinity of Jammy Joe's disco. Nobody saw them there of course, but you know the reign of terror these thugs have imposed on the social life of this city.' Peter Inglis pipes up:

Peter   Bruce, I just had an anonymous call. Male, young, tells me these guys definitely were in the club that evening.

Bruce   Anonymous call, male . . . 'young'. That'll be our blond-haired stoat-the-baw chum, Ocky, cowardly wee ratbag. Worse than useless unless he grasses up in court,

which he won't as it would mean the end of the cunt's sorry
life. I point this out to Inglis, crushing his moment of shiny-
faced glory. He's had the audacity to put himself in the
promotion stakes. Against *me*?

He produces a big black and white surveillance photo . . .

Sad loner, Peter Inglis. There's something – queer about
um. Twenty per cent of heterosexual couples enjoy anal sex.
Only fifty per cent of homosexual couples do. (*He seems to be
losing the plot . . .*)

Last night I stayed home and watched one of Hector the
Farmer's videos. A sci-fi effort about two extraterrestrial
space dykes who kidnap nubile virgin schoolies from an
American town, from schools, discos, outside shopping
centres et cetera and condition them into lesbianism
through forcing them into repeated sex acts. The long-term
plan of the crafty alien dykes is to make men superfluous
and Earth into a lesbian planet, ruled of course by them. A
stud detective and his crew of sexual athletes have to save
the young schoolies from carpet munching and bring them
back over to the right side, through the power of their cocks.
Eventually, after fucking the schoolies back into
heterosexuality the ace detective faces his greatest challenge
in a conflict with the superpowered cosmic lesbos. He hus
tae bring them ower tae the other side. It turns out to be a
happy ending for all. The dyke spacegirls find out that they
love cock, but the cop admits that lesbianism is a turn-on for
men, provided the women are good-looking and the men
can watch. So they decide to join forces and exterminate all
homosexual men.

He sticks up a Page Three girl from the Sun *. . .*

I take April from Newcastle to the bogs with me.

(*Masturbating*) C'mon baby, Bruce is here. It's your big night,
that's it come on . . . Phoa, come on baby. Oh, oooh, ya
fucker that ye are. Bingo! (*He comes . . .*)

*With **Bruce** carried away by his orgasm, the **Worm** slips out: it's voice is a girl-boyish one . . .*

Worm   I let ma spunk drip on to ma thighs. Its alkaline properties might do the rash good . . .

Bruce *recovers and writes on the lavatory wall: 'INGLIS – SICK DISEASED QUEER'.*

Bruce *(raising a stink)*   'Peter! Peter! Have you seen the *filth* in the toilet?'

Peter   Thir's eywis somethin thair. I nivir take any notice.

Bruce   'Maybe ye should. I'm gettin a bit fed up of this shite. Some cunt's playing silly fuckers here. Just hope ah dinnae find oot whae it is! Gaffer, I want you to come and see something in the toilet. As Federation Rep ah'm no having people's character defamed in this way.'

Peter   It's . . . just a loaday bloody nonsense . . .
It's . . . just a loaday bloody nonsense . . .

Bruce *(washing hands)*   'See, Bob, Peter's a lonely guy. What he gets up to is his own business.'

Toal   Come on, Bruce. How can you have confidence in a man who's constantly undressing you with his eyes?

Bruce   'Aye, but I'm not standing by while a brother officer is harassed for his sexuality. The force in some parts of the country advertise in the gay press.'

Toal   This isnae some parts of the country. This is Scotland!

Bruce   The concept 'Inglis' is now firmly in bed with the concept 'poof'. The concepts 'Inglis' and 'promotion' are just waiting for the divorce papers to come through. *(Idea!)* Speaking of which . . .

He dials a phone number and produces the puppet . . .

The worms are on the run. The worm called Inglis is being flushed out of the system, outed and routed before further infestation can take place. And now –

Bunty   Hello?

'Frank'   Awright, Coontay?

Bunty   Go away!

'Frank'   I've been tellin Little Frank about yaw. E wants taw give your fanny a lickin, e does.

'Puppet'   Ah do not.

'Frank'   Yes yaw do!

Bunty   LEAVE ME ALONE! (*Hangs up.*)

Bruce (*sings*)   'I am the Antichrist! I am an anarchist! I know what I want and I know how to get it . . .'

The telephone rings.

Bruce   Bladesey!
She's what?
Oh no.
Bladesey, listen, would it help if I came over and had a wee word with the both of you. An experienced polisman's view might help to, uh, allay fears . . .
Consider it done. I'll be there!
I'll be there – for you . . . (*End.*)
'I'll be there, with a love that will shelter yooo!
I'll be there, with a love that will see you throo!'

He seats the puppet 'at a table' . . .

Music: a cascade of sitar music . . .

He takes me for a curry in the Burning Ruby. He has a chicken korma which is par for the course for a wee fuckin pansy. I rip through a beef vindaloo like there's nae tomorrow. Couplay pints of Kingfisher . . .

We have been with Bunty. As arranged, Bruce called to pick up his old mucker Cliff, and meets – The Wife. She's a big woman, hefty . . . The place is immaculate, not a smidgen of dust. Make a good polisman's wife. Or fuck. About five-five, but eleven stone plus, on the voluptuous side of fat, black hair curled and twisted into ringlets, quite a bit of flash jewellery, earrings, necklace, bracelets, giving a tarty hint under her haughty tones. 'Pleased to meet you, Bunty,' (*a shade Sean Connery*) I smile, extend my hand, giving hers a full wholesome grip. She returns my smile:

Bunty   Bruce, isn't it?

Bruce   Yes it is, you meaty-thighed bit-titted whore. 'Yes.'

Bunty   Cliff's told me all about you.

Bruce   Ooh . . . This cow respects power. 'I understand how unsettling this must be for you, Bunty. Try not to worry unduly. I've dealt with creeps like this one before. Most of them, if you'll pardon the expression, are all mouth and no trousers. Slamming the phone down only goes to show them that you're frightened. They feed off that fear. Stay as cool as you can, and talk to them . . .'

Bunty   Your officer said not to get into it with them.

Bruce   'Yeah. We generally tell our younger less experienced officers that. And you'll find that works, if you want them to stop. But, if you actually want to catch the bastards, if you'll pardon my French, you have to use different methods.'

Bunty   Oh, I want him caught, don't you worry about that. I want him to suffer.

Bruce   Phoa . . . (*Hard-on!*) 'Well, Bunty, ehhhmmm, the best thing you can do is offer a bit of self-disclosure.'

Bunty   What do you mean by self-disclosure?

Bruce   'Tell him something about yourself. Play along. Turn up the heat. That way you have *control*. He becomes the victim. Force him to confront his own need.'

For a while, he relishes being both of them, wordless . . .

Bruce   'We'll nail this creepy bastard, Cliff. No danger. We'll get him, Bunty. Cliff – (*still gazing at* **Bunty**) – I want you to take special care of this lady, this very, very brave lady . . .'

Bunty   I feel so much happier now. Thank you so much, Bruce.

Bruce   'Not at all. Thank your good hubby here, my pal Cliff.'

Music fading away . . .

(*To* **Bladesey** *at the table, toast:*) 'Low friends in high places, eh?' (*Drinks lager . . .*)

Bladesey   Bruce, d'you mind if I ask you a personal question?

Bruce   'Fire away.'

Bladesey   What made you join the force?

Silence. It's a big question . . .

Bruce   'Why did I join the force? Oh I'd have to say that it was due to police oppression. I'd witnessed it within my own community and decided that it was something I wanted to be part of.' (*Smile.*)

He goes to the bogs.

(*Rant*) You sad little cunt! He needs to be confronted with what he really is. He has to feel, see and to acknowledge his inadequacy as a member of the human species, then he has to do the honourable thing and renounce that membership. And I will help him. (*Mirror . . .*) 'Reach out! Reach out . . . !'

He retches . . .

Worm (*slipping out of jacket*)   Ooo-oo! I'm growing! I eat
through my skin n hang on with my jaws. Slowly slowly I'm
consuming the matter that surrounds me, ingesting *and*
excreting – through my skin. Does that make you want to
scratch your erse? (*Mirror*) I've come a long way since my
gala-pie days, sweetheart. They say, if you drink whisky,
you'll never get worms. Wrong!

He starts chopping coke on the mirror . . .

Do you know they picked one that was forty fit long out of a
boy's arse? What a way to die! . . . So I'm hanging in there.
Bruce eats a pile of shite, but speaking as an intestinal worm
the important thing at this stage of *ma* life is quantity. Call
me old fashioned but, size counts. And Brucie gives it to me
big, hot n greasy, don't you lover? Vindaloo! Vindaloo!

Telephone rings . . .

Shirley   Broooss . . .

Worm/Bruce   Fuckoff. (*Snort . . .*)

Shirley   Brooose!

Worm/Bruce   Fuckoff-fuckoff! (*Snort . . .*)

Bruce   That's Shirley. Carole's sister. Wants shagged.
Fuck off! (*He brandishes a claw hammer, bagged and labelled.*) All I
can think about is that boy's skull bashed in, the way his
head was caved in and how it wasn't like a head at all, just
like a broken silly puppet face, about how when you destroy
something, when you brutalise it, it always looks warped
and disfigured and slightly unreal and unhuman and that's
what makes it easier for you to go on brutalising it, go on
fucking it and hurting it and mashing it until you've
destroyed it completely, proving that destruction is natural
in the human spirit, that nature has devices to enable us to
destroy, to make it easier for us: a way of making righteous
people who want to act do things without the fear of
consequences, a way of making us less than human.

I tell you, this job. It holds you. It's all around you, a
constant, enclosing, absorbing gel. Early on, there are wee
areas of your life that are free of it. But slowly, slowly it
invades them. See, the gel is intelligent, a life form, and it
gradually dissolves and sucks up your human essence like a
Venus fly trap absorbing a fly.
Or like . . . (*He can feel his worm* . . .) Bastard!

He produces a pharmacy bag containing a bottle.
Vermolax! (Drinks)

Meanwhile: Sound of distant police sirens . . .

I can't remember why I'm here . . .
You just have to keep playing the games . . .

'Good King Wenceslaus looked out
On the feast of Stephen . . .'
'Twas the night of the Christmas Curry.
For the Lothian CID.
Once more the Burning Ruby! Vindaloo!
And then I lead my happy crew
Through sawdust bars with oyster shells
To greasy pubs with hoorish smells
And onward through the driving snow
Towards a club I happen to know
Is closed for refurbishment following a nasty fire.
'Shite,' I moan, 'It'll have tae be one ay they arse-bandit
places!' And I point to the Top of the Walk.

Music: The Tamperer, 'Feel it' (intro) . . .

'Ah'm no gaun thair,' Inglis scoffs. 'What have ye goat tae
hide, Peter? Ray laughs.

Peter   You sayin ah have got anything tae hide likes?

Ray   Naw, I'm sayin nothin.

Bruce   'Look, c'mon, it's jist for a fuckin drink!' I lead
them in, brooking no dissent. [(*Optional*): The bouncer
tipples we're polis and nods us through.]

Music: 'Feel it' kicks in, all drum and bells . . .

The lights go clubbing . . .

Bruce (*shouts*)   The place is full of all sorts of sad buftie
boys, scene-queens and tourist puffs, and a good few
hardened ex-cons who got a taste for it in Saughton.
I spot the man of my dreams (*displays nude photo*): Sinky, a
mercenary wee Calton Hill rent boy. He dives downstairs,
but I catch up with him in the bogs.

He mimes a wordless encounter . . .

We huv a wee . . . blether, likes . . .
And I rejoin ma lads, who are huvin a good crack. Big
Dougie Gillman's already bust one queer's mooth in the
lavvy for giving him the glad eye. No accounting for taste, I
suppose. We're hearing all about it when Sinky appears and
heads down the floor towards Peter Inglis, camping wildly
on cue.

Sinky   Pea-tihr! Oh Pea-tihr! Long time no see, darlin!

Bruce   Inglis is stunned.

Peter   Ah dinnae ken you!

Sinky   Oh . . . Oh sorry, Peter love. Didnae realise.

Bruce   Sinky flounces away, pouting at Ray Lennox.

Sinky   Och, he can be so immature . . .

Bruce   Shock, embarrassment, fear and loathing . . .

Peter   Ah fuckin dinnae ken him!

Bruce   Inglis squeals and makes to go for Sinky. I grab his
shoulders manfully. 'Fir fucksakes, Peter, we're polis!
Dinnae cause a fuckin scene in here!'
But too late: Dougie Gillman says something about
boyfriends. Inglis calls Gillman a cunt, punches are swung,
heads bang, and pished polismen stagger messily on to the
snowy street. Inglis is away down Leith Walk, alone,
despised and rejected of men.

Ray   Fuckin arse bandit!

Music fades away . . .

Dougie   BIG FUCKIN NANCY BOY!

Bruce   Big Dougie's tasted fag blood and he won't let go now. We bay mocking lynch-mob laughter at the broken figure of the sodomite Inglis as his hunched figure is lost in the snow.

Bruce   'Who'd have believed it, eh? In the Craft n aw,' I muse, as we head doon tae Shrubhill tae the Masonic. (*Sings*) 'We three kings of Orient are. One in a taxi, one in a car . . .'

He farts wet . . .

Fuck. Fuckin laxative!!! Woooaaahhh . . .

Water drops on him . . .

Worm (*screech . . .*)   Fuck! Fuckin laxative?! You're trying to kill me! What's your fuckin problem?

(*Shivers . . .*) Ah'm so fuckin cold . . .

Reverting to **Bruce** *he shivers and puts on* **Carole***'s robe . . .*

Music: Curtis Stigers, 'Keep Me from the Cold':
'When the snows come and the wind blows cold,
Will you hold me, like you'll never let go?'

Firelight . . .

He sits and stares at the fire and listens to Curtis sing:
'Will you kiss me so sweetly,
And whisper you love me so?
I have wandered through the mountains,
I have searched the streets below,
But all I ever really wanted
Was someone to hold me
And keep me from the cold.'

Mirror. He becomes **Carole** *. . .*

Carole   It's Christmas,
But the streets were cold and grey,
Like many streets in many towns
In this cold country.
The wind cuts through you.
And the people: nosy, predatory,
Ready to revel in others' pain.
I saw a man look at me.
I know the type.
Repressed.
You have to pity them.
That was me before I met Bruce.
He knew how much I needed, to come out.
That was what our sex club was all about.
Wee flirtations and wee games,
But they serve
To strengthen a true love.
I'm a different woman now.
O God . . . it's Christmas Eve . . .

Bruce   . . . Christmas fuckin Eve! Need to get something
for the bairn . . .
I start early. With Ray Lennox. Sound guy. Fuckin good
polisman. There's a blizzard, but it's behind the blinds
inside his bachelor flat. Snow . . . (*Sniffs.*) Jingle fuckin bells!

Music: The Flaming Lips, 'The Observer' . . .

And I have to listen to cool Ray's trendy fuckin CDs.

Ray (*in full flow*)   Sure there are laws which are shite. The
problem is, most people are weak, so if you don't have laws,
even shite ones, then you don't have any order. Ah think the
best solution to the whole fuckin mess would be if we could
jist go around and shoot any cunt we felt like at any time.
Imagine! All the scumbags wid be gaun roond wi big
apologetic smiles on their faces. (*He clowns*) Birds comin up n
giein ye a blow job in the street for the privilege ay no gittin
their heids blawn oaf . . .

Sniff . . .

Bruce   'But maist of all, just fuckin well shootin spastics stone dead.'

He forms a gun out of his hand, puts it to his head and makes a loud exploding noise as he jerks head and hand away from each other; he does it a few times, going into slow motion . . .

Then he has the audacity to chuck me out, into the snow, the cold wet snow, cos he's off to the paternal home for Christmas. Fuck'um. I need to Christmas shop anyway . . . They're open late tonight. I have a pint in Alan Anderson's old boozer, then repair to the bogs where I chop up a huge line on the cistern and snort it back. I need to use the energy of coke to brave this shopping hell. Down to the St James's Centre. C&A! I need some new slacks. I refuse to wear jeans. It is the mark of a schemie. The credit limit on my Visa card is fucked. (*Humiliation!*) I pay by Switch and get the fuck off out.
'Cash flow that's all. Professional. Not a schemie! Man of wealth! Man of wealth!'
Vultures are circling. Uh . . . (*i.e., where now?*)
Toys R Us? Uh! (*i.e., can't face it*)
Fuckin John Lewis! JOHN LEWIS STORE GUIDE: LADIES FASHIONS. Something for Carole. Christmas Carole . . .
I can't hack this, the crowds and all that shite.
Do another big line in the store bogs. (*Sniff . . .*)

The music dominates the scene, desolately . . .

See . . . they're flying past! Eyes every place but mine. Just please look at me. See: the procession of sheep up the escalator . . . the big cow you want to just scream GIES A FUCKIN SHAG at or even just look at me please police please please look at me . . . Aargh!

He feels a hand on his arm . . .

Staffer   Allrightsir?

Bruce (*ID out*)   'Police! Please me like I please you!' Move away through the house of the Lord, this great temple of

worship to our God of Christian givingness spendingness
consumer-expenditureness business-competitiveness shop-
and-cheat-deathness and into the street where the excluded
jakeys beg for pennies! Nnnnnn . . . (*a heart-groan like worm-
mew . . .*)

Back by the fire, he shrinks inside **Carole**'s *robe . . .*

*Music cross-fades to the mid-section of Pink Floyd's 'Echoes' from
their album* Meddle: *wind moans, rooks caw, etc.*

Worm (*Bedtime story-ish*)   In a little mining town outside
Edinburgh, you were the first son, born in troubled
circumstances to Ian Robertson and Molly Hanlon. But
there was no joy at your coming, no warmth or tenderness
from your father. You wanted him to love you, but he
looked away. When he came into the house covered in black
coal dust, he'd see you picking nervously at the food he'd
put on your table with his sweat, see you not eating. 'Eat!'
he'd roar. Your mother looked away as the man pulled you
up to the fireplace and pointed at the coal in the bucket.
'Ah've been fuckin diggin this shite aw day for you! Eat!'
But you still couldn't eat the food. So he'd pick up a lump of
coal and make you eat it. 'Eat . . .' Making you taste the
coal, taste the filth. Oh why? You mammy came when you
cried in the night. 'You're a good wee boy, Bruce, you're
Mummy's wee boy,' but you could taste the pity, you knew
there was something wrong with you. Something so wrong
that when your baby brother Stevie came and you looked in
the cot and touched the bairn's small hand, your father
pulled you away, wrenched the arm in your socket, 'Don't
you ever lay a finger on him!' and your mum led you away:
her pitying look, your father's sneers, the way the villagers
glanced at you as if you were a freak; parents told their
children not to play with you. But Stevie always played with
you. Everyone loved Stevie, he grew up into such a bubbly
wee boy, and then it was you and him together, inseparable.
And when the great coal strike came, the power cuts, the
long dark nights, then your father sent the pair of you out at

night in the cold, down to the byng to steal coal . . . (*Softly*)
'I'm the king of the castle . . .'

Bruce *wakes as if from a nightmare.*

Music fades, loops and mixes with passing-car sound effects . . .

Bruce   Drummond! I am out on patrol with Amanda
Drummond of Bulldyke and Drumstick. Why? I don't know
why. She's going on about the effin fuckin worry case:
victims, suspects, SHERPA, crime scenes, forensics,
analysis, I want to scream SHITE! I DON'T FUCKIN
CARE ABOUT THIS! I'M FUCKIN WELL DYIN
HERE!
Cause I am. Somebody phone the police . . . Pleasssss . . .

Amanda   Are you okay, Bruce?

Bruce   'Yes. Okay I certainly am.'

Amanda   Look you can say it's none of my business.

Bruce   'I'm fine . . . honest. I've just been having a bit of a
bad time.'

Amanda   If you want to talk about it . . .

Bruce   'Don't put on your personnel hat, Amanda. This is
real poliswork.'

Amanda   It's not my personnel hat. I'm concerned about
a colleague, that's all.

Bruce   'Is that all?'

Amanda   Oh! don't flatter yourself.

Bruce   'You fancy me. I can tell.'

Amanda   Bruce, you're a silly pathetic man, you know
that? You're very possibly an alcoholic and God knows what
else. You're the type of sad case who preys on weak
vulnerable women in order to boost his own shattered ego.
In the sexual marketplace you're not even Poundstretcher.

Bruce   Wha – ?! Look at me. I'm not so good at my job now. Been in it too long. I was the best. My family don't talk to me. Cause of the strike. Miners, see? They don't let us in the house. My father . . . It was my brother. The coal, the dirt, the filth. I hate it all. They won't let us in the hoose! Ah wis only daein ma fuckin joab –

Amanda (*snap*)   Accept it. Deal with it. You have a wife, a daughter . . . don't you?

Bruce   Don't I? Don't I (*Shows wallet photo.*) Carole, see? See, wee Stacey! (*Pulls out other photos.*) Women? Weak, vulnerable women? Chrissie: 'Broosss! Turn ma gas off, Bruce!' Shirley, Carole's sister Shirley, cervical fuckin smear! Bunty! Coontay Boontay, look at the cow's arse! See this, fae Helga fae Amsterdam, nipples like a fighter pilot's thumbs! (*Rips and tosses photos.*) There's something wrong with us now. Something bad. Something inside.

The music has gone. A car sweeps past.

Bruce   Happy New Year. (*Picks up photo bits . . .*)
Carole . . .
'The road leads back . . . it always leads back to you.'

Music: intro to Michael Bolton's 'Georgia on my Mind' . . .

Bruce   I'm going out – with Carole.

Song: 'Georgia, Georgia, the whole day through
Just an old sweet song keeps Georgia on my mind.'

*He sits a while, then slowly changes into **Carole**'s clothes . . .*

'Talkin 'bout Georgia, I'm in Georgia,
A song of you comes as sweet and clear
As moonlight through the pines.
Other arms reach out to me,
Other eyes smile tenderly,
Still in peaceful dreams I see,
The road leads back to you.
Georgia, sweet Georgia, no peace I find,
Just an old sweet song keeps Georgia on my mind.'

Then there's the make-up . . . and wig . . . And a drink . . .

Other eyes smile tenderly,
Still in peaceful dreams I see,
The road leads back to you.
Georgia, sweet Georgia, no peace I find,
Just an old sweet song keeps Georgia on my mind.'

Then there's the make-up . . . and the wig . . . and a drink . . .

Music: Georgia segues to Regular Fries, 'The Pink Room' . . .

'Carole'   Oops!
It's freezing. I'm glad I've put my warm coat on. The city is
thronged with revellers. I turn off a side-street and head
towards a little bar I know. It's . . . special. Then I see the
car: it comes cruising alongside of me, curb-crawling – as if I
was a hooker! One guy's hanging out of the window making
signs. I ignore him. I don't like talking to strangers. It stops a
little way in front of me and two young men climb out.
They approach me and block my path.

Lexo   Happy New Year, doll.

Bruce   Setterington!

Ghostie   Ye comin fir a wee ride, sweetheart?

Bruce   Gorman!

'Carole'   'No . . . I . . .' They start to laugh. I start to
laugh. We start to laugh . . . They push me into the car!

Ghostie   You're a fickin sick fairy. Ah'm goony fuckin
cripple you!

Another   You shag guys like that, ya fuckin freak?

Lexo   Need a bag ower its heid before ah'd fuck it!

Ghostie   Ah'm no gonny fuck it wi ma cock, am ah, ya
daft cunt! Wull see whit we kin find tae stick up its queer
erse, see how much the cunt kin take!

Lexo   Move yir queer erse!

Bruce is pushed out and across the floor . . . .

'Carole'   They bundle us out of the car and push us up a set of stairs. The place is derelict: we see broken glass under our feet. They throw us into a room and pile in. We have to take control now. (*Wig off. Now* **Bruce**:) 'Police! Workin under cover. Detective Serg –' (*He is punched.*)

Ghostie   We ken aw aboot you, pal.

Another   Any keks you are wearin may be taken doon and used in evidence!

Bruce   Ocky! (*He is kicked.*)

Lexo   The thing is, boys, we huv tae go aw the wey wi this pig. N ye ken what that means.

Ocky   Dinnae be daft, Lexo, ye cannae waste a pig!

Lexo   Shut yir fucken mooth!

Ghostie   Lexo's right. Deid cunts tell nae tales. We can torch this place wi the cunt in it. Or what's left ay the cunt.

Bruce   'Fuckin villagers! Ah ken you, Gorman. You hide in the mob. You are one shtein cunt. Ah'd take you. Ah'd take any one ay yis in a square go! Fuckin shitein cunts!' Oh, we've cracked their code! We're in control!

Ghostie   Right this cunt dies. Ah'm takin um. Leave um t'me!

Lexo   Let's jist dae the cunt now n'stop fuckin aboot.

Ghostie   Naw! Ah want um! Personal.

Bruce   He signals for the others to leave us, leave us alone. Yes! And they go, like sheep! Yes! And he has an old key which he uses to lock us in the room together.

Ghostie (*crooning*)   The key to the house of love . . .

Bruce   'Fuckin donkey!' (*He attacks, stilettos flailing.*)

But **Bruce** *takes a beating and ends up bent over backwards.*

Ghostie   Ah've always fuckin hated cops. No in the normal way everybody hates cops. Ah've eywis hated the cunts in a special wey. You're different though, sweetheart. You kin be saved. Ah'm gonny make an honest woman ay you yet! Fuckin wide poof polis!

He kisses **Bruce** . . .

Bruce   He kissed me!

Ghostie   Ye liked that, eh sexy. Ye liked it eh?

Bruce   Yes. We know that we want him to do this again, this is our last wish. We want to say, please, let us be together like that again, just one last time . . .
He does.

Bruce *bites* **Ghostie**'s *tongue off* . . .

Ghostie *squeals* . . .

Bruce Push!

Music: scratch two-second repeats . . .

Bruce   Watch him falling backwards crashing through the rotten windowpanes trying to grab the curtains but the material tears in his hands and he looks at us with hate and incomprehsion, his own blood spilling from the severed tongue in his mouth, as he slides out the window and crashes down on to the concrete court below. A huge heart-shape puddle of blood forms round his head.

Smoke . . .

Bruce (*climbing* . . .)   Who's fuckin next, spastics! Schemies! Villagers! Youse die! Youse git the same as that fuckin spastic! YOUSE DIE! Cummoan, cummoan, cummoan!

Sirens . . . *lights* . . .

Music: mix to Meddle: *wind, rooks, banshee cries* . . .
A red emergency light continues to flash . . .
Smoke drifts like mist . . . *or snakes out through air vents* . . .

Bruce/Carole/Worm *is perched somewhere strange . . .*

Worm   'I'm the king of the castle, and you're the dirty
wee rascal!' You and Stevie slipped through the corrugated-
iron fence. You gasped at the huge big mountain of coal.
'Let's climb the mountain!' Wee boys, silly wee boys . . .
Wee Stevie rushes lightly up to the top ay the byng in a
cloud of coal dust and sings down at ye: 'Ah'm the king of
the castle and you're the dirty rascal!' Ay, you're the queer
one here, darlin! So up you go, starting a shower of loose
coals under your heavy feet. 'Fuck off!' you curse as you
grab Stevie and push the wee laddie back down the side of
the mountain. Watch him falling back and crashing down.
Fuck, he's going down into the hatch of the bunker! The
mountain's shifting round him. He's trying to climb out . . .
but see the mountain shifting down around him! You don't
mean to make it happen but it does: it all slides down on top
of him, it hits Stevie in the face, it wipes Stevie out, it seals
Stevie in, it buries Stevie. You tried to dig him out, the
nightwatchman came and tried to dig him out, and all the
other people came, the lights came, the oxygen pipe came,
the ambulance . . . Your father came, he arrived just as they
were pulling out the wee black broken dead body. He's
crouching, crying, beside his son's dead body, and he looks
up at you and he points. The villagers fall into a silence.
'That thing killed him, that bastard spawn ay the fuckin
devil killed ma laddie! You're no ma son! You've never been
ma fuckin son! You're filth!'

He drops down and goes to the wash basin . . .
The effects die, leaving the domestic fire . . .
He strips and washes himself . . .

The answer machine begins, speaking in Other Voices . . .

Bunty   Bruce. Bunty. Please call me.

Beep.

Bunty   Bruce, Bunty. I'm worried about you. They said
you were ill. I called but you weren't in. Call me.

Beep.

Chrissie   Broosse! It's Chrissie! Call me sometime, sexy.

Beep.

Gus   Hello, Bruce. Gus here. Hope all is well and that you'll soon be fighting fit again. Gie's a wee tinkle!

Beep.

Toal   Bruce, it's Bob Toal here. If you're home from hospital and you're needing anything, just call me. I – uh – I understand the situation. Just call.

Beep.

Shirley   Anybody home? Oh well . . .

Beep.

Gus   Bruce. Gus. Ah didnae get it, Bruce. The promotion. I want tae take this up with the Federation. Ye ken who they did give it tae! Fuckin Lennox. Ray Lennox.

Beep.

Ray   Hello . . . It's Ray. 'What's she gonna look like wi a chimney oan her?' Give me a bell. Give me a –

Bruce *switches on domestic light and stops the machine. What can he say? Time to go . . .*

He kneels down and gets out a cardboard box. It contains his old police uniform. During the next speech, he puts it on . . .

Bruce   My mammy's family came fae Ireland to work in the pits of Midlothian. She fell in love with Ian. He loved her. Well, he was willing tae get married in a Catholic church for her sake. And he stood by her too when the man attacked her. She was putting flowers on the grave of her dead brother when she was attacked by a man, and beaten . . . And raped. He was caught, and tried and convicted of multiple rapes and sexual assaults on women and men. He had mental problems: schizophrenia and that.

Voices . . . And she was pregnant by him. She went to the priest, but he said, Father Ryan said, that it was her duty to bring this life into the world. So . . . they brought forward the wedding . . . and the child was born . . . and bore the name of Bruce. Bruce. Ian Robertson stood by his wife, but every time he looked at the baby he saw the face of the man from the front page of the *Daily Record* and the caption 'THE FACE OF THE BEAST'. The Beast . . .

Sometimes I took time off from my job in the pits and made the pilgrimage to Glasgow to read the old *Daily Records* in the files . . .

I left the pit and joined the force.

Dressing complete. He produces a framed photo . . .

Wee Stacey . . . Poor wee lassie, what a fuckin legacy. And Christmas n aw. It makes ye think . . .

He finds lights and winds them round the Christmas tree . . .

If you haven't got a family, you haven't got anything. That night . . . Aye, it was Jammy Joes that night. You know what they're thinking: a woman drinking on her own. All those men . . . And there was a black laddie, a nice-looking black laddie . . . The trouble with people like him is that they think they can brush off people like me. You pushed me away, mister. You rejected me.

I reach into my bag and I pull out my claw hammer. Part of me is elsewhere as I'm bringing it down on his head. After two fruitless strikes I feel a surge of euphoria as on my third his head bursts open. His blood fairly skooshes out, covering his face like an oily waterfall and driving me into a frenzy: I'm smashing at his head and his skull is cracking open and I'm digging the claw hammer into the matter of his brain and it smells but that's only him pissing and shitting and the fumes are sticking fast in the still winter air and I wrench the hammer out, and stagger backwards to watch his twitching death throes . . . and I feel myself losing my balance in those awkward shoes but I correct myself, turning and moving down the old steps into the chilly street. Merry Christmas.

He plugs in the fairy lights, puts the others off, and switches the tree on: the lights flash very slowly . . . He moves towards his locker . . . and gets a sharp pain in the guts . . . But he gets the shotgun out.

Worm   Naw! Naw, Bruce, look, nothing is so bad it can't be made better! All you need is love! Everything's gonna be alright!

Music: Sweetbox, 'Everything's Gonna Be Alright' . . .

Worm   Brooose! What about me? It's not fair! (*Ad lib al fine . . .*) *He shoots himself.*

Dawn comes . . .

End.